DRA

C000221416

Saiswaroopa Iyer holds an MBA from IIT Kharagpur. She worked as an investment professional before turning to her passion for storytelling. Her love for epics, Puranas, and philosophy encouraged her to become a full-time author. Before *Draupadi*, she has authored three novels, all based on strong female characters from the ancient past of India. She also possesses a certificate in Puranas from Oxford Centre for Hindu Studies.

She lives in Bangalore.

DRAUPADI

The Tale
of an Empress

Saiswaroopa Iyer

RUPA

Published by
Rupa Publications India Pvt. Ltd 2019
7/16, Ansari Road, Daryaganj
New Delhi 110002

Sales centres:
Allahabad Bengaluru Chennai
Hyderabad Jaipur Kathmandu
Kolkata Mumbai

Copyright © Saiswaroopa Iyer 2019

ISBN: 978-93-5333-315-7

First impression 2019

10 9 8 7 6 5 4 3 2 1

The moral right of the author has been asserted.

Printed by Nutech Press Services, Faridabad

To Krishna Vasudeva,
the eternal inspiration

To Krishna Dwaipayana,
the guru who gave us the immortal epic of *Mahabharata*

To Krishnaa Draupadi,
the embodiment of feminine strength, courage and resilience

Contents

Introduction

Mahabharata was my first literary love, at the age of five or six, when my parents introduced reading to me. And it did not remain just a literary indulgence. Those immortal personalities occupied a permanent space in my conscience. They became a part of my dreams, fantasies, joys and misery. This inseparable connection with those who existed millennia ago and continue to exist in my life, made me take to storytelling. One can imagine my elation when I was asked to write a novel based on *Mahabharata*. And the character was none other than Draupadi—the propelling heroine of the undying epic.

Along with the celebration came a challenge. I was to write the story of a character on whom volumes had been written, from academic to pop literature. I wanted my story to be unique and yet highlight the core of Veda Vyasa's brilliant heroine.

Draupadi was a woman who had the brains to propel the future, spine to stand up for truth, will to fight, and the heart to love despite the cruel games of fate. Many of the previously written expositions portrayed her only as the wronged woman in a man's world, stuck in a polyandrous marriage, drawn into one intrigue after the other, helplessly calling out to Krishna. On the other hand, to the common Indian consciousness, she is a person who could strike fear in the heart of a prospective wrongdoer. The compelling contrast between the intellectual and the popular world views was a fascinating topic to dwell upon.

Within traditional schools too, a spellbinding variety of interpretations exists. Dvaitic traditions extol her compelling devotion. Scholars regard her as an aspect of Shri herself. Some regard her as a manifestation of Sachi, the wife of Lord Indra. Those engaged in shastraic discourses praise her as the wife who took the institution of vivaha (marriage) to a new level. Of all the interpretations, one struck a chord with me. It was the scholarly premise driving *Andhra Mahabharatamu*, the Telugu recreation of *Mahabharata* composed between eleventh century to fourteenth century CE. The poets of this composition regard Draupadi as the Ichha Shakti, the propelling force of initiative that was powered by the Jnana Shakti of Lord Krishna, taken to fruition by the Kriya Shakti of the Pandavas. Delving into the story also gave me an opportunity to revisit some medieval folklore-inspired beliefs and contrast them against the spirit of Veda Vyasa. Draupadi, being a woman thirsty for vengeance, capable of no emotion other than anger, was one myth that I was motivated to counter. As Yudhishtira says about her in the critical edition of *Mahabharata*, Draupadi is the embodiment of compassion, but not a pacifist. Quoting Rudyard Kipling, she was that woman who managed to keep her head while everyone around her lost theirs. Naturally, hers was the earth and she, the immortal empress.

My reference list includes BORI's critical edition of *Mahabharata*, translated by Dr Bibek Debroy, Kisari Mohan Ganguli's translation of the Calcutta edition, and *Andhra Mahabharatamu* published by Tirumala Tirupati Devasthanams. My understanding of various characters was influenced by discourses by Bhagawan Sri Satya Sai Baba, Swami

Chinmayananda, Brahmasri Samavedam Shanmukha Sarma, Brahmasri Garikipati Narasimha Rao and Brahmasri Chaganti Koteshwara Rao.

Keeping with the vibrant storytelling tradition of India, this narrative too takes creative liberties that may seem to depart from the literary narrative at places, but strives to bring the reader closer to the characters.

I should mention the inspiration I drew from the works of Sri K.M. Munshi (*Krishnavatara*), Sri S.L. Bhyrappa (*Parva*) and Sri Bankim Chandra Chatterjee (*Krishna Charitra*).

With the blessings of elders and inspiration from the one above, I present this offering, in the hopes that you enjoy the tale of this immortal empress of ancient India.

Prologue

The cool monsoon river breeze blew against her face, making her curls flutter. She loved the sight of clouds clearing the sky, making way for the rays of the sun. After the customary sun worship, Rajmata Uttara would always linger to feast her eyes upon the red ball before he turned into a ball of flames, too bright to cast an eye on. Sensing the maids waiting for her, Uttara tore her gaze away from the sky and turned to return to the royal rest house on the banks of Yamuna, close to the city of Indraprastha. This was a site she had carefully chosen for the privacy it provided her in the Vanaprastha stage of her life, and because it was close to the city. The errand boy bowed to her before leaving for the city on the humble horse cart to get provisions for the next couple of days. The young maid extended her hand to support Uttara on her walk back. A commotion at the end of the usually quiet path leading to the city drew her attention. A grand chariot approached the rest house with the charioteer reining in the Gandhara-bred shell-white stallions to a gentle trot. Uttara's face brightened for a moment before a frown wrinkled her sunburnt forehead. Leaving the maid's hand, she turned the other way, without staying to welcome the visitor. Unmindful of her maid who stood rooted to the spot, facing the biggest dilemma of her life, Uttara turned to walk back to the rest house.

'Grandmother!'

It had been more than a month since she had heard the call. The voice did not lack even an ounce of affection and reverence. But Uttara decided that she was allowed this privilege to sulk against the emperor of Bharatavarsha—the vast expanse from the southern seashores to the heart of the cold snow mountains in the north. Though the original empire under the celebrated ancestor Bharata was much bigger, this was the biggest that the empire had been in recent generations. To his credit, her grandson had proved a worthy successor, carving his own journey in the midst of the agony of losing his father. But the affairs of an emperor could not be an excuse to not visit one's own grandmother. Uttara did not pay heed to his pleas, not until Janamejaya overtook her, blocking her way.

'Grandmother,' he twinkled. 'We both know that you cannot stay angry with me.'

Uttara folded her hands on her chest. That boyish spark only surfaced in his eyes in her presence.

'But tell me, am I the only one to blame? Why do you insist upon staying here instead of your older mansion in Hastinapura? That way, you could command me to present myself in front of you anytime you wished, Grandmother.'

Thanking the gods and ancestors for the simple pleasures she enjoyed, even after nearly losing everything she had loved, Uttara gave in with a majestic wave of her left hand. 'Like I should give up my ashram dharma just so that your horses are saved a ride here.' Turning to the stupefied maid who had not yet decided her course of action between the emperor of the land and the only woman she feared, Uttara instructed her to serve the meal.

After affectionately asking about Rajmata Iravati, her daughter-in-law, the queen of the late emperor Parikshit, and about the well-being of Bhimasena, Ugrasena and Shrutasena, she proceeded towards the spacious portico where she usually had her morning meal. Janamejaya told her about the other developments in Hastinapura and his desire to perform the Ashwamedha. The conversation veered towards the Ashwamedha Yajna conducted by his great-grand-uncle Yudhishtira. The impact of the recollection of the erstwhile empress, Draupadi, was visible on Uttara's face.

An awestruck silence overtook them, each drowned in their own memory. Uttara was remembering her association with her enigmatic mother-in-law, and Janamejaya was thinking about Rishi Vaishampayana's narration of the exploits of his ancestors and their much-celebrated queen. He saw Uttara fiddle with her silvery white plait, still long and lustrous, despite her ripe age of nearly eighty springs.

'You lost a lot in the great war, Grandmother,' he murmured, shuddering while he imagined the dance of destruction at Kurukshetra. 'Was there ever an occasion when you felt your life would have been better had you not married into the Pandava household?'

'Depends upon how one defines the word "better", Janamejaya,' Uttara replied, still staring into space, as if she was viewing the incidents of her past right there.

Janamejaya moved closer, taking his place by her feet. 'After listening to the most learned rishis of Bharatavarsha for days, I have still not been able to come to terms with my father's death, Grandmother Uttara. How can I even dare to imagine how it must be for you who lost...' he could not complete the sentence, partly out of the numbness his empathy generated and partly because he did not want to refresh her moments of bereavement. Uttara had lost her father, brothers, and a very young husband with whom she had hardly spent a year of marital life, to the war at Kurukshetra. Her unborn child, Parikshit, Janamejaya's father, had escaped from an episode of horrific midnight slaughter.

'Everyone lost someone dear to them in the war, Janamejaya,' Uttara sighed. 'My marrying into this household at least gave me the satisfaction of bearing an heir to this empire. In fact, I am proud that the thought of unborn Parikshit gave the much-needed hope and strength to Uncle Yudhishtira to take up the reins of this devastated land. I had the good fortune of being a daughter to Mother Draupadi when she lost everyone born of her womb to that midnight slaughter.'

Janamejaya's eyes filled with a sense of admiration. 'Old men and women at Hastinapura still blame Empress Draupadi and her anger for their losses in the battle.' With a pained shrug, he added, 'The gap of understanding that exists between the wise and the mundane.'

'As the emperor, it is your dharma to dispel misunderstandings surrounding the history of this land, Janamejaya,' Uttara's voice was stern. 'The whole point of reciting the records of the past is to learn from the exploits of our ancestors, take pride in their valour, strength and courage, while gaining wisdom from the stories of their tribulations. If people judge their ancestors because of false notions about history, it is only a matter of time before the population is uprooted from the values their ancestors fought for, and falls apart.'

Janamejaya nodded. 'That is the reason why I have impressed upon the rishis and acharyas to impart the timeless record of Bharata to students while they acquire education from their gurus. I have also appealed to the erudite disciples of Bhagavan Veda Vyasa to conduct recitation sessions in public gatherings during the festivities.'

Uttara smiled in satisfaction at his genuine attempts. 'Janamejaya, lazy intellect puts the blame of the Great War on one person. Those who truly understood what led to the eighteen-day-long slaughter at Kurukshetra would reflect on the events and choices of three of the four generations that led the entire empire to war. Blaming someone like Mother Draupadi is not only foolish but also a disturbing sign of misogyny that would be frowned upon by the learned rishis who recorded history and composed the timeless story. Mother Draupadi, in fact, saved the empire from many disasters with the sheer power of her desire to protect this land.'

Janamejaya listened to her animated discourse and smiled. 'Grandmother Uttara, I have never seen a woman defend her mother-in-law with the passion that you did just now. Pray, tell me the story again, this time through her eyes.'

Uttara rejoiced at Janamejaya's undying enthusiasm to listen to the tale of his ancestors repeatedly. Very few were fortunate enough to carry the legacy that he did and even fewer realized and strived to live by it as he did. She was more than delighted to narrate the tale, especially from the perspective of the woman who had captured her respect, awe and love for this life and the lives to come—from the perspective of Draupadi.

Part One

Princess *of* Panchala

One

The Banishment

She woke up with a start.

The nightmare seemed real. The senior nurse ran to comfort the little princess.

'You are safe, my princess…'

'Where are they?' Princess Draupadi demanded. Traces of defiance surfaced on her face and fear had no option but to bow out. She saw the nurse exchange an uncertain glance with the other female attendants.

'Who do you talk about, my dear?'

'Father, Shikhandi, Satyajit, Dhrishtadyumna… They have to be saved!'

The nurse held her by her arms, brushing her lustrous curls. 'They are all in the court, Princess. You must go to sleep.'

'But they were in danger!' Draupadi protested, attempting to jump off the bed. In the lamplight, the attendants who blocked her way saw her eyes turn crimson. There was something about the anger of this ten-year-old princess that made them shudder. The only person in the royal household of Panchala they feared more than her was King Yajnasena Drupada himself. Even the Crown Prince Dhrishtadyumna, who was quick to anger, did not inspire the awe that she did. The very friendly Shikhandi and the quiet Satyajit, not more than Shikhandi's shadow, came nowhere near in wielding the authority that she did at her age.

'That was just a nightmare, my lady,' the nurse smiled. 'Come back to bed, or else your father will get angry.' She hoped to convince the princess using her father's name, but tonight, the ten-year-old Draupadi was too possessed by her nightmare to fear anything else. The nurse shrugged when she saw the princess bite the arm of the female guard who was trying to stop her.

'You cannot go to the court like this!' the nurse hissed, pointing at Draupadi's crumpled silks and dishevelled hair. Even this attempt to stop the princess was futile. 'Idiots! Catch her!' she shouted at the sleepy guards. 'If she reaches the court in that state, some of us are going to lose our jobs!' she screamed at the two guards who were pursuing her.

The guards outside the entrance of the courtroom were also surprised when Draupadi stormed in. She saw her father and brothers stop their conversation abruptly to look at her.

'Father!' she screamed.

Drupada opened his arms to take her into a comforting embrace. What Draupadi missed was his discrete nod to Satyajit. Draupadi sat on his lap and turned to face her brothers, all of them sporting a smile. Fake smiles to fool her into thinking that everything was fine. Shikhandi's smile faded earlier than the others. Something told her that everything was not all right.

'Go back to bed, little one,' Drupada kissed her on the forehead and looked at Satyajit who came forward. 'You must sleep now. Else, the boys will go off to ride the horses at dawn without you,' Drupada added with a grin.

Draupadi could not protest. She studied Dhrishtadyumna's face and then Shikhandi's, letting Satyajit lead her away. There was an undercurrent of sibling rivalry between the older princes of Panchala and she was not a stranger to it. But today, it seemed much graver than anything that had happened before. 'Tell me the truth, Satyajit,' she pleaded. 'Did they fight again?'

Satyajit shook his head and tried to smile her question away. Halfway through the corridor, behind the courtroom that led to the inner compartments, Draupadi loosened herself from his grip. 'Something is wrong! Isn't it, Satyajit?'

The youngest prince of Panchala sighed. He could not lie to her. She wielded a strange power over the men of the family. Many had dismissed the trait by calling it the typical pampering of the youngest child, something that doubled in magnitude if the last child was a girl after three boys. But Draupadi was very different from a pampered princess. Satyajit feared she would sulk if he lied to her and she found out about it. She was bound to know sooner or later.

'Listen to me, little sister,' he knelt down, holding her arms. 'Shikhandi is going away. For good.' Satyajit saw her pupils dilate and lips part. He held her tighter. 'We can't do anything about it. He risked doing something stupid. Stupid enough to earn us the wrath of Hastinapura.'

To his relief, Draupadi did not make a dash towards the courtroom again. But her limbs froze, and so did her eyes, till tears fell from them.

'Will the armies of Hastinapura attack us?'

'Not yet,' Satyajit assured. 'Not if they know that Shikhandi was banished for his folly.'

'Can we not meet him ever? Ever?'

Satyajit thought quickly. Secretly, he liked Shikhandi more than Dhrishtadyumna. He felt Draupadi shared the sentiment. But there was little they could do now. Dhrishtadyumna would not be of much help. He pursed his lips for a while, wishing he had a solution. 'Guru Upayaja might know. He is sure to watch over Shikhandi.'

'Can we ask Guru Upayaja to help us meet Shikhandi?' Draupadi's voice broke at the end.

'As soon as this matter dies down,' Satyajit assured her. He saw her rush to the latticed window that overlooked the courtroom, just in time to see Shikhandi leave the courtroom. He shared a glance with Draupadi and they rushed to the terrace of the palace to see the departing figure of Shikhandi move towards the gates.

'I hate Hastinapura. I hate everyone associated with that place!' Draupadi hit her fist against the wall.

'Not a word about Hastinapura!' Satyajit covered her lips with his right palm. 'I beg you, Draupadi.'

More tears flowed from her eyes. Wrath and grief alternated on her tender face. Satyajit himself was in no position to console the child.

'What did Shikhandi do? Why can't father save him?'

'Something got into him!' Satyajit wrung his hands. He dreaded telling her the details of what Shikhandi had done in the frenzied belief that he was the reincarnation of a mad princess of the past.

'Reincarnation of whom?'

'Amba of Kashi,' Satyajit whispered.

Satyajit told her the bizarre stories of the past that he had heard the previous day. They were about the princess of Kashi who had been in love with someone else, but had been abducted by Bhishma—the patriarch of Hastinapura—for his brother. The headstrong princess had protested the wedding, citing that her heart belonged to someone else. But when Bhishma had sent her back to her lover, it had been futile as the false pride of the man had come in the way of accepting his beloved. The norms of the day had left Amba at the mercy of Bhishma who had also refused to marry her because of his vow of celibacy. She had then spent the rest of her life trying to woo warriors, kings and sages, to kill Bhishma—as revenge.

Satyajit then recounted the various speculations about whom she had approached. 'Father still remembers the day she came to our Kampilya. She was in her sixties, spent with rage and frustration. But the feeling of vengeance had only grown with her age. Mother was pregnant with Shikhandi then and had fainted, hearing Amba's scream for revenge,' Satyajit narrated what Guru Upayaja had told him.

'Amba wanted Father to fight Bhishma?' Draupadi frowned.

Satyajit nodded. Draupadi guessed that Drupada had rejected her plea, which had made her curse his family.

'She cursed the unborn Shikhandi first. Then, she threatened to kill herself so that she could be born in our household to take revenge on Bhishma. Father asked his guards to take her away. A few days later, her corpse was found in the outskirts of Panchala, in a half-burnt state, allegedly attempting some ritual that had gone wrong.'

Satyajit bit his lip, realizing he had gone too far in narrating the details. But he saw her listen in quiet pain instead of shock.

'But what did Shikhandi do to bring the past back?'

'He started believing that he indeed is the reincarnation of Amba…' Satyajit tried, unsuccessfully, to shield the last bit of detail from her. 'We can no longer call him our…brother.'

Two

The Defeat

Three years later...

Satyajit suppressed a groan when Draupadi applied the medicine over his wounded arm. The burning sensation, however, did not dampen his elation, or that of Dhrishtadyumna. They had returned victorious. Draupadi looked longingly at their battered armours. Her own armour lay aside, as if it had come from the forge the day before. Dhrishtadyumna laughed, sensing her desire. 'Not while we are alive, little sister.' He kissed her on the forehead. It was a rare act of affection and Draupadi gauged that her older brother must have been overjoyed to express his love this way. 'In fact, those Kuru princes proved to be disappointing opponents.'

'Why did they attack us in the first place?' Draupadi asked. She had just learnt from Acharya Upayaja that the neighbours on the banks of Ganga had been Panchala's allies.

Dhrishtadyumna shrugged carelessly. 'Their senses had taken leave of them, I guess.' After a loud chuckle, he looked at her. 'I am sure the poor descendants of Kurus now have a reason to feel ashamed every time this incident is thought of.'

Not satisfied by his rhetoric, Draupadi looked at Satyajit. But before the younger prince of Panchala could oblige her, the attendants announced the entry of King Drupada. The king of Panchala was in an even better mood than his sons. 'Now now, where is the embodiment of all my good fortunes?' he grinned, looking at Draupadi, who ran into his arms. Over thirteen autumns, she was still his youngest, and he held her as he had when she was a toddler.

'What should we do with the prisoners, Father?' Dhrishtadyumna asked, earning a frown from Satyajit for worrying over tasks when celebrations were due.

'Feed them well tonight and send them back home wiser,' Drupada guffawed. 'Perhaps the cooks at the Kuru kitchens did not feed those poor boys well. Why would they? Their parents, the king and queen of Hastinapura, are blind to the world. The servants must have the time of their lives there! This also explains the folly of the boys!'

Draupadi looked at her brothers chuckling at Drupada's rhetoric. But nothing explained why the princes of Hastinapura had attacked Panchala. It was not surprising that her father and brothers had won the battle with ease. The inexperienced princes lacked in all aspects, right from strategizing a battle to fighting in one. She heard her father and brothers discuss the battle in detail; at times, their voices betrayed their feeling of triumph.

The palace maids appeared, carrying sweetmeats in enormous plates. Drupada's eyes lit up on seeing the arrangements for the celebration. He brushed Draupadi's hair tenderly. 'So, you've assumed control of the palace in our absence, little one.'

Draupadi nodded, pleased. It meant a lot when the compliment came from her father. Drupada was not a tough

9

taskmaster. But he expected one to be committed to the tasks and deliver as promised.

'Even the arrangements at the temple of Lord Mahadeva for the evening worship are done, Father,' Draupadi beamed. 'I know that we share the moments of joy with Him before we celebrate publicly.'

'As you wish, Your Highness!' Drupada bowed in mock courtesy and laughed when she frowned. 'After all, you are *my* daughter, Draupadi. I expect you to adhere to what we stand for.'

Drupada and his sons went for a quick bath before starting for the temple of Mahadeva, at the outskirts of Kampilya, the capital of Panchala. The spacious temple premises had been cleared for the evening worship. Drupada and his children descended from their chariot and entered the temple, accompanied by minimal security. Drupada had learned from his ancestors that one never went to the temple of Mahadeva with royal pomp. The god believed in humility. Drupada himself was dressed in modest clothing and jewellery and carried just a sword. His children had done the same. The priest started the elaborate ritual while the royal family sat patiently, their eyes closed in gratitude and devotion.

It was Satyajit who first felt the movement behind him. Opening his eyes, he found nothing. He turned back to participate in the puja. But something kept nagging him. Perhaps, it was just a remnant feeling from the battlefield.

Suddenly, he felt a hand upon his shoulder. Turning left, he saw Dhrishtadyumna put a finger on his lips. There was surely someone else in the premises of the temple. Making no sound, the brothers shared a glance and rose to their feet. Grabbing their weapons, they hurried out of the garbhagriha—sanctum sanctorum—in search of the intruder.

Draupadi felt a movement behind her and turned. Finding the boys missing, she shook Drupada. But the king of Panchala frowned at her and closed his eyes again.

'The boys are not here, Father!' she whispered, knowing that they would not leave a puja midway without a good reason.

Drupada opened his eyes and felt for his sword beside him. Unsheathing the weapon, he pulled his daughter closer. Something indeed felt wrong. He was about to stop the priest and ask him if he had noticed anything unusual. But Drupada decided against it. If there was nothing, he would appear paranoid. He relaxed his hold on the weapon and waited for his sons. There was silence everywhere, except for the chanting of the priest.

Then, many things happened at once.

'Father!' Draupadi shrieked when she saw a weapon pointed at Drupada's neck. A strong hand pulled her away from her father's side, and she saw two boys—one as young as herself, and the other, a bit older but giant-like. They held Drupada by his arms and pinned him down. Draupadi struggled against the strong grip, calling out to Satyajit and Dhrishtadyumna. But she could hear shouts and clangs of blades outside. The sons of Drupada were also engaged in a tussle!

Draupadi dug her teeth into the one who held her and bit hard. The hands clenched her more tightly, but did not let go of her. 'Shhh! You will not be harmed, Princess.'

Frowning, Draupadi pushed hard, digging her nails into his hands, and almost managed to break away. But he held her arm before she could get far enough to raise an alarm. To her dismay, she saw Drupada, overpowered by the two boys, being taken out of the temple.

'Let us go, Eldest,' one of them called out.

11

Then, the hands let go of her. Grunting hard, she attacked her captor, taking her sword. But he caught it and beamed, patting her cheeks. 'You father must be proud of you, Princess. But now, be wise and go home.' The kindness in his voice caught her unawares. Taking advantage of her daze, he slipped away, following his younger brothers.

Recovering from the daze, Draupadi rushed out, towards the great bell in the courtyard. There was no trace of Satyajit or Dhrishtadyumna. She wondered if they had been captured as well. Even then, they would not have crossed the border of Kampilya. She could still raise an alarm, directing the soldiers in to protect Drupada. But before she could ring the bell, a hand clasped over her mouth. Draupadi fought back, but recognized the touch. More than the strength of the person, shock overcame her. She felt angrier with him than with the strange boys who had captured Drupada. In fact, they had been able to do it only because of this...

Traitor!

Three

Drona and Drupada

'What is happening?' Satyajit's voice was frantic. He got no response from Dhrishtadyumna who paced across the hall, waiting for the generals and the wise Upayaja to join them for the emergency council. The brothers, in their desperation, had not noticed the stoic Draupadi who was thinking of something else.

'For all their morals, the Kurus turned out to be back-stabbing rats!' Satyajit added and then turned to the entrance when Upayaja entered. Dhrishtadyumna collapsed on his seat, a multitude of speculations clouding his mind. With the king of Panchala captured by the Kurus, they were soon going to face high demands. In the light of the events of the past few days, chances of retaining his life seemed bleak.

'Crown Prince Dhrishtadyumna, Prince Satyajit, Princess Draupadi! Not the time to panic,' Upayaja counselled. 'A war with the Kurus will only cause more damage to the already questionable relationship.'

'Why was he captured when we had nothing against the Kurus, Acharya?' Draupadi asked, her calmness contradicting her brothers' emotions.

'The capture was a result of the whimsical demand of the Kuru preceptor Dronacharya,' Upayaja narrated. 'In his younger days, your illustrious father and the warrior Brahmin Drona were friends, seeking tutelage under Bhagavan Rama of the Bhargavas. In one of his boyish moods, your father had promised to share half of his kingdom with Drona.' He paused, seeing the look of disbelief on Dhrishtadyumna's face.

'Obviously, the promise was not kept when Drona turned up at Panchala's door to claim his "share". I was one of those who advised the king against keeping such ridiculous "promises",' Upayaja recounted. 'But the king went overboard in ridiculing the Brahmin over his unrealistic expectations. That did not go well.'

'But Dronacharya must have nursed his anger for long enough to respond this way,' remarked a surprised Draupadi. Upayaja could not help but smile at her perceptiveness— something that the boys did not possess. 'His offer to allocate land for a gurukul and extend patronage for life came after the damage was already done to the Brahmin's ego.'

Dhrishtadyumna's impatient grunt drew their attention. 'Those upstart Kuru princes had come to avenge their beloved "guru". We taught them a lesson for life. But *this* has to be the result of treachery.'

Draupadi looked at him, eager to share what she had discovered during her fateful encounter with Drona's disciples. Before words could escape her lips, a sense of foreboding stopped her.

If she spoke the truth, she knew things would get worse.

'The Kuru elders are reasonable people, who will be open to negotiation,' Upayaja's counsel interrupted her thoughts. 'Besides, I think we badly need someone to be back with us this moment.'

Draupadi turned towards the door. Satyajit and Dhrishtadyumna too looked out for the solution Upayaja was hinting at. The brothers were shocked when a familiar figure strode in. So shocked that they failed to notice Draupadi's lack of enthusiasm.

'Shikhandi!' Satyajit rushed down the couple of steps and threw his arms around the long-lost sibling. Even the usually hostile Dhrishtadyumna came forward in an open welcome.

'A very unfortunate occurrence indeed!' the eldest child of Drupada spoke even before he took the seat offered by Dhrishtadyumna.

'Where were you all these days?' Satyajit enquired.

'Hastinapura. In disguise, of course!' Shikhandi replied, fatigue showing in the darkness under his eyes. He saw Satyajit and Dhrishtadyumna look at him with renewed hope.

Like he could save their father.

'As soon as I heard the news, I had to reveal myself to the Kuru elder, Vidura. He assured me that the royal council of Hastinapura had nothing to do with this capture and he would urge Guru Drona to release our father,' Shikhandi's words were hurried. The confidence in his eyes, however, evaporated when he met Draupadi's unforgiving gaze. He broke away from the guilt that hit him and looked at Satyajit. 'However, it is the noble Vidura's well-meant advice that we part with a principality of Panchala as a token apology and make peace with Drona.'

'No way!' Dhrishtadyumna cried. 'We should demand that our father be released without conditions!'

'It is not a condition, brother. And when will you start appreciating the nuance here?' Shikhandi chided. Probably, for the first time in his life, he prevailed over the otherwise favoured Dhrishtadyumna. 'Say, we convince the Kurus to release our father. Say, the good Kurus even manage to do that. In return, that would only anger Drona who will leave them in a moment, and possibly join a common enemy. Maybe Jarasandha of Magadha,' Shikhandi's voice assumed a new level of authority with every sentence. The ensuing silence only encouraged him. 'And that military teacher knows secrets that the Kurus hold dear. Like the strengths and weaknesses of each of their princes, defence strategies and what not!'

Dhrishtadyumna was about to say something when Upayaja intervened. 'And we need to be careful because if things happen as per Shikhandi's speculations, Drona's angry exit will damage both our kingdoms.'

'But, Acharya, parting with a principality—it will cost Panchala her pride!'

Shikhandi sighed, signalling Upayaja to stop. 'A bit of pride is worth a long-term friendship with the Kurus who are bound to feel apologetic for what their princes did to satisfy the preceptor's whims.'

Disgust had not left Dhrishtadyumna's face. Satyajit remained unconvinced too. But in the long wordless debate for a better solution, the sons of Drupada lost. 'Get our father back, Shikhandi.' Dhrishtadyumna's shoulders slumped at last. 'I shall relinquish the position of his heir in your favour. Do whatever but bring him back safe.'

Shikhandi's eyes blurred for a moment. 'Where did the relinquishing part come from, brother?' He saw Dhrishtadyumna's eyes soften for the first time. 'It was never about the inheritance, brother. You shall remain the heir.'

Dhrishtadyumna, known to be stoic, needed all his strength to keep his tears at bay. 'Welcome back, Shikhandi.' He left abruptly and they all knew why.

Shikhandi saw Draupadi rise and follow Satyajit. 'Little sister.' Her footsteps showed no signs of slowing. 'Unhappy to see me return?' he called out but in vain. He saw Satyajit disappear into the adjoining corridor. 'Why did you keep quiet when you knew?'

Draupadi halted. The masked traitor who gave away their father. She had known who it was, all this while! She pursed her lips for the words that raged in her would only hurt him. She wanted to hurry out but could not. Shikhandi had caught her arm.

'Don't you walk away, little sister.'

'Don't you call me that!' she tried to break away.

Shikhandi did not let go and pulled her towards the empty room. 'Draupadi, you need to hear me out!'

'Another tale of assumed righteous revenge. Forgive me, Shikhandi, My heart can't melt for traitors!'

'It is not about revenge, sister. I can't be angry with our father. I only wanted to come back home.'

'Stop cheating yourself, brother!' Draupadi shook his grip away. 'Relationships—they don't heal or build upon falsehoods, Shikhandi! Or upon treachery.'

Shikhandi dropped to his knees. 'You don't know what it means to be *me*, Draupadi.' He tenderly brushed her cheek, her stern expression no longer bothering him. 'And I wish you never know. But thank you for not blurting out the truth.'

'I only saved a fight between my siblings,' Draupadi remained unshaken. 'You don't know what this will lead to, Shikhandi.'

Four

The Fire Pledge

Three years had passed since Drupada's capture and subsequent release. Upon intervention from the Kuru elders, Drona agreed to let him go in exchange for a principality called Ahichatra, carved out of the northern part of Panchala. Soon after his return, Drupada sent Draupadi to be trained under Upayaja in statecraft. Draupadi now saw her father less frequently. Even during their precious meetings, she could see that he was not himself. The wounds of insult and defeat refused to heal. Worse, they festered in his heart, giving rise to a dark side Draupadi never knew existed within him.

At the end of her training, she was given an affectionate farewell by the indulgent acharya and his wife. With Shikhandi being away from Panchala, only Satyajit arrived to take her back to the palace. She remembered the days of the past when Drupada would personally bring back his sons after the completion of gurukul training. She wondered why he hadn't come for her.

'Where are Father and Dhrishtadyumna?' she asked Satyajit, unable to conceal her disappointment.

'They await your arrival, Draupadi,' Satyajit's tone was graver than usual. Affection and the joy of reunion showed in his eyes, but clouding his characteristic tenderness was a dark tension. Knowing how Drupada and Dhrishtadyumna had become in the recent years, Draupadi could not help feeling sorry for Satyajit. The third son of Drupada drove the chariot towards the yajnashala, where she saw her father and brother dressed in red. A row of palace women waited to extend her a ceremonial welcome.

Ever since she remembered, Drupada would always stop her midway from touching his feet and would embrace her warmly. But today was different—he only stroked Draupadi's head. There was no lack in the affection, but Draupadi could swear that something else had taken over her father. Dhrishtadyumna seemed the same.

Drupada turned around, leading her inside the yajnashala. Draupadi noticed his greying hair. In the past months, he had aged many years. She realized that irritability had become his second nature when she heard him chide the servants for delay in arranging the seats.

Taking her seat along with everyone else around the sacred fire, she sensed the grimness in the air rise. The palace attendants left without daring to seek any gifts on the occasion of her return. Soon, it was only King Drupada, his children, and the priests who sat in the yajnashala.

'My children,' Drupada started. The newly-developed hoarseness in his voice did not escape Draupadi's attention. Something about it shook her from within. 'It has been fifteen springs since the queen, your mother, left this world. I have tried to fill her place to the best of my abilities.' He paused to suppress the lump in his throat.

Draupadi saw Satyajit's eyes moisten at their mother's mention. Even the ever-stoic Dhrishtadyumna's face softened.

19

Having been too young when she had lost her mother, Draupadi had only seen her father care for her and had always thought that he had done his best. Even the palace nurses, she remembered, were wary of his protective aggression for his children.

But why was Drupada talking about those times today?

Drupada continued, 'I hope I get the opportunity to sire children like you in the coming life and the next. Perhaps, play the role of a parent better than I did in this life. But you make me proud, the way each of you have blossomed.' His gaze lingered on Draupadi for a long moment. 'Today, I ask of you, my children, to share my burden, to end what has been consuming me since the fateful spat with the Kuru princes.' To Draupadi's shock, his tone became harsher. 'Unite with me in teaching those Kurus a lesson they will not forget. No, a lesson even their descendants will not forget for aeons to come!'

Dhrishtadyumna's eyes turned crimson, mirroring Drupada's rage. Satyajit nodded as if a ghost had possessed his body. Shikhandi was conveniently absent and Drupada did not even seem to care. She squirmed when he turned to her, seeking her affirmation.

What did he expect her to do?

Drupada beamed as if reading her thoughts. 'The boys will do their bit when the opportunity graces them on the battlefield. But you, Draupadi, the dearest of my children, young as you are, your role is going to be critical. More critical than theirs.'

A sense of foreboding overcame Draupadi. She dearly wanted to support Drupada and help him rid all the worries. But the mention of a battlefield and her involvement in 'more critical areas' signalled something wrong.

Drupada stared at the delay in her affirmation and frowned. He then turned to Dhrishtadyumna, making no attempt to hide his displeasure. 'Battlefield might or might not be a possibility. But if it is, will you two fight by my side and claim the lives of those who insulted your father?'

If there ever came a possibility of a battle, the sons of Drupada would undoubtedly fight by their father's side. Any other possibility, Draupadi knew, was unthinkable.

Why was their father asking explicitly?

She saw Dhrishtadyumna move restlessly.

'Would you pledge by the sacred fire, princes of Panchala? Will you end the life of the one who tore your motherland into pieces?' Drupada roared.

Dhrishtadyumna could sit no more. Springing to his feet, the heir of Panchala strode towards the fire and extended his right hand towards the flame. The heat of the fire caught the hair on his arm. But neither the heat, nor the burning pain seemed to deter him. Draupadi winced, seeing his fair palm darken and shake. 'I, Dhrishtadyumna, son of Drupada, take this oath in the presence of Agni, the eternal messenger of the gods. May the God of Fire carry my words to the gods above; let those bear witness to my pledge to avenge my father, my motherland. Let them oversee my endeavour to restore the honour of Panchala by ending the life of that wily Brahmin, Drona. None of my other responsibilities shall come in the way of dispensing this duty of mine. Not even the sin of killing a learned Brahmin will deter me from keeping my word. I shall welcome and bear the consequences, but not let my father's anguish continue. I shall not let my motherland remain unavenged.'

Draupadi saw her father smile in satisfaction, but only for a short moment. He turned to Satyajit, who repeated Dhrishtadyumna's words, but with lesser intensity.

Drupada finally turned to Draupadi who looked at him

21

with mixed feelings. It was endearing, the commitment that her brothers reiterated to regain their lost honour. Shikhandi would have probably laughed at the mention of motherland. But Draupadi knew that he had his own inexplicable ambition to beat the Kurus in some way, and spent any time he could, collecting information about each of the Kuru family members.

But would killing Drona really restore Panchala's honour? Draupadi was not convinced. Drupada called her and she went to sit next to him. A pang of guilt shot through his dark eyes when he brushed her hair. It was a visible struggle between a vengeful king and a doting father. Draupadi dearly hoped that the fatherly side of him would win. But fate decided otherwise. Drupada's festered anger got the better of him. 'You, princess of Panchala, can wreak damage that these boys can't even think of. You shall enter the Kuru household as their daughter-in-law. You shall have the power to shake the very foundation of their arrogance. You shall be the coal that will burn their peace to ashes. That self-righteous, pompous patriarch, Bhishma, will have a good reason to fear us.'

Draupadi felt words desert her at Drupada's schemes, filled with bitterness. Every word of what he said was against the shastras she had learnt in the gurukul. How could she marry into the household that had insulted her home, her father, and her kingdom? Even if the call for vengeance had legitimacy, did it warrant subverting the institution of matrimony? Draupadi was not a believer of doctrines. But narrow-minded subversion of that which bound and propagated humanity and civilization sounded unbecoming of Drupada. It was even more disappointing to see such a downfall in the thought process of a man who had been a loyal husband and a doting father.

Draupadi rose to her feet and walked away from the

yajnashala. She heard Dhrishtadyumna's angry voice calling her back. She heard Drupada telling him to give her time. Boarding the chariot outside, she did not respond to the charioteer's repeated question about her destination. The old charioteer sensed her daze and drove the chariot towards the royal mansion.

For the first time, Draupadi did not feel at home.

Five

Drupada and Jarasandha

'Can we not restore the honour of Panchala without resorting to this?' Draupadi had repeated this question to herself, her brothers, and her father, multiple times in the last one year. She had learnt to ignore Dhrishtadyumna's pleas and taunts. The crown prince had initially made the grave mistake of thinking that she feared setting her foot into enemy territory. His presumptuous assurances of protecting her had only annoyed Draupadi further. Satyajit had gently tried to reason with her and the conversations had always ended without a resolution. Drupada alone had desisted from pressurizing her. But his continued agony worried Draupadi.

She had visited Acharya Upayaja multiple times to discuss the contents of shastras, revisiting the tenets of statecraft, diplomacy, governance, and even the social issue of wedlock. Everything seemed correct from each individual's point of view. Draupadi empathized with Drupada's boiling need for revenge. She understood Dhrishtadyumna's absolute devotion to his father. She accepted Satyajit's silent, unwavering desire to walk with his father, unmindful of the consequences. Yet, the fire pledge to destroy the Kurus seemed wrong. Upayaja could not support her beyond voicing the gravity of the situation and providing an occasional word of encouragement at her determined stance.

Sleepless nights had become a norm in Draupadi's life. Even the senior women of the palace and their advice regarding her blooming youth did little to provide her the peace her mind yearned for.

Through their vast spy network, she also collected information about developments in the Kuru household. All did not seem well at Hastinapura too. She heard about the grand convocation ceremony of the Kuru princes that had taken place about two years ago. She heard about the duel between Prince Bhima and Prince Duryodhana becoming so bitter that they had to be dragged away from the arena and face ridicule by Drona. She heard about the skills that Arjuna had exhibited in archery and how the citizens of Hastinapura had been spellbound. She also heard about the inappropriate challenge he had faced from the son of one of the charioteers at Hastinapura. Vasusena was the name of the archer—popularly known as Karna—who had dared to challenge Arjuna. When his credentials, including his social status, had been questioned, Prince Duryodhana had grabbed the opportunity by making Karna the lord of one of the Kuru principalities, and in the process, he had won Karna's loyalty for life.

Draupadi's keen investigation went beyond what the common people saw. Karna had only a spring or two to go before he saw thirty. He had been an early student in Drona's ashram and had even pursued advanced archery under the tutelage of Rama, the Bhargava himself. Did it seem fair on the part of an experienced archer like him to challenge an archer who was a good twelve or thirteen springs younger to him? Draupadi remembered that Arjuna was only a spring or two older than she was.

Draupadi's interest in the Kuru dynamics grew. The growing hostility between the sons of King Dhritarashtra and the five sons of Pandu, the very princes who had defeated and captured her father, was a reason of worry to every elder in the Kuru household.

'Pray, tell me more about the late King Pandu of Hastinapura,' she asked Acharya Upayaja, one day. 'Why do the spies of Panchala hold him in such high regard? They don't show that kind of regard even for the current king!'

Impressed by the observation, Upayaja answered, 'King Pandu was the hope this broken land of Bharatavarsha was looking for, Princess Draupadi. You have heard enough of Jarasandha of Magadha, who would be the undeclared emperor of this land if not for the vast kingdoms of Panchala and Kuru.' He paused, seeing Draupadi frown. 'King Pandu was a promising nemesis of Jarasandha. He had the charisma that could persuade other kings to grow a spine to stand against the imposing king of Magadha. He proved his valour through various campaigns, keeping death and defeat at bay on the battlefield...' Upayaja sighed midway, betraying his own liking of Pandu. 'As fate would have it, a pleasure trip changed his fortunes.'

'And the five brothers are his sons.' Draupadi continued, 'No wonder the citizens of Hastinapura like them.' It was difficult for her to express admiration for the very brothers who had captured Drupada. But Draupadi knew how to keep personal rivalry away when analysing people.

'That is the mystery,' Upayaja raised a finger. 'They are not Pandu's biological sons. But those begotten through the process of *niyoga*. *Niyoga* was an unconventional process of begetting children, sanctioned by the shastras under exceptional conditions. A childless couple could conceive an heir with the woman seeking the seed of another man and bearing the child who her husband would then take as his.'

Draupadi arched her brows. 'So, did the sons of Pandu face resistance in being accepted by the Kuru household after King Pandu's death?'

'The elders, I hear, love the five brothers—Pandavas, as they are collectively known as—and so do most of the citizens,' Upayaja narrated. 'The resistance is from their cousins, the sons of Dhritarashtra, who see them as contenders to the throne.' He shrugged, 'Citing *niyoga* as a disqualifier sounds petty, given that Pandu and Dhritarashtra were obtained by *niyoga* themselves.'

Every detail about the Kuru past and present seemed to increase Draupadi's fascination. But her enthusiasm had to take a break when the chariot from the palace came to take her home. That day, Draupadi found it difficult to shake off thoughts about the Pandavas. When she shared pleasant moments over the evening meal with her brothers and father, Draupadi could not help wonder how the Kuru dining chamber was like, with the growing animosities.

On one such occasion, when Draupadi was too preoccupied to participate in the conversation between Drupada and Satyajit, they were discussing Jarasandha.

'King Jarasandha seeks a free pass through the highways of Panchala to attack Mathura,' Satyajit shrugged. 'To avenge his dead son-in-law.'

'One free pass, and you never know the damage he might wreak on the way,' Drupada said. Drupada had always maintained his distance from the king of Magadha. Historically, his ancestors and the older rulers of Hastinapura had been allies and this alliance had kept Jarasandha from trying to increase his sway. But with Drona in the picture, Drupada hesitated going against Jarasandha. 'Is that king of Magadha so drunk with vengeance that he wants to attack an insignificant city like Mathura?'

'He has apparently asked the Yadavas of Mathura to surrender the killer of his son-in-law, Kansa. But they seem to love Krishna too dearly.'

Draupadi looked up, startled at the mention of Krishna. It almost never happened that somebody called her by this name. 'Krishnaa' was the fondest name she had been given, because of her dusky complexion. But due to Drupada's extreme attachment to her, the palace nurses had started calling her Draupadi. The pride on the king's face whenever she was called 'Draupadi' was visible.

It was only after some time that Draupadi understood that the subject of conversation was someone else.

'Krishna?'

Satyajit beamed and then shook his head. Before he explained more, Drupada had made up his mind on how to tackle Jarasandha's request. 'The season of harvest is upon us. If we give a free pass to those barbarians from Magadha, they are sure to antagonize our farmers. Things might spiral out of control.'

Satyajit and Dhrishtadyumna nodded. There was a time when they could reject Jarasandha's overtures without worrying about the diplomatic damages. But not anymore. Draupadi could see their faces pale under the weight of the decision.

'Wasn't Jarasandha's son-in-law unpopular among the citizens of Mathura?' Draupadi asked. The news of Kansa's death was too small in Panchala's scheme of things. But Draupadi had enquired about the developments among Kuru neighbours and Kansa's death was something significant there. It meant that the Kuru sway to the east of Ganga till the banks of Yamuna had increased. Now Jarasandha's plan to attack Mathura would challenge the Kuru pride too.

Draupadi felt that it was a boon in disguise. The situation required Drupada to put his desire for revenge aside and become friendly with them to take on Jarasandha. To her dismay, Drupada did not think the same.

'Send for Acharya Upayaja. Let us convey to Jarasandha that they are free to pass through the Panchala lands a month past the harvest,' Drupada smiled meaningfully—the same smile that curved his lips when he secured a diplomatic victory. Draupadi understood why. A month post harvest would mean that the armies of Magadha would land at the doors of their enemy post summer—something Jarasandha would not prefer. Monsoon was not a season suitable for a battle. A delay of an entire cycle of seasons meant a lot of uncertainty for Jarasandha.

'If Jarasandha is shrewd enough, and he is,' Drupada continued, 'he will read more into our message and see the intent beyond the words.'

Did this mean that Drupada was thinking of allying with Jarasandha in the future? Draupadi looked at her father in dismay. Even Dhrishtadyumna and Satyajit weren't pleased. They had all grown up with the idea that Jarasandha represented everything that was wrong in the land of Bharata.

Draupadi knew that Drupada would not consider allying with Magadha if he could find a way to exact his own revenge from the Kurus, and she, Draupadi, was standing in his way by not agreeing to marry into the Kuru family. She retired with mixed thoughts, to another sleepless night. She dearly wanted to

29

stop her father from walking on this path of destruction. Hope was not something that graced her that night, but Draupadi's determination was ready for a fight—with hopelessness, with destiny, with anything that could put a halt to this adharma.

Six

Rukmini

Kashi

The river breeze brushed her face. Draupadi gazed at the million lamps that swayed to the resonating rhythm of the hymns sung by the devotees and pilgrims on the banks of Ganga. The perennial river that cradled the civilization in the northern plains flowed through Panchala too. But the grandeur she acquired at the abode of Lord Vishvanatha was incomparable. The royal family's visit to Kashi, however, Draupadi knew, had nothing to do with devotion. At eighteen springs, her understanding of the power struggle in northern Bharatavarsha was beyond her years.

Drupada's participation in the festivities of the Kartik month at Kashi spoke of his inclination towards Jarasandha who had called for this ostentatious festivity as an excuse to consolidate his power. The king of Kashi played the role of a mute host in the event. Draupadi saw her father and brothers immersed in the ritual aarti after their conference with the kings. The encampments erected for each royal family stood to her right, Panchala's being one of the most luxurious ones. Unable to concentrate on what she felt was everything but a show of devotion, Draupadi walked on the decorated path around the encampments. The path was adorned with pots of flowers, and various fragrances greeted her.

Something disturbed her about this visit to Kashi—the kings and their power games, all under the pretext of the holy festival of Kartik.

'Is the god of gods also a mute spectator?' Draupadi wondered to herself, almost aloud, unmindful of the guards of various royal retinues. Her attire and the shining Panchala medallion got her reverential bows and nods from everyone she encountered. The nods turned into frowns behind her as each of them wondered what a princess like Draupadi was doing without her personal guard, away from her encampment. But her decisive gait deterred them from approaching her.

Lost in her troubled thoughts, in pursuit of a solution that did not seem to exist, Draupadi strode on—until a scream fell upon her ears. It was the scream of a woman. Draupadi instinctively walked towards the enormous tent, which belonged to one of the royal families.

'Shame on you all! I am ashamed to be called your sister! You are no more than Jarasandha's concubine!'

Draupadi flinched as she heard a resounding slap, followed by another scream.

Concerned, she darted towards the entrance of the tent. The woman she saw was of her age, struggling against the man's grip on her hair. Draupadi's fingers curled. The man saw her and let go of his sister. Draupadi witnessed a dramatic change in his demeanour.

'Welcome, Your Highness,' he beamed, signalling to one of the attendants to bring refreshments. 'Welcome to the home of Vidarbha. A temporary home though,' he chuckled at what he thought was a joke.

Draupadi's gaze was, however, on the maiden, the princess of Vidarbha who was fixing her hair without looking at her guest.

Prince Rukma, as he introduced himself, turned to his sister. 'We can expect esteemed guests anytime here, dear sister. You cannot afford to roam around with dishevelled hair like this,' he grinned.

Draupadi saw the princess of Vidarbha glare at her brother for a moment before acknowledging her arrival with a polite nod.

'It must have been a long walk from your tent to here,' Prince Rukma said, looking over Draupadi's shoulder in search of her carriage.

Draupadi smiled back and said nothing.

'I shall escort you back, Your Highness,' Rukma volunteered.

Draupadi was about to reply when she saw the princess of Vidarbha frown and then turn to Rukma. 'Brother Rukma, isn't sister-in-law, the future queen of Vidarbha, waiting for you to join her for the evening worship?'

Rukma's smile faded at the mention of his wife. His sister responded with a measured smile and turned to Draupadi.

'After the esteemed princess of Panchala is refreshed, I shall stand by our word and escort her in my chariot.' The tinge of triumph in her tone was not lost on Draupadi.

Strange dynamics between a brother and a sister!

'I would hate to delay Your Highness when your better half awaits you,' Draupadi bowed as Rukma left, making little effort to conceal his displeasure at being hustled out by the women.

When the princess of Vidarbha excused herself after instructing the maid to fan the guest, Draupadi followed her to the inner section of the tent. A strange feeling of camaraderie drew her to the feisty princess of Vidarbha. Draupadi smiled, seeing her struggle with braiding her hair.

Probably someone used to maids grooming her.

Draupadi, proficient in braiding, stepped forward and took the bejewelled comb in her hands.

'Your Highness!'

'Call me Krishnaa,' Draupadi grinned. None except Shikhandi called her by that name. She saw the princess of Vidarbha stare at her for a long moment.

Like the name melted something in her.

'I'm Rukmini,' she sighed, her gaze turning warmer. 'Please don't trouble yourself, Krish...naa!'

But Draupadi's attention was on Rukmini's hair. Well-oiled and braided hair dishevelled by a violent encounter. She knew that asking about it or about the welts on Rukmini's cheek would be venturing into tricky waters—it would be interfering in family matters. But the pain that shot up in Rukmini's eyes when her fingers brushed across her cheek was enough for Draupadi to speak out.

'Why was your brother manhandling you that way, Rukmini?'

Rukmini shook her head and let Draupadi braid her hair. Tears of fury dropped now and then from her eyes until a resolute calm took over her. It was only when they were alone in the chariot that Rukmini spoke up. 'I protested, Krishnaa. I protested against a complete stranger deciding my fate, and placing my hand in those of his protégé in marriage.'

Draupadi listened, remembering what she had heard the preceding day—about Rukmini's engagement to Shishupala, the prince of Chedi. The match had been made by Jarasandha of Magadha, the de facto emperor whose name caused awe or fear among every ruler of Bharata.

And her own father, who had stood up to Jarasandha all these years, had accepted the latter's invitation to this 'festival'!

Both of them moved towards the chariot outside.

'Was your consent…?' The rest of the question remained on Draupadi's lips as she saw Rukmini shake her head and whip the horses into a canter. 'How could they do that?' A part of her marvelled at Rukmini's hold on the horses. The frown on Rukmini's forehead became more pronounced as she debated discussing her mind with Draupadi.

'This is my battle. If I do not protest, I shall become a misplaced example of an "ideal daughter" by the sold-out bards who surround that monster Jarasandha! If they succeed in sealing my fate, more princesses of Bharata shall fall to his devious plans! He has to be stopped and it has to be now!'

Jarasandha's crafty strategies to dominate other rulers through marital alliances was not new to Draupadi. A generation of princes and noble maidens had given into his plans and indirectly ceded control to him. But a princess standing up to his plans was a first. Draupadi dearly wished she could help Rukmini somehow.

'How long will you protest, Rukmini? And how far can you go?'

Rukmini beamed, 'I am not alone, Krishnaa.'

Draupadi wished Rukmini would tell her more. But the princess of Vidarbha remained tight-lipped. When the camp of Panchala arrived, Rukmini politely refused Draupadi's offer to return the hospitality. 'Krishnaa, had my brother escorted you back in his chariot, in the view of everyone here, can you imagine what kind of statement it would have made?'

Draupadi chuckled at Rukmini's speculations. 'My father

and brothers are yet to come under Jarasandha's influence and barter my hand this easily.'

'King Drupada, I know, is far too principled,' Rukmini's gaze turned stern. 'But do not underestimate the craftiness of the king of Magadha, Krishnaa.'

Rukmini's warnings could not be taken lightly. But Draupadi could not imagine Drupada giving into Jarasandha's wishes when it came to her own marriage. Her father, who had patiently waited for her to agree to marry into the Kuru household, and was still waiting, would surely not seal her fate without her consent. She could not help feeling bad for Rukmini who seemed all alone in her fight. She affectionately patted Rukmini's arm before alighting from the chariot. 'If and when the need arises, remember you have a sister in Panchala.'

∽

Rukmini remembered her promise soon enough. Two days later, towards the end of the festivities, Draupadi found a desperate Rukmini at the shrine of Lord Vishvanatha.

'The prince of Chedi wants to visit Vidarbha in the coming month of Magha!' Rukmini whispered so that the maids could not overhear. 'I don't want to get stuck hosting him!'

Draupadi thought fast. 'Would you like to join me for a pilgrimage to the northern shrines of Lord Mahadeva? I am sure my father's scribes know how to compose a compelling invitation which your father and brothers won't be able to deny.'

Rukmini's eyes shone with gratitude.

Seven

Krishna, the Friend

Panchala

Draupadi stayed back after the court was dismissed. Drupada's stern brows did not deter her from broaching the topic he had forbidden her from talking about. Drupada was not in one of his best moods and knew of her persistence—a quality he was sure she had inherited from him. But pride was not the emotion Drupada felt for her today. 'I already told you to leave the diplomatic affairs to me, Krishnaa. Very unlike you to meddle into things that don't concern you!'

The lines on his forehead did little to shake her resolve. 'How can an unfair conquest not concern me when my father stands to be a part of the wrong side, My King?'

'If you consider yourself a better judge of fairness than me...' Drupada shrugged, his eyes narrowing in contempt.

'I learnt to separate the fair from the unfair from you, Father. How did we part ways so much that now we support opposing sides?'

Drupada was capable of being angry with anyone until his

death, but when it concerned his daughter, that emotion was an unreliable partner. The mix of earnestness, faith, and persistence in her tone was far too endearing. 'There are no sides here, My Princess,' he assured Draupadi, brushing her hair when she knelt before him. 'It is just about a powerful neighbour, like Jarasandha, wanting a free pass through Panchala to attack a petty province, Mathura, where his son-in-law was murdered. It is about letting a father avenge his widowed daughters.'

'Rukmini of Vidarbha tells me that Jarasandha's son-in-law resorted to all sorts of heinous acts, including killing defenceless infants!' Draupadi looked straight into his eyes.

Drupada sighed, 'Brutal as it might seem, little one, we cannot afford to investigate everyone's crimes. It is Panchala's safety that is paramount when decisions like this are concerned.'

'How long can Panchala remain safe if it lets smaller provinces fall prey to the likes of Jarasandha, Father?'

'It is a tricky decision as far as ethics is concerned, I admit, Draupadi,' Drupada leaned back against the ornate backrest of his throne. 'But with a reduced army, post our ceding Ahichatra to that wily Drona... I have to explore alternatives.'

'Jarasandha can't be your alternative, Father!' Draupadi rose and sat on the hand rest of the throne, on the king's right.

Drupada smiled sadly, a wave of nostalgia overcoming him. 'Idealism, Draupadi, is a luxury you can afford as long as you sit here, on the right of the throne, the rightful place for the children of a king. Come to my place, on the throne, little one. The bitter realities render that luxury unaffordable. Besides, I waited for you to consider turning our fortunes for two years. You aren't ready to become the daughter-in-law of the Kurus. The alternative I am left with is Jarasandha's grandson.'

Draupadi stared at him; she recognized the streaks of

helplessness in his tone. Drupada's final statement had left her mouth dry.

Jarasandha's grandson!

The shock left her rooted to the spot even after Drupada left the throne room.

Restlessness engulfed Draupadi that night. She could not even spend a cordial evening with Princess Rukmini whose visit to Panchala was ending. It did not help when she found out that Rukmini had in fact eavesdropped on her conversation with her father. Even though the princess of Vidarbha apologized, Draupadi was far from feeling at ease. The political turmoil, Drupada's thoughtless reactions, and the undesirable consequences that would ensue, made her toss at night. Realizing her helplessness, Draupadi could only pray for a solution to manifest itself. It irritated her—the sheer lack of control over events. With sleep evading her that night, Draupadi sensed the movement when Rukmini slipped out noiselessly. Partly annoyed and partly curious, she leapt out of the bed and followed her guest into the garden. Rukmini headed out to one of the streets behind the palace garden. Her footsteps seemed to grow frantic with each moment. Draupadi continued shadowing Rukmini and saw the latter come to an abrupt halt by the unguarded gates. She was about to raise an alarm, on finding the guard absent, but stopped when she saw Rukmini throw her arms around a man. A stranger. A stranger who had managed to hoodwink the security ring of Panchala and enter the palace garden. A stranger who, despite breaking into her garden, did not rouse her defences. Curiosity overcame any remnant of concern and Draupadi sneaked closer to the couple, keeping herself hidden in the shadows.

'Forgive me, Krishna!' Rukmini's voice was frantic. 'The king of Panchala does not want to block Jarasandha from attacking Mathura.'

'Shh... Don't blame yourself. You've already risked a lot.'

The voice made Draupadi want to peer out of the shadows and catch a glimpse of Rukmini's lover.

'Enough of all this. I shall come with you right away,' Rukmini sounded determined.

'Not like this, love.'

'Listen to me,' Rukmini insisted. 'If you take me with you, you can threaten my brother, and even Jarasandha might hesitate before he attacks your city.'

The response was an amused laughter. Draupadi could not see them clearly but she felt Rukmini's vehemence rise.

'Rukmini, by eloping from Panchala, we shall only be creating newer animosities, dragging Drupada's family into this political vortex. He has suffered enough. We can't add to their troubles now.'

'Why would you worry about them when they don't care about you?'

Draupadi found herself waiting for the answer as much as Rukmini. Moments seemed to grow longer with his silence. She could not comprehend why she felt that the response would bear any significance. But it came.

'Our mind cares for our limbs. But our limbs don't care for the mind. Do they, Rukmini?'

Draupadi could not help but come out of the shadows. Rukmini did not see her, but she felt that the uninvited guest surely did. However, for some reason, he showed no signs of retreating. In fact, for a moment, she felt small for hiding and eavesdropping on their conversation.

Rukmini remained quiet until restlessness overcame her. "So...you wish that I go back to Vidarbha. Even though...

there are risks.'

His voice turned tender. 'I disappoint you, princess of Vidarbha. Don't I?'

In the dim moonlight, blurred by the clouds, Draupadi could see Rukmini shaking her head.

'You make me stronger, Krishna. I know the risks that follow my return to Vidarbha will affect you as much as they affect me.'

Rukmini took a step backward, her gaze still fixed upon him. Then she retraced her steps towards the palace. She paused when she saw Draupadi but the latter found no traces of guilt on her face. Draupadi wordlessly gestured towards the palace and Rukmini left.

Draupadi turned the other way and had the first glimpse of her namesake that Rukmini swore upon. She saw him smile at her. She was compelled to smile back.

Like she would when she saw the dearest of her friends.

Closing the distance between them with measured steps, she had to put an effort to look solemn. He shared not just her name but also her dusky hue. 'Too brave for an intruder, aren't you?' she said.

'Or too sure that a friend will not be harmed for trying to meet one, where someone like you are in charge, Krishnaa.'

It was the first time that the stranger had taken her name—without a formal salutation. Instead of offending her, it only added to the cordiality between them. Draupadi grinned to herself. She glanced at the retreating form of Rukmini.

Walking back without a care about what she would face at home once she returned.

'What kind of a friend would risk sending back his beloved to face risks?'

'The one who is confident that his beloved can tackle those risks, given her courage and will.'

'Courage and will,' Draupadi repeated, frowning. 'Friendship with someone like you can only invite trouble, it seems,' Draupadi teased.

'You don't seem to be someone who likes a boring life either, Krishnaa.'

Flirtatious flattery was something Draupadi could immediately see through. But his words were much more.

Like a challenge. A challenge she would enjoy.

A thought struck her and her lips flattened. 'If the utility of this friendship is to somehow block Jarasandha's passage to Mathura, I have tried my best, Krishna. And failed.'

'Heard of the folklore? Those with the name can't afford to fail!'

The quip failed to make Draupadi smile. A part of her was sadder than before for not being able to help him. 'You should have instead taken Rukmini with you and left Panchala to deal with the consequences.'

To her surprise, she saw his eyes turn grave. 'A union causing loss of innocent lives cannot be dharma.'

'Can a union against the wishes of the woman be dharma?'

The response was an emphatic shake of his head. 'I shall not take Rukmini with me before securing her future home from Jarasandha's whimsical raids.'

'I love Rukmini like a sister,' Draupadi replied. 'If there was a way to convince the king of Panchala...'

'There is. I know that King Drupada is a reasonable negotiator,' his frown was meaningful.

Draupadi wondered if he knew much more than he seemed to. Before her lips parted, he added, 'You love your father dearly, princess of Panchala. When he realizes that his partnership with Jarasandha caused only meaningless violence, his moral self will be broken. And you would want to do anything to save him from that.'

Draupadi was convinced that he knew a lot about their private lives. That he cared for them as much as he did for his own. And that it was safe to lay bare details before him.

'I don't think you are ignorant about what I can offer him in return to convince him,' it was her turn to sound grave. 'And you just said that a union must not cause violence. It should also not cause a rift in a family, Krishna.'

'King Drupada's anger against the Kurus can be allayed. Only if we allow time to heal his wounds and empower him to see reason. And you, Krishnaa Draupadi, are a strong woman who can protect your home from the gravest of dangers,' Krishna said.

'Be clear about what you seek from me, prince of Mathura,' Draupadi insisted.

Her new friend said, 'I desire that you consider not just Panchala, but the whole of Bharatavarsha as your home, Sakhi.'

Eight

House on Fire

The large hall in Drupada's mansion was quiet except for the rattle of the brass chains that held the huge swing. The king of Panchala had received news that had forced him to rethink all his plans. The five sons of Pandu along with their mother had perished in a fateful fire at Varnavata and rumours claimed that their own cousins, the sons of Dhritarashtra, were the culprits.

'I release you from the pledge, little one,' Drupada looked at his daughter who sat by his side, taking her hand. 'I know about the eldest son of the blind Kuru king. He does not deserve your hand…'

Draupadi held his hand tenderly. The release from the pledge should have relieved her. But the news of the fire accident at Varnavata saddened her. 'They were famed warriors, the sons of Pandu. They did not deserve to die this way.'

Drupada let out a deep sigh. He remembered the moments when the brothers, Bhima and Arjuna, had overpowered and captured him. Despite his best efforts, he could not remain too angry with the two chivalrous lads. His anger had been against Drona. Even against the Kuru patriarch Bhishma for letting the injustice happen. But beyond the initial indignation, he had taken a strong liking to the young warriors and had hoped to turn them to his side by offering Draupadi's hand in marriage. But the death of the five brothers brought a slew of political uncertainties with it. He had risked his relationship with Jarasandha by refusing the king of Magadha a free pass. In turn, the act had won him a note of acknowledgement from Bhishma. But now, with the option of allying with the Kurus not available anymore, there was an urgent need to revive his worsening relationship with Jarasandha. Drupada realized, to his own dismay, he had unwittingly cast Draupadi's future into a morass of power thirst. He looked into her understanding eyes, his chest constricting at the thought of how he had failed her as a father.

And how she had stood by him as his daughter.

Holding back the lump in his throat, he brushed her long curls. 'Forgive me, little one.'

Draupadi tried to respond with a playful pat on his arm, 'You did not kill my future groom, Father.'

Her father shook his head. 'It took his death to make me realize how I used my little one's future as a tool to achieve my shallow aims.'

Draupadi looked up. She knew her father loved her dearly. She also knew that he often forgot himself in his frenzied emotions, be it rage or excitement. Yet, this was the first forgiveness he had sought from one of his children.

'For once, forget the political struggle, Draupadi. Take charge of your future and carve it out to your fulfilment,' Drupada declared. He had able sons who could take up the reins of power. He owed his daughter a life of her choice. But, unfortunately, there was little time left. Something had to be done before Jarasandha came up with another shady attempt to dictate the future, and dragged Draupadi into it. 'How about a swayamvara? Say, a gathering of all eligible suitors where you can make your final choice—square and fair, without allowing for any speculations?'

That very moment, a guard interrupted the conversation, informing them about the arrival of guests from the newly-built port city of Dwaraka.

Draupadi beamed and took Drupada's leave to welcome Krishna, and possibly, his newly wedded bride. A lot had happened since her last meeting with him. She rushed out of the royal mansion into the sprawling garden where the fragrance of seasonal blossoms greeted her along with the spring breeze. Her heart leapt when she saw the familiar figure alighting from the chariot, which was sporting the majestic eagle banner. Draupadi saw a couple of commoners as well as guards and palace folk, men and women, gather around the chariot. Krishna Vasudeva's meteoric rise had made him a household name. He was heralded as a god, a hero, a leader, and a much-loved and loving friend.

She stopped her guards from hurrying the little crowd and watched Krishna walk towards the mansion, talking to all who sought him.

'Welcome, hope of the aeon,' Draupadi grinned when he reached her.

'Sakhi!' he extended his right hand to brush her curls and held out an intricately crafted wristlet of pearls. 'From your dear friend.'

'Hope she is being treated well in Dwaraka,' Draupadi mocked a frown, clasping the jewel. 'Lest you think Rukmini is now estranged from her natal home, she has an elder sister in Panchala who will not hesitate to pummel down whoever

46

causes her any pain.' Her finger shot up in mock warning and they laughed. A thought struck Draupadi when she remembered the complex familial relationship that existed between the Kurus and Shoora Yadavas, Krishna's family. 'Sakha! You don't look like someone who has lost a dear aunt and cousins to a horrible fire.'

'If my mourning could bring back the dead...'

'No, Krishna!' Draupadi stopped him mid-sentence. 'You have the right to hold back a detail you don't wish to divulge. But pray, don't try humouring me with one of your philosophical arguments.' It was a request, earnest in tone, but firm in stance. The princess of Panchala would not appreciate anything less than an honest admission of what he knew.

Krishna discretely signalled to her and she led him towards her chamber in the western wing of the mansion, out of the earshot of palace folk and possible spies.

'Sakhi, they could be alive. They could be alive and in disguise,' he lowered his voice to a whisper and saw relief in her eyes. But it was short-lived. 'I expect that the king of Panchala is thinking of announcing a swayamvara for you?'

This got Draupadi thinking and Krishna chose to not prompt her thoughts. Rays of the sun fell through the latticed window, making her dusky complexion glow against the reddening light. 'If what you say is true and if there is a swayamvara...it has to have something that can draw them out of disguise. It has to be timed well, giving them a sufficient breather after this heinous attempt to kill them. But it has to be quicker than Jarasandha's next attempt at his expansive ambitions. And if they don't turn up, we have to ensure that undeserving hands don't get to dominate the swayamvara.'

'Should the contest not eliminate such suitors, Krishna?'

Krishna tilted his head. 'If skill and valour was the mirror of one's character, Jarasandha would be a god equivalent, Sakhi.

47

On the other hand, character without skill and valour...' he shrugged, leaving the rest to interpretation.

Draupadi frowned, thinking of the various contests that could challenge the valour of the Pandavas enough to make them come out. But stakes were high and Bharatavarsha had many warriors who equalled them in valour. It did not take her much time to think of the possibilities.

'I should be able to stop a suitor from participating in the contest if I deem him undeserving.'

'It is *your* swayamvara!' Krishna raised his eyebrows. Sharing a knowing glance with her, he added, 'And swayamvaras are meant to make the process of choosing easier. It will be *you* who will set the rules.'

They were interrupted by Satyajit and Shikhandi, who took Krishna with them to the weaponry. A thoughtful Draupadi followed them. Often the power to choose made things more complicated. She was not petty-minded and could not see things just for herself. She had to keep in mind the long-term effects of the alliance.

The men began to talk about the latest developments in forging and breeding of horses in Panchala. Draupadi kept examining the weapons that her brothers used. The mace was Shikhandi's favourite. Even Dhrishtadyumna made efforts to excel at it. The warriors known to have mastered wielding the mace were Balarama, Krishna's brother, and Duryodhana. The only other warrior who could equal them was Bhima, whose whereabout was unknown, and his coming to the swayamvara, almost improbable. The sword was a weapon which never lost its relevance, even in the era when the ability to fight on a chariot was the dominant war skill. The skill of the blade required ultimate courage to take on the enemy at close quarters. But this was a skill learnt by every warrior, right from emperors to foot soldiers. Selecting the best swordsman would be like searching for a garnet lost in a heap of stones.

Draupadi's gaze veered to the bow placed on a pedestal at the centre of the weaponry. It was her father's. The last time he had used it was in the skirmish against the Kuru princes in which he had defeated them all with ease, only to get captured by deceit later. Arjuna. He was the one her father had hoped she would marry. Draupadi kept staring at the bow. If Arjuna really returned as Krishna speculated, she would make this difficult enough to exert his full mettle. Unknowingly, her lips curved while she planned the level of complication for the contest. That would also eliminate many mediocre warriors who would seek her with an intention to ally with Panchala. Standing in front of the bow, Draupadi lost track of time, until Krishna's hand waved before her.

'Decided already?' he let out a gasp of surprise.

She grinned. Jerking her head, she asked, 'Are you planning to take part in the swayamvara, in case...?' She shrugged, prompting him to comprehend her unspoken sentence.

Krishna's eyes widened; he pretended to consider. If Draupadi had not known him enough, she would have easily thought he was interested.

She nudged him, 'You lost it. Don't even dare trying!'

'Trying to make peace between you and Rukmini in case... no, not even in my dreams!' he laughed, earning a glare from her. Sensing something beyond the façade of mock anger, he held her palms, almost cold with an unknown fear.

'You will be here on that day, won't you?' she asked.

'At all costs, Sakhi.'

Nine

Swayamvara

The open court of Kampilya swarmed with royalty from various corners of Bharatavarsha. Decorated extensively for the occasion with exquisite clay art and floral frames, the venue of the swayamvara mirrored the importance of the occasion. A pair of detached eyes scrutinized the place from an overhead balcony, high enough to give her a view of every participant who vied for her hand. Draupadi's gaze toured around the open court and then came to a halt at the centre. The *matsya yantra*. A dummy fish installed on a rotor, overlooking a pool of water reflecting the same. Any suitor who desired her hand in marriage had to string the bow placed there and shoot the moving fish, looking only at its reflection in the water below.

A daunting challenge!

Draupadi could not help but notice that she lacked the trepidation a bride in her place would have experienced. The news of the tragedy at Varnavata had, in a strange way, liberated her from her father's expectation. She was not interested in accepting the alternatives, be it Jarasandha's grandson or the Kuru Crown Prince Duryodhana.

Magadha. Panchala. Kuru. The three powerhouses of

northern Bharata. An alliance between any two could neutralize the third. For this reason alone, Draupadi hoped to not marry either of these suitors. But to her dismay, the other suitors failed. Some were not even able to lift the heavy bow provided for the purpose.

Her gaze fluttered when it fell upon the less ostentatious retinue of Dwaraka, on the man who led the retinue—someone who could win the challenge if he willed so, but chose to remain a spectator today. She could not help but feel a pang of envy for Rukmini.

Suitor after suitor tried and failed, some of them eyeing her with a mix of disappointment and vengeance. Like she was the reason behind the humiliation they faced, and not their desire. She stood there unflinching, a slight curve fixed on her lips. Krishna's words rung in her ears. She looked like a coy bride under her heavily bejewelled attire, but she was seeking a groom who would take her to where she was meant to be—a position where she would stop being a tool and start being an inspiration.

A sudden silence among the crowd shook her out of her reverie. Draupadi saw that the prince of Hastinapura had just retreated after an almost successful attempt at the *matsya yantra*. But the suitor who followed made her lips part.

Vasusena. Radheya. Karna.

The earls announced his exploits. The right hand of Duryodhana. King of Anga.

The radiant archer betrayed his confidence and ease in the way he lifted the bow. But the kingdom he controlled was neither a result of his valour, nor his inheritance. It was a result of charity by the royalty of Hastinapura.

Would he be able to...?

Draupadi strained her eyes as she saw Karna examine the

51

target and then proceed to nock the arrow. She had to act fast.

'Stop!' Draupadi's words reverberated from the high balcony, moments before Karna drew the string. Draupadi exhaled, 'I, Draupadi, cannot marry you, Lord of Anga.' The might of Panchala could not ally with someone who was a shadow of his patron. Draupadi knew that only she could stop it. A murmur rose among the crowd as people exhibited a range of reactions.

Karna froze in his position; his eyes were void of any expression, but his characteristic smile had faded.

'You heard my sister, Sutaputra,' Dhrishtadyumna stepped forward when he saw that the archer showed no signs of withdrawing.

But contrary to his expectation, his words only infuriated Karna. Throwing a contemptuous glance at the crown prince of Panchala and the princess, he resumed his stance.

Draupadi glared at his stubbornness. 'I made myself clear…' The rest of her sentence dissolved in an inaudible gasp at the sound of the twang. The arrow had missed the target by the breadth of a hair! Draupadi as well as the might of Panchala had been saved from allying with a mere yes-man.

A maid came forward to wipe the beads of perspiration from her forehead. Draupadi frowned and fell back. The crowd was too distracted to notice her open relief. With Karna's failure, there was little hope of anyone else succeeding in the daunting task. He was the best archer. The best archer alive. That's what everyone at the swayamvara thought. Everyone except one. Draupadi's eyes moved back to see his suppressed smile. He was the only person who was not shocked at Karna's failure.

'Stay seated, revered Brahmin,' Dhrishtadyumna's words drew Draupadi's attention. She saw her brother call out to a youth clad in white. 'Just because no suitor succeeded does not mean we will not host you for a sumptuous meal,' Dhrishtadyumna grinned.

But the Brahmin approached the *matsya yantra*. For reasons unknown to her, Draupadi's gaze locked on his form. The confidence in his gait—there was something about the Brahmin.

'Can a Brahmin try his luck, noble prince of Panchala?'

The request left Dhrishtadyumna speechless. The Brahmin turned to look at Draupadi. The pronounced curve on his lips drew a smile from her too. 'If I succeed, would the esteemed princess of Panchala be ready to hold the hand of this humble Brahmin, who at the moment, has nothing but his skill of the bow, the love of his family, and an undeterred faith in dharma.'

Draupadi saw the crowd break into laughter. Dhrishtadyumna was trying his best to suppress his grin. She could not laugh. Still locked in his gaze, she nodded. For the first time in her life, the maiden in her dreamt of her future. A future free of political intrigue. A future as a proud bride of a skilled archer. A future as a revered matron of an ashram he would start to train the archers of the next generation. A fulfilled future where she could influence and shape the destiny of Bharata. Her gaze followed the archer who gracefully lifted the bow. The dexterity he displayed in stringing the bow silenced the crowd. Her lips parted at the sight of his arms flexing when he drew the string. She prayed. She prayed for his success and her freedom.

Freedom to break out of the vicious circle of power games.

The anticipation that widened her eyes spoke of the arrows that had already struck her heart. Striking the *matsya yantra* was just a formality now. Only for the best archer alive.

And he, the nameless youth, was the best archer!

Draupadi, to her disappointment, noted that the spectacular achievement did not get the applause it deserved. She saw her father freeze with shock. Her brothers appeared devastated and her sisters-in-law looked at her as if a tragedy had struck her. With a smile fading into a frown, she turned to the musicians who were supposed to announce the groom with resounding trumpets. They hurried to make up for the delay. Ignoring the silent pleas of her female companion to reject the suitor, Draupadi took the heavy garland and approached her groom with measured but proud steps. She could see his eyes widen and then fix upon her in a mix of reverence and admiration. His form was covered in dust, his white garments faded with use. Stepping closer, she noticed the bristles of his beard. Most brides, she had heard, looked away in conventional bashfulness. At the moment, she could look nowhere but at him. She felt he needed her to be by his side when the royal world acted hostile at the feat he had achieved.

She would not let him feel alone, not now. Not ever.

She promised herself, garlanding him.

'Stop insulting the Kshatriya honour, Drupada!' The words came from one of the suitors, impudent enough to take the name of the king of Panchala, despite the age difference. Before Draupadi could see who it was, her husband pulled her behind him. Draupadi remembered being greatly annoyed when Satyajit had, in the past, displayed this level of protectiveness. At this moment, however, she was only amused at his enthusiasm. She saw her brothers gather to pacify the angry guest. But the anger only spread from one suitor to the next. Draupadi suddenly felt movement and turned around to see four men flank her. The slight resemblance between them told her that they were her husband's brothers. Three of them strode ahead of her, while one of them, the eldest, as she realized, stayed by her side. By now, the guards, too, had formed a protective circle around them. But the anger among the guests seemed to rise with each moment.

'Our soldiers shall handle the dissenters,' Draupadi looked at the eldest brother. 'I can take you to safety,' she pointed towards a passage.

The eldest brother beamed in response and declined her offer with a polite shake of his head, his etiquette making her doubt his origin.

'Worry not, Princess,' he smiled. 'If my brothers were not sure of handling the charged opposition, we would not have taken part in the first place. In fact, request your father and brothers to fall back and withdraw the guards too. Let us prove that we truly deserve you in our household.'

The thought of the five brothers with nothing but their weapons pitted against the angry royals seemed bleak. But Draupadi was touched by the confidence the eldest had in his brothers.

With them, she felt safer than ever before.

∽

Draupadi frowned, sensing movement in the humble backyard. She was alone in the small room, wondering what was transpiring between the five brothers and their mother, who had a mixed reaction to the big news. She was taking off her jewellery and smiling to herself, when she sensed a presence in the dimly lit backyard.

'Satyajit!'

'Little sister!'

'Are you spying on your brothers-in law?'

Dhrishtadyumna joined Satyajit, his face stern and decisive. 'Enough of this, Draupadi. Come back home with us.'

'Brother...'

'We shall find an amicable way to compensate the Brahmin brothers,' Dhrishtadyumna declared. 'We can't let you walk into misery…'

'Enough!' Draupadi snapped. She glanced at the entrance where her new family was deep in discussion and turned to glare at her brothers. 'Enough with these absurd ideas. And with spying on my home like thieves.'

'This is madness, little sister,' Satyajit held her. 'You are destined to become a queen, not the bride of a beggar.'

'A beggar indeed! A beggar who took on the entire host of angry royalty and their frenzied soldiers without asking for your help.'

'We promise his valour will be compensated,' Dhrishtadyumna persisted. 'They won't feel slighted.'

'Forget him, I am slighted. By my own brothers, who think their sister values palatial life over a life of austere dignity,' Draupadi turned her back. 'Go away, Dhrishtadyumna.' She stopped in her steps when she saw who had overheard a part of their conversation.

'Go back with your brothers, Princess,' the woman, who was in her fifties, was gentle.

'Mother…'

Draupadi saw the woman smile tenderly and approach her. 'This shack is no place for you, daughter of Drupada.'

'Mother, do you think the daughter of Drupada will shy away from what is right?'

'No, child. Nor shall I let things go wrong. Go with your brothers. I shall seek the king's audience tomorrow to claim my daughter-in-law.'

Draupadi waited for her husband, realizing she had not even asked his name.

'Just this night, Princess. For your honour and mine,' the woman smiled. Draupadi felt compelled to obey.

'For a poor Brahmin woman, she is too regal,' Satyajit remarked later as he helped Draupadi climb his chariot.

'I think they are not who we think they are...' Draupadi spoke as if in a trance.

Satyajit found himself wondering.

'Who are they?'

Part Two

Queen *of* Indraprastha

Ten

Kunti

'The sons of Pandu?' Draupadi's jaw dropped. Never in the wildest of her dreams had she thought that the assumedly dead sons of the great Pandu and his widow would manage to appear at her swayamvara. She stared at the erstwhile queen of Hastinapura, clad in humble clothing.

'I know that the first encounter of my sons with your father was less than friendly,' Kunti beamed, brushing Draupadi's hair. 'But there are always fresh starts. You, as the bride of the rightful heir to the Kuru throne, will propel this new beginning, Draupadi.'

Draupadi pursed her lips. The political intrigue she had thought she had escaped was back, putting her right in the middle of the swirling vortex.

Draupadi was not prepared for what came next.

'The bride of the five famed brothers,' Kunti added.

Bride of five!

Draupadi knew that Kunti would not joke. Suppressing her shock, she stared back at her mother-in-law. 'I am sure you must have thought of the slander that will follow, Queen Mother.'

'Slander,' Kunti's lips curved on one side as she repeated

the word. 'It follows whoever tries to question the conventions. But you, daughter of Drupada, don't seem like someone who would fear slander.' The widow of Pandu looked at her with an intensity that conveyed a lot more than her words.

Ambition?

'Besides, will you be satisfied with being anything less than a queen? Then, you should be the bride of my first born, Yudhishtira.'

Draupadi's eyes narrowed at what she thought was blatant manipulation. But she knew Kunti's words could not be taken lightly. Draupadi had heard of her tumultuous journey, as a coy princess who had briefly enjoyed the status of the empress of Bharata before destiny had thrown her into a life of uncertainty, misery, and peril. But the lioness of a woman had survived it all, bringing up five warrior sons, all of whom Draupadi had taken a strong liking to. But at the same time, Draupadi refused to play into manipulative arguments.

'Queen Mother Kunti,' Draupadi leaned forward, 'a wise survivor like you would know a lot about trusting the right people. When you trust someone to make her a part of your lives, it is also fair that she knows what she is getting into.'

Kunti's gaze softened and she clutched the hand rest, almost unwilling to let go of her heart's secrets. She finally said, 'Together, they survived. Together, they prevailed. Together, they will overcome their enemies.'

She saw Draupadi's eyebrows arch and drop as the younger woman considered her words. 'My demand is unreasonable. But so are the intrigues that face us, that will face you, if you choose to enter the *Pandu* household.'

Draupadi did not miss the subtle emphasis Kunti put on her late husband's name.

Why would she say Pandu household and not Kuru household?

Draupadi knew that the five brothers had been conceived out of *niyoga*, with Pandu being only their namesake father. It did not take her long to figure out that powerful parts of the Kuru household did not accept them. It explained the fire 'accident'.

She could choose to walk out of these intrigues by rejecting Arjuna's hand. She knew that the five brothers were not petty and would not persist if she did so.

'You can weld them together, Princess. Like the mind that unites and controls the limbs. They would stay bound to your word and not let your honour be compromised.'

Kunti betrayed a pang of guilt as Draupadi nodded, unaffected by the radical proposal. 'Of course, slander will follow, my child. But trust the vibrant legacy of our land. We shall figure out a way to convince the conservative minds. There are wise elders who would stand by you.'

For a woman at the threshold of Vanaprastha, a stage when people renounce material attachments, Kunti seemed too driven. For a moment, Draupadi questioned her own lack of ambition. But the meeting with the erstwhile empress of Bharata kindled a new flame within her. Bidding Kunti a polite farewell for the moment, Draupadi spent the rest of the day contemplating. It was time for the evening meal when she sought Drupada's audience.

The king of Panchala was close to ecstatic upon knowing the identity of the winning suitor. Draupadi had not seen him in such a good mood since many years.

'Believe me or not, I always dreaded the day you would leave us for your marital home,' he beamed, serving her sweets.

'With Duryodhana becoming the crown prince of Hastinapur, the place will not treat you with the respect you truly deserve if you enter as Arjuna's bride,' Drupada spoke, looking at her intently. 'It would be wise to carve out a principality and crown your husband as its king. It will please me immensely to have you both settle down in Kampilya itself.'

Years of observing her father's statecraft had trained Draupadi to maintain an unaffected demeanour while her mind furiously decrypted the unspoken intent. Drupada, unaware of Kunti's proposal, had made his own plans—of somehow convincing Arjuna to leave his brothers to their own fate and possibly make a tool of his son-in-law to achieve his own aims. Drupada, she knew, was not capable of wicked ambitions like Jarasandha. But stuck between the Kurus and Jarasandha, and after losing a significant portion of his own kingdom in an ego battle, Drupada was a prisoner of his own mounting insecurities. Draupadi averted her gaze and carefully gathered her words, 'The one who weds me shall claim his rightful inheritance from the Kurus, Father.'

'And I don't doubt his capabilities even for a moment,' Drupada nodded vigorously. 'But you, with your wisdom, can see that he will be better positioned to carve out his own share once he is backed by a portion of Panchala's might. You could be the queen of the combined principality and enjoy the comforts of your natal home.'

Draupadi did not continue the conversation. Drupada would back his son-in-law with a principality and would expect him to claim his inheritance from the Kurus. The combined principality, as per her father's desire, would then come under Panchala's control—his response to losing Ahichatra.

Drupada refused to grow up.

Draupadi knew better than to argue when her father was in one of his ambitious moods. She knew she had to dodge his move without hurting him. Giving an excuse of fatigue, which was not entirely false, she retired to her chamber. Probably at Kunti's behest, Arjuna had not tried to seek her out yet. Solitude helped little when faced with intriguing demands from both her natal and marital homes.

Strange as it seemed, adhering to Kunti's demand seemed the better choice.

⌣

'You made the right decision, Princess,' Kunti's voice betrayed her triumph.

'Pray, don't ever belittle the complication of this choice, Queen Mother,' Draupadi made no attempt to hide her scepticism regarding the polyandrous marital life.

'Not for a moment, child,' Kunti smiled—this time, the smile showed the mother in her. 'My sons shall be worthy of your decision. Consider this my promise. But I am sure you have thought about some conditions for your own protection.'

'Conditions to keep the Pandu household and its reputation intact, Mother Kunti,' Draupadi's lips corrected Kunti's suggested intentions. 'You must know that the households where women are given their due survive the tests of fate.'

Kunti nodded, examining Draupadi's face—the determination in her eyes, her placid forehead, and the subtle grit in her well-formed jawline. The Pandu household had at last found a daughter-in-law who could take on her mantle.

'People wonder why I insist on calling my sons, the Pandavas, undermining the traditional lineage of the Kauravas.' Seeing Draupadi's curiosity piqued, she continued, 'The Kuru household has always been proud of its legacy, being descendants of the great emperor Bharata, the founding father of Bharatavarsha, Princess

Draupadi. But I am not here to praise our marital household. I value our history and the achievements of our ancestors. But more important is the effort to be worthy of our ancestors.'

Draupadi did not interrupt Kunti even when the latter paused. 'Pandu could not reproduce. My sons were born by the sanctioned method of *niyoga*. But after Pandu's death, their very identity was mocked by their cousins. My sons were told that they were not eligible to name Kuru as their ancestor. They were not called Kauravas, like their cousins. I told them to bear the identity of Pandu with pride, for Pandu, despite not being their biological father, loved the five brothers with all his heart. He had made all plans to return to Hastinapura and claim the throne for Yudhishtira. But…'

Knowing about Pandu's ill-timed death, Draupadi gently patted Kunti's shoulder. But the older woman's determination overcame any traces of bereavement. 'They are Pandavas, Draupadi. They do not believe in the oppressive ways of their ancestors! They do not subscribe to the norms which allow princesses to be dragged from their swayamvaras, or bartered away in exchange of political benefits. Pandu dreamt that they would challenge the rotting belief systems of the Kuru household. I want them to fulfil their father's wish! I wait for the day when Pandu's sons will be the leaders of the land, more than the so-called Kauravas.'

Draupadi had heard of rebellious women challenging the hegemony of dogmatic chauvinism from her Guru Upayaja and his wife. But in Kunti, she saw a living rebel, a manifestation of the blazing desire to change the old order. It was fascinating. It was then that Kunti's face withered.

'Challenging the hegemony of the Kurus is not a straightforward task, Princess of Panchala. The most crucial thing needed to achieve this is unity,' Kunti paused and turned to face Draupadi. 'Be the force that binds them to each other, Draupadi. I know you have it in you.'

'Mother Kunti,' Draupadi spoke, not attempting to hide her scepticism now. 'You have been an illustrious mother. But what you're asking me to do is something no mother-in-law has asked of her daughter-in-law. I have some conditions too.' Her stern demand impressed Kunti, who beamed in response and asked her to continue. 'The social ridicule or slander that will follow is of little consequence to me as I have made this choice. But your sons must honour my choice at all times. I will live with only one of the brothers for a stipulated period, say, a year. The other four cannot desire me as a wife during that time.'

Draupadi paused for Kunti's reaction. But the older woman simply nodded. Draupadi was aware that her demand was not a small one, but it was the only way she could enforce a routine in her marital life, which would soon be ridden with complications. She expected Kunti to talk to her sons once before promising on their behalf. But when Kunti nodded like she had almost expected this condition, Draupadi felt better about the situation.

'I assured you even before you consented, Princess Draupadi. My sons would never let you down,' Kunti beamed. In that curve of her lips, Draupadi saw the woman who was once the empress of Bharata.

Eleven

The Wedding

Draupadi's fingers pensively rubbed against each other. And against the soft silk that covered the bridal bed. The wedding ceremony had been unique. Her husbands, Draupadi had noticed, had looked at her with varying emotions—tenderness, awe, disbelief, and perhaps, love. She laughed to herself. Considering the situation, it would take a long time before she found love. Kunti's truth about the five brothers kept ringing in her ears. She knew she sat upon a throne of immense power.

Only she had no idea how to wield it!

Yudhishtira, the eldest. Focus on him for a year.

She told herself this, looking at her image in the small pool of water, big enough to reflect her entire form. But it was not her appearance that bothered Draupadi. It was the belief that Kunti placed upon her.

To preserve the legacy of Pandu! To inspire his sons. To gather their strengths.

Blankly looking at her reflection, she suddenly found another face staring at her from the placid water. 'Yudhishtira. I mean, Arya…' She saw a slight smile on his lips when she took his name. The silks of royalty suited him. A sense of calm played in his eyes. Something in them commanded respect. She looked directly at him. She remembered the short conversation she had with him at the swayamvara. Not breaking the lock of gazes, she turned towards the bed.

Yudhishtira remained where he was, even after she had taken a step towards the ornate bed. He saw her turn again and look at him. Her large eyes spoke of courage. Something quite different from what he had expected. The questions that had raged in his mind ever since the polyandrous wedding was decided, seemed to evaporate. The guilt of 'usurping' his little brother's rightful bride, even for a year, subsided, and he dearly hoped it was not just his reaction to her beauty. While it could be said with reasonable confidence that the princess of Panchala was a peerless beauty, there was something more about her that connected to him.

She seemed like someone who would share his burden.

'Draupadi!' he said suddenly.

But where could he begin?

She tilted her head, expecting him to say more. He seemed to be at a loss for words. Pursing her lips, she remembered the lessons of the senior women at the palace that evening. She had been told that the groom becoming speechless at the first sight was the beginning of her dominion at home. Draupadi was sure that it was just a myth. Yet, she could not help the smile and the mischievous glint in her eyes. However, the contemplative hesitation on her husband's face signalled something else.

'I remember seeing you when you were...perhaps twelve or thirteen autumns old...when...'

'When the five sons of noble Pandu conspired with Shikhandi and captured my father?'

He had not expected her to come to the point with that lightning speed. Her eyes showed neither approval nor reproach. Possibly some questions. He nodded in affirmative, thinking of an explanation that would not offend her. 'Let us say, it wasn't one of my proudest deeds and we were blind in our devotion to Drona.'

'I suppose, after the defeat of your cousins on the battlefield, the back-door attack was the only way left for you to render your gurudakshina.'

He had expected a tinge of hostility. But she put forth only her observations. Perhaps it was because of the light from the multiple lamps shining through the latticed partitions, but her dusky skin glowed. Yudhishtira felt his heart miss a beat when his gaze moved over her supple curves. He ached to lay his soul bare in front of her.

'Not very proud of the means we had to deploy. But from the limited scope of a disciple, indebted to his guru, it seemed heroic then,' his eyes narrowed sheepishly.

The eldest Pandava had no qualms in admitting his mistake. But a tinge of pain reflected in his eyes. Draupadi sensed more than regret. 'The realization of being just a tool in pursuit of personal revenge must have hurt later.'

Yudhishtira's brows rose at the perceptive deduction. There was a time when he, as the newly crowned heir apparent of Hastinapura, had sought the support of his guru, Drona. He had banked upon the preceptor to oppose the idea of their 'short' stay at Varnavata. Yudhishtira had sensed danger the moment he had been asked to visit the place on a flimsy pretext. But the guru whose wish he and his brothers had fulfilled by putting their lives at risk had deserted them when they had needed him the most.

'The guru failed to reciprocate when you needed him to?' her tone suggested her eagerness to understand his predicament.

Yudhishtira responded with a slight nod but turned away, not wanting her to see his pain. Draupadi walked closer and squeezed his arm. His other hand clasped hers, holding her close to him. They remained that way for a while. He had almost lost track of time when he felt Draupadi snatch her hand away and press her head. 'Princess, are you all right?'

She nodded, trying to smile. But soon, she cringed again. She wished the nagging headache would choose some other time and not bother her when her groom was about to bare his soul in front of her. 'Just the early morning rituals and the excitement of the night before...' Draupadi tried to dismiss it when he held her hand and led her to the bed.

'Lack of sleep. By Mahadeva, I hope you are not the kind who keeps awake and suffers these nagging headaches.'

She hardly had the time to answer before he made her sit on the bed and began pressing her temples. His arms brushed against her shoulders now and then. There was something comforting about his proximity.

Something pleasurable too.

Her sigh was audible when she leaned her head against his chest. She felt him pause abruptly; his heart was pounding. Looking up, she saw his eyes, still brimming with concern. 'It felt good, Arya.'

'I am hardly done,' Yudhishtira smiled. 'And the rituals were harsh on you.' He noted the casual shake of her head. That very moment, he realized the strength in her shoulders. Like many princesses, she was trained in combat. It came as no surprise. He still remembered her angry eyes, trying to protect her father. If not for Shikhandi's intervention, she might have even succeeded in slowing them down that day.

'I must say, it was brave of you that day when you were defending your father. Perhaps things would have been different, had you succeeded.'

'Very different,' she responded, not showing any emotion. Had she held them off until the guard had arrived, the five brothers would have possibly been captured instead. Knowing her father, Drupada would have let them go. In all probability, she would have been married to Yudhishtira when the two royal families would have sat down to reconcile. But Drupada would have been saved from the agony and needless rage. 'Even though the result would have been the same, the journey would have differed,' she added after some more thought. Yudhishtira's massage had relieved her of the ache. But she did not feel like stopping him.

'You seem to steal words right out of my mouth!' Yudhishtira chuckled. He held her close to him. She turned around to face him. He descended upon the bed, still holding her in his arms. Beneath her coyness, he saw her readiness to step into his life.

'Something holds you back, Yudhishtira.'

A cloud of melancholy passed over Yudhishtira's face. His efforts to seem normal were not working. He had to ensure his new wife knew what she was getting into.

'Do you know what awaits you, Draupadi?'

'If you mean the intrigues and slander that surrounds a polyandrous marriage...'

Yudhishtira shook his head. 'I won't even try and downplay the complications there. But there are more pressing issues in your marital home. If you happen to have one, that is,' he said sadly.

'You were the heir apparent at Hastinapura before the

incident at Varnavata. And now that your cousin Duryodhana holds the position, you worry about our future at Hastinapura?'

Yudhishtira slowly rose to his feet. 'I am also worried about exposing you to the dynamics there. You must know that the fire "accident" at Varnavata was, in fact, a wilful attempt. The resthouse constructed for our stay was made of highly inflammable lac called "siva".'

'You expect more attempts like the fire "accident"?' Draupadi asked.

Yudhishtira said, 'My brothers are restless to speak in the language that our "cousins" understand. I am sure that my cousins who left no stone unturned in demeaning us will talk about this polyandrous marriage and subject you to slander as well. Think of living with the possibility of a familial clash.'

Draupadi rose and tugged at Yudhishtira's arm. 'Vengeance has far-reaching consequences, Arya. So does jealousy.' She saw him look at her with a knowing smile. 'A clash between both can be disastrous, Yudhishtira. What can we do to avoid that?'

Yudhishtira stepped closer. 'That would require me to relinquish the Kuru throne and settle for a much smaller principality, Draupadi.' He added, 'And I am sure my beloved uncle will try his best to ensure that we get a raw deal.'

There was something in his wry smile that made Draupadi feel protective of him. If they chose to stay back at Panchala, a similar fate awaited them. At least, going out to claim a province of the Kuru kingdom could bring them newer fortunes.

'It is your rule that matters, Arya. Besides, the size of the principality need not remain small for life, noble Pandava,' Draupadi beamed.

If it was ambition that shone in her eyes, he yearned to be the one to achieve it. Before he knew, Yudhishtira had drawn her into his arms again. It was a long and pleasurable night for both. At the end of it, the eldest son of Pandu fell asleep as his new bride looked at him fondly. Draupadi felt a new surge of power. She had to find out how far it could go.

Twelve

Khandava Prastha

The view from the window of the hill mansion overlooked the wilderness of Khandava. Having moved there in early autumn, Draupadi enjoyed gazing into the yellow carpet of leaves that the season left in its wake. She was overjoyed to see the onset of spring with wild blossoms. The villagers had begun to look up to her and Yudhishtira. The lack of luxuries did not bother her. With Yudhishtira by her side, she felt right at home.

The weather, however, was not congenial when the rains started. One day, during monsoon, Draupadi was filled with a sense of foreboding. She tossed the entire night, sleep deserting her, despite Yudhishtira's warm embrace. He noticed her waking up earlier than usual, and followed her. He was surprised when she chose to visit the chamber with the weaponry.

'Something is bothering you, My Queen.' Even his gentle words startled her.

'Draupadi! What is wrong, love?'

She did not have an answer. Yudhishtira's doubts about her health and enquiries about her wish to visit her natal home only annoyed her. She loved it when Satyajit or Shikhandi visited them, but for reasons unknown to her, she did not miss Panchala at all.

'Or is it me?'

'Yudhi?'

Yudhishtira withdrew with a sad shrug. 'The absence of Arjuna. Have I not been…?'

'No, My King,' Draupadi frowned. 'I do miss Arjuna, but that's not what worries me. Nor do I blame you for his departure.' Looking closely in his eyes that betrayed hurt, Draupadi felt at a loss. Yudhishtira had more than once expressed that he felt like an intruder in her life, which he believed, was rightfully to be shared with Arjuna. Draupadi had initially felt touched with his sensitivity, but it had been *her* choice to enter into this polyandrous marriage.

With her stipulated period with the eldest Pandava ending, she was actually beginning to fear missing his gentle warmth. With a start, she realized that she would soon be sharing her bed with the giant Bhima who, she feared, did not have even an ounce of his elder brother's sensitivity.

'This is our last week together. I fear I will miss you!' she blurted out. She saw a flicker of affection pass Yudhishtira's face. 'I…I fear being with…'

'Bhima?' Yudhishtira called out, sensing a presence outside the room, almost making Draupadi gasp. 'Come in!'

'What is with you two and the weaponry chamber?' The giant entered with a sly grin, unaffected by the solemn expressions he saw on both their faces. Looking at Draupadi's unforgiving frown, he lifted his hands. 'All right… I just wanted to ask Draupadi if she wants to accompany me to Sire Aryaka's place the next fortnight.'

'Our mother's grandfather, the Naga chief…' Yudhishtira explained.

'…who refuses to die even after a hundred and twenty autumns,' Bhima added, chuckling again.

'A very dear and important ancestor of ours, Draupadi,' Yudhishtira did not have to explain further as she nodded with a slight smile.

'There is a shorter and a more adventurous route to his hamlet through the wilderness!' Bhima said, and was pleasantly surprised when Draupadi nodded with certainty. Observing her in the past months, he had come to know that that she liked riding. 'I shall have the steeds groomed for the journey,' he beamed and left.

There was something in Bhima's parting smile that made Draupadi rethink her earlier opinion about the giant.

∿

The journey to Aryaka's hamlet was longer than Draupadi had expected. Fortunately, the skies were clear and the small retinue did not have to worry about rain. She and Bhima were accompanied by only three guards as Bhima did not want to take a battalion that would disturb the peaceful hamlet.

There was something troubling about the hamlet. Looking at it, a frown marred Bhima's usually exuberant face. 'Something has gone wrong here,' he muttered when Draupadi asked him. 'I think they fear someone.'

'Who?'

'Brother Bhima!' a chirpy voice called out. The couple turned to see a girl of barely thirteen springs wave.

A grin broke on Bhima's lips and he spread out his arms. Instead of running into them as he expected, the girl stopped by the threshold of her humble home and kept waving at them.

'Is this our sister-in-law?' she asked, looking at Draupadi

77

with wide eyes. Draupadi beamed at her and asked her name.

'Vikadru, the youngest great-granddaughter of Chief Aryaka,' Bhima introduced her, brushing the girl's long curls. 'Where is your sister?'

'Saurasi...' the girl began, her greyish pupils dilating, betraying terror. Draupadi drew her closer, concern mounting for her new-found family. Their simplicity had already won her heart.

'Vikadru!' the voice was feeble but authoritative.

Bhima and Draupadi turned to face the chief of the hamlet. His wrinkled face broke into a feeble smile after seeing Bhima. Draupadi knelt at his feet, introducing herself.

'It has been a good couple of months since we shifted to Khandava Prastha, Grandsire. 'How come you did not visit us?'

Tears filled Aryaka's eyes. He broke into sobs when Bhima enveloped him in an embrace. Bhima realized that in happier times, he and his bride would have been given a warm welcome at the Naga hamlet. The settlement now looked like a ghost of its former self. 'What is wrong, Grandsire Aryaka?'

'It is that rogue Takshaka again,' Aryaka whispered, ushering them inside his home. The sight shocked Bhima. Aryaka's grandsons lay on the floor, tending to fresh injuries. Bhima's eyes fell upon a girl, sitting huddled in a dark corner of the room.

'Saurasi?' Bhima was about to rush to her when Draupadi stopped him and approached the girl. Injuries showed on the girl's neck and shoulders.

'Who did this to her?' Draupadi exclaimed, trying to console the girl, but in vain.

'Kalasena, the son of Takshaka,' Aryaka collapsed into Bhima's arms again. 'I saved your life when you were defenceless, Bhima. Now, please help this old man and save my people from that abomination of a naga.'

Draupadi looked at Bhima, her eyes red due to shock and anger. 'Our own family suffers this way and we don't even have a clue?'

She could not help but blame her husbands, and at that moment, it was directed towards Bhima, who did not miss the ridicule.

'Stay here,' he growled at her and stormed out.

'Bhima, wait!' Aryaka and Draupadi called after him. But the departing giant did not look back. Draupadi spent the next couple of hours trying to enquire after the other nagas who seemed to have suffered similar atrocities. But she remained distracted with the thought of Bhima. An hour before sunset, she saw the giant Pandava stride in, dragging a man mauled out of shape and covered in blood.

Barely yet painfully alive!

Blood splattered on the floor when Bhima threw him at Saurasi's feet. The man tried to plead but only vomited more blood.

Draupadi and Aryaka cringed at the sight. Saurasi clung to Draupadi, her terror multiplying.

'Bhima! She is just a child!' Draupadi gasped at the rage and vengeance that had taken over her husband.

'Yes, a child!' Bhima growled, making everyone freeze. He stomped on the injured man's neck. 'Whose innocence was defiled by this...abomination!'

'Kalasena!' Aryaka gasped.

Draupadi, however, remained unimpressed. Her tongue felt bitter, and her throat, dry. Taking a quick leave of the Naga family with assurances from her side, she left without bothering to see if Bhima was following her. She could hear him call her.

But she could not turn back. It was not that bloodshed was new to her. But something felt wrong about the way Bhima had meted out retribution.

Thirteen

Bhima

Riding back to the imperial mansion, she sought out Yudhishtira to secure a quick shelter for Aryaka's family. After Bhima's killing of Kalasena, she was sure Takshaka's faction would attack the already weakened people ruled by Aryaka.

Though disturbed at the turn of events, Yudhishtira ordered his attendants to start building a new home for the persecuted nagas. 'It is not just Aryaka's faction that is suffering, Draupadi. Other villagers, too, have faced Takshaka's brutality. The rogue naga hides in the wilderness with his minions and raids the other nagas as well as the villagers. Now, they have gone beyond looting and…' his pause was pained. 'It will be a shame to let them continue unabated. They *have* to be stopped.'

Draupadi shook her head.

'It is the first time I am seeing you talk about action without thinking of any attempt to reform, My King.'

'I wish there were a chance for reformation, Draupadi. But the chance died the moment they resorted to brutally forcing themselves on young girls to terrorize the villagers.'

Nodding her assent, Draupadi began thinking. It was something she needed to ponder over on her own before she shared it with the brothers. Perhaps discuss it with Krishna. Yudhishtira expected her to leave but she sat down.

'Draupadi, is it about Bhima?'

Blood left her face at the mention.

'I know how it must have felt,' he sighed, noting the struggle on Draupadi's face.

'He…he is my husband now…' the sentence trailed as she debated whether to face her demons on her own or seek the support of the only husband she knew well enough.

'Would you have felt this disgust if Kalasena had been killed by my spear or Arjuna's arrow or by the twins' swords?'

No, she would have felt proud.

Draupadi had to admit to herself that it was just Bhima's unhindered display of emotions that disturbed her. Kunti's words rang in her ears—'Each of my sons is what he is because the other four are what they are.'

Yudhishtira's sensitivity or Arjuna's finesse was because of Bhima's crudeness. If she desired the other two, she had to make peace with this. Or maybe it wasn't crudeness at all.

Smiling, Draupadi left the throne room. Her attendants had spread out the silks and jewellery for the evening. Shaking her head, Draupadi sent for the cooks. Bhima, whatever was his approach, deserved a sumptuous meal that would convey her approval of him punishing a wrongdoer. Despite some reservations by her attendants, she cooked the meal with the greatest care, knowing Bhima's enthusiasm for food, before retiring to a perfumed bath. She had almost finished decking herself when a resounding voice from the kitchen made her attendants jump.

'You call this a meal?' she heard Bhima thunder at the cook, unaware that it was she who had prepared the meal. Her feet froze at the threshold when she heard him call the cook a few more names. It was when the cook noted her presence and backed away in fear that Bhima realized what had happened. The giant turned around, sheepishly biting his lips.

When a single tear threatened to break her wrathful expression, Draupadi whirled around and walked towards the terrace. There was no way she could bear the insult to her hours of hard work and attention to detail. Unable to hold more tears of frustration, she decided to spend the night alone, on the terrace, hoping that the cool monsoon wind would soothe her. After glancing at the door a multiple times, expecting Bhima to turn up to apologize, she closed her eyes—disappointed.

The breeze from the thick peacock-feather fans that her attendants held stopped abruptly. Sensing a familiar presence, Draupadi pretended as if she had fallen asleep on the stone couch.

'Open your mouth.'

Her eyes opened.

'I said, open your mouth. You don't really have to look at this monster.'

Draupadi's gaze softened and she saw Bhima break into a grin. It took her a good deal of effort to not respond to his infectious smile. But the fragrance from the sweet dish he had brought was enchanting and her lips could not help parting. Bhima took the opportunity to thrust the sweet into her mouth. His grin only became more pronounced when he saw the appreciation in her eyes.

'You...you prepared this...right now?'

Bhima nodded, a smug grin accompanying his dismissive shrug. He made no attempts to hide his pride.

Or show off that he was a superior cook.

Draupadi's frown returned. 'Still, that was no way to mock

my culinary skills.'

Bhima's lips parted in disbelief. 'But, that was just…inedible!' His shoulders slumped to see her turn away.

Disastrous start! But then, he was Bhima! Nobody could remain angry with him for long.

Draupadi walked towards the parapet overlooking the wilderness. A part of her silently cursed Kunti for putting her in this mortifying position. But perhaps Bhima was right and her culinary skills were really not that good, and Yudhishtira had just been too gentle to point that out. But no, the eldest Pandava had always relished the food made by her and his praise had always been more than diplomatic! Before she could say more, she felt a strong tug at her arm. The next moment, she found herself wrapped in Bhima's embrace, the sweet dish thrust in her mouth again. The abrupt hustle shook her from inside.

Bhima held her close and kept the bowl down. His words assumed a gentle tone that she had seldom heard him use. 'Look at what my brother has done to you! Made an ascetic out of a chubby princess. I need to fatten you up!'

Draupadi felt a new wave of warmth envelop her and she stopped fighting his grip. But she would not submit just to his strength. 'To "fatten" me up, you need to cook every day!' she challenged. 'Every single day, this whole year.'

'Every single day, this whole life if you wish so!' Bhima raised his right hand.

'That is tempting!' she blushed without realizing. With that earnestness in his eyes, he was a different Bhima. She smiled tenderly and pulled his forehead towards her lips.

The next moment Bhima swept her off the floor, carrying her with ease. Midway towards the bedchamber, he shook his head. 'Make it twice every day. You are lighter than…' he saw her frown, expecting him to take names of other women he had bedded. Mischievously, he pretended to try and remember the name of a woman in comparison. Her mounting indignation was obvious the moment he lay her on the bed and he had to block her exit with both his arms. 'A Kunda flower!'

'Too predictable!' Draupadi narrowed her eyes.

Bhima pretended to think, scratching his head. But not for long. Pinning her to the bed, he leaned close. 'Words aren't my strength, princess of Panchala. My real strength lies somewhere else!'

'Try and show me, son of Pandu!'

Cautiously relaxing his weight upon her, Bhima closed his lips on hers. Her hands interlocked with his, her long fingers pressing into his knuckles, as he broke the kiss and buried his head in the hollow of her neck. 'I promise you, my gentle queen. Tell me when to stop and I shall.'

'You overestimate yourself, Bhima!' she hissed, digging her nails into his back. 'Gentle queen indeed! Who knows, you might have met your match!'

With a powerful wave, Bhima put off the lamp by the bedside.

Her legs wrapped around his waist and the night seemed too short.

Fourteen

The Takshaka Menace

Activity around the hillock where Draupadi lived with the Pandavas picked up pace in the following months. Along with Aryaka's clansmen, other nagas and villagers who had been persecuted by the rogue naga faction of Takshaka, sought refuge in the nascent Pandava settlement. Yudhishtira ordered for the path to the riverbanks to be cleared and secured, so that the women and young girls could find a safe place to bathe and procure drinking water from. The twins started gathering able-bodied villagers to form hunting groups who would keep a watch against wild animals. But the dangers were not just from wild animals.

Once, in the month of Magha, the sound of an alarm horn before dawn made all the brothers rush down to the riverbanks with their guards, only to find out that members of Takshaka's faction had hidden themselves to abduct helpless naga girls who had come there to bathe. An old woman who was carrying a horn had saved the day. But the miscreants still succeeded in escaping death by the hands of the Pandavas.

'Arjuna's arrows would have claimed the lives of all those cowards!' Draupadi said. Looking at Bhima's emphatic nod, she missed the momentary cloud that passed over Yudhishtira's face. But the priority, all of them understood, was a permanent solution to the menace.

A messenger from Hastinapura sought audience. He brought a round of cheer conveying King Dhritarashtra's affirmative response to building a city on the banks of Yamuna. Securing the new settlement with a wall would provide a greater sense of security to the villagers and possibly attract more talented men and women. Draupadi nodded at Yudhishtira who dwelled upon the plan with Sahadeva.

Her mind refused to calm down, imagining Kunti's scorn at the thought of depending on grants from Hastinapura. The little settlement had begun to show the promise of sustaining itself but Draupadi's patience was at its end. The characteristic nausea of early pregnancy only added to her discomfort. Walking across the corridor overlooking the wilderness, she thirsted for a permanent solution. A solution that would make the villagers feel secure and trust the name of the Pandavas. Lost in thought, she felt the presence of Yudhishtira who had come to check on her morning meal.

'Burn the whole treacherous forest down,' she spoke in a fierce whisper.

Yudhishtira almost chuckled at the absurdity of the idea but then frowned at the crimson that had spread in her eyes. 'Draupadi!' Compassion was her foremost characteristic. He wondered if she even knew the number of lives that would be lost if the forest was burnt down. 'Tell me you did not mean it. You are asking for the destruction of an entire ecology, My Queen.'

Draupadi nodded. 'Let us not deceive ourselves, Arya. Destruction of the natural ecological balance started much before

87

the day we came to settle here, My King. Takshaka and his rogue followers have made this forest their slave. We only need to free the land caught in their clutches. Besides, our settlement will claim more land in the days to come. With the settlement growing in size, we are bound to destroy the forest bit by bit, Yudhishtira. I am only calling for an accelerated process because that will render the enemy homeless.'

She saw Yudhishtira stare at the forest, speechless for a long moment.

'We can always grow newer and safer ecosystems within the new city,' she smiled.

'Are you sure, Draupadi?'

'I have seen the wilderness closely, Yudhi. To take on Takshaka's forces without harming the forest, we need a larger force. We will have to ask for help from Hastinapura again. My father would be more than happy to oblige, but I trust your competence and that of your brothers.'

'Yudhishtira would never refuse anything you ask for,' Kunti had told her before they had left for Khandava. It had come partially as an assurance and partly as a warning that Draupadi now had the power and responsibility of what Yudhishtira did. At that moment, she hoped that Kunti had been right.

Yudhishtira responded with a slight smile and then walked away, still non-committal. 'Let Arjuna return. This is too big a decision to be taken in his absence,' she heard him sigh before he left.

✧

Arjuna did return and Yudhishtira could not delay the issue any longer. The attacks from rebel nagas on villagers had increased. The most painful cause that hastened the need for action was the merciless slaughter of twenty-two faithful guards who had taken to sleep after three nights of patrolling. The wailing of their wives and children still echoed everywhere.

The incident left the villagers in shock, and with the rising fear of the rebels, trust on the Pandavas was eroding. Travellers did not dare to travel through the forests of Khandava. The economic activity slowed down too, further incapacitating the population. The vicious cycle continued to worsen and the Pandavas had to do something drastic to break it.

'Three years of hard work gone down the Yamuna!' Draupadi clenched her fists, her nails tearing into the embroidered cushions beside her.

'Hate to admit it, Eldest. Even a mild gale evokes a sense of insecurity, even in the palace,' Nakula added. 'We are left with no option but to eliminate the rebels completely!'

Sahadeva and Bhima agreed. Arjuna, who had returned from his journey only a few days ago, was unaware of the terror caused by Takshaka's rebel nagas. He blankly stared at his outraged brothers and felt compelled to agree. Yudhishtira's hands pressed against the lion-shaped bolsters of his seat. Robberies, harassment of innocent villagers, rape of defenceless women, and now, the killing of his own guards. He had let things spiral out of control. He could not help but feel responsible for the murder of men who had protected him and their territory day and night. He and his brothers could not afford the guilt of inaction anymore. The land that vouched for dharma had no place for bloodthirsty terrorists.

'The forest shall be burnt,' he uttered. 'Along with the rebels. Every last man among them.' A quiet followed his decree; even Draupadi looked up in wonder.

Yudhishtira's brows arched. 'I am telling you all to go ahead.

89

Burn them. What stops you?'

Draupadi nodded, but saw the other four still stare at him in visible disbelief. She could not help a smile, knowing that each of them had expected their eldest brother to try and restrain them from taking the drastic step. Another voice came from the door, expressing what she felt.

'When the man, lauded as the Ajatashatru—one with no living enemy on this earth—who is known to not even sulk, passes this order, one can't but pause at the havoc that will take place in its wake, Eldest.'

'Krishna!'

The mood in the room transformed instantly and the five brothers rose to their feet.

'Welcome Vasudeva,' Draupadi beamed, without rising from her seat.

'Greetings, Maharani,' Krishna said, amused because of her changed demeanour.

'Some prior message about your arrival would have helped us arrange for a suitable welcome,' she gestured at an ornate seat. She knowingly ignored the five stupefied faces wondering what was wrong, and called for the cook to ready the meal with special instructions to please the unexpected *guest*. The emphasis on the word 'guest' was too obvious to ignore.

'What in the name of Mahadeva is wrong with you two?' Bhima felt compelled to break the cold silence.

Draupadi ignored the question and pretended to go over the temporary plan made to round up the rebels—a roughly inked scroll that included the number of deployable forces, supplies, and other contingencies. Without looking up, she added, 'Meet Subhadra and check on whether your little sister is happy in her marital home. The meal will be ready soon.'

Realizing the reason for her annoyance, Yudhishtira shrugged, signalling Bhima, Nakula and Sahadeva to step out. Arjuna stayed back, his eyes exhibiting hurt. 'Draupadi, we have been over this.'

'We both have indeed been over this, Arjuna,' Draupadi's eyes softened when she looked at him. 'But not *us.*' She jerked a thumb at herself and then at Krishna, her dark lashes straining against her brows.

Krishna patted Arjuna's shoulder and the latter left the room to join his brothers. Once he had exited, Draupadi frowned at Krishna and went back to pretending to look at the scroll. 'And you aren't going to meet your little sister?'

'It looks like the little sister can wait,' Krishna beamed, walking over to stand behind her seat. 'Did I take you for granted, Sakhi?'

Draupadi did not flinch when his hand gently pressed her shoulders. But turning to her side, she looked straight into his eyes. 'You don't know the hurt you have caused, Krishna.' Taking a deep breath, she walked towards the window, staring into the wilderness. 'She is a child and you influenced her.'

'It was not a bad choice that she was "influenced" to make. Was it, Sakhi?' Krishna replied, taking the scroll she had placed beside her and giving it a quick glance. 'At least, she could save the Yadava warriors from being "obliged by marital relationship" to serve Duryodhana.'

Draupadi remained unimpressed. 'We started out trying to defy those who indulged in this abominable practice of using marital alliances to establish hegemony. Doesn't it hurt to realize that we are doing the same?'

'Are we?'

'Aren't we?'

91

Krishna looked at her, his lips missing his characteristic smile. 'Only Subhadra can answer. You can ask her when you feel she is sufficiently "grown up".'

Draupadi remained thoughtful. In her heart, she felt repulsed at the idea of making marital alliances tools in power games. But Krishna's decisions meant much more to her, beyond the definitions of the rights and wrongs that bound the world. This was because in him, she saw a person who owned this world without seeking to control it; someone who felt one with the world, and yet, was beyond it.

The dilemma, she figured, could wait. A more dire challenge awaited them, hidden in the treacherous woods of Khandava, and that commanded their attention.

Fifteen

Indraprastha

Black smoke filled the horizon. Draupadi surveyed the burning forest, coughing at the occasional whiff of smoke that blew her way. She felt different. It was not like her to wish for the destruction of an entire forest along with most of its denizens. There were times when her conscience interrogated her about the wisdom behind this move. Yudhishtira's condition was not very different. Draupadi was aware that his brothers, too, felt the same—Arjuna most of all. She could see that in the passionate appeals he made to save some of the rebel nagas who surrendered in the crucial moments, caught between the unforgiving fire and the menacing warriors. Some of them, fearing for their lives, also offered to labour for the new city that was proposed on the site of the burnt forest.

It was in these troubling moments that Draupadi sought the opinions of the villagers downhill. The villagers and the nagas belonging to Aryaka's clan, however, unanimously celebrated the gutting of the forest. Having borne the brunt of Takshaka's atrocities, they could still not believe that it was a thing of the past. She could sense the agony they had gone through in the last few months when they opposed the suggestion of rehabilitating the surrendered rebels.

She remembered the incidents of the morning, swallowing a lump in her throat. The wife of Takshaka and her young son, Ashvasena, had tried to surrender to protect their lives while the cursed Takshaka was nowhere to be seen, even in the crisis facing his own family. The mother had pleaded with Aryaka to accept the young Ashvasena and had even offered to serve his family.

'Your other son brutally raped my granddaughter!' Aryaka had lashed out. 'Who knows what this son of yours will do if I let him stay in my home?'

Aryaka had not budged when the woman had fallen at his feet. Draupadi would have concluded that Aryaka was a harsh and selfish patriarch had she not seen the terror that his family had been through earlier.

Who would risk the safety of his own family to rehabilitate the son of a sworn enemy?

But how could the son be responsible for the acts of his own father?

Perhaps, his tacit support of his father's atrocities itself warranted this castigation.

The mental battle had raged within her until she had heard the hysterical cries of the woman who had been so heartbroken at Aryaka's anger that she had chosen to run back into the flames.

Arjuna had caught Ashvasena from following his mother at the nick of time. But the woman could not be saved.

Despite trying as hard as she could, Draupadi could not shake away the image of the woman caught in the forest flames.

'You haven't eaten anything, Sister,' Subhadra's chirpy voice came from behind her. 'I have prepared your favourite Kadamba delicacy!'

Draupadi forced herself to smile. Having never had a

younger sister, she could not decide whether Subhadra's frequent liberties with her were interferences or just expressions of familial intimacy.

'How will you feed little Sutasoma if you do not eat yourself? And what if you are pregnant again?' Subhadra gasped.

Suppressing her annoyance, Draupadi ate a little. But even the delicious preparation felt bitter to Draupadi's tongue when she thought of Ashvasena's wrathful face as he had walked away rejecting the Pandavas' offer, asking him to stay in the palace.

Subhadra coughed uncontrollably when another strong gale blew in, carrying the burning stench. 'So, we are building a new city!'

Draupadi beamed at Subhadra's incessant efforts to take her mind off the morning's tragedy. 'Subhadra, do you think we can build a flourishing city upon the burnt corpses of those rebels?'

'...robbers, molesters and other abominations of human race? Very well, yes,' Subhadra replied with no hesitation. 'When I spoke to brother Bhima earlier today, he told me about the incident at Lord Aryaka's place. Why would we want to spare the lives of those monsters?'

It was not as straightforward as Subhadra felt, Draupadi knew that. But still, she could not help feeling envious of the way Subhadra stood by her view.

Subhadra smiled, reminding Draupadi of Krishna immediately. 'Elder Sister, you are my brother's best friend, I am sure you know how he had to kill our uncle Kamsa, fight Jarasandha, and then lead an exodus to Dwaraka.' Pausing to see Draupadi nod, she continued, 'I heard people decry his every decision and action. They decried him when he killed Kamsa. They decried him when Jarasandha fell upon us. They decried him when he spared Jarasandha's life on the battlefield. They cursed him when they had to abandon the city of Mathura for a shore city that was still to be built. They owed their very existence and sustenance to my brother. Yet they denounced him at the first opportunity,' Subhadra's voice shook towards the end. 'Now that the Yadava confederation has flourished on the shores, people sing paeans of praise for him. Because he saved the present for the future, Elder Sister.'

It wasn't that Draupadi was not aware of Krishna's exploits, but Subhadra's passionate recounting of her brother's life was charming. With an indulgent smile, Draupadi let her continue.

'I meant to say, the future generations will respect those who take action. The present has to be saved for a future to exist. Had we let those forest-dwelling rebels terrorize the people of Khandava Prastha, limiting our action to just meek defence, it would have caused the population to either get disheartened or get influenced to join them.'

Draupadi chose to go with Subhadra's explanation of what had happened. Subhadra suggested going through various plans for the city.

'We should be ready with something impressive when our mother-in-law returns from her pilgrimage!' she said, enthusiastically.

∽

But contrary to their expectations, Kunti was less than impressed with the developments in her absence. Sending Subhadra away on some pretext, she stared at Draupadi, disappointed.

'How did you let this happen, Draupadi? New city? Will that not tie down the five brothers to the barren lands of western Kuru Kingdom? Will that not make them look like mere recipients of their so-called uncle's benevolence?'

Draupadi did not let her disappointment show. The decision to settle for the principality of Khandava Prastha, despite the region's failings, had been taken so that they could secure a solution to the continuous clashes between the cousins. Furthermore, she was hopeful of the Pandavas' ability to transform the region.

Kunti, though, was not in a frame of mind to appreciate the merit of the decision. 'Secure a solution to the problem of continuous clashes? By Mahadeva!' she exclaimed. 'Their father was once an emperor of this land, Draupadi. Yudhishtira suffers from an obsession for peace. To the point of restraining his brothers from doing their best. I had hoped that you would remedy that...' she paused when Draupadi held both her arms, breaking her volley of rants.

'Mother Kunti, you were the one who inspired me to challenge the old order,' she beamed like she would at a child. 'That is exactly what I seek to do. But superfluously challenging and rebelling against the dynasty and their obsessions serves no purpose. We have to establish dharma, and emphasize to the world that the driving tenet of this land, dharma, is not a static code of unintelligent rules, but a dynamic counter-balancing force.'

Kunti heard her out and smiled sadly. Draupadi chose to not press further. Perhaps the older woman, too, was obsessed with seeing her son upon the very same throne on which her late husband had sat and ruled over the land.

Mahadeva willing, there would be bigger thrones!

Draupadi wanted actions and results to speak louder than just assurances. She knew her husbands would make it happen. She looked out the window, surveying the site of the erstwhile Khandava, now cleared of the waste, and presenting a magnificent golden sight under the midday sun. If only Kunti saw what she did. A city that would make the gods descend to be a part of the flourishing land. A city that would equal that of the gods! A city the true lord of the land would rule.

Indraprastha!

Sixteen

Jarasandha and Krishna

'Not again!' Draupadi sighed to herself when little Shatanika called out to her from his cradle. She had not expected that juggling the lives of a queen and a mother would be an easy task. But using motherhood as an excuse to postpone her queenly duties was not something she could come to terms with. By the time she hurried from the spacious portico back to the inner chamber, she saw her firstborn, Prativindhya, vigorously shaking the silver rattle to draw Shatanika's attention. 'He is a little too old to be interested in a rattle,' she smiled and told the bewildered Prativindhya.

Having crossed a couple of months after his first spring, the son of Nakula had a reputation of being too agile, rebelling whenever he was put in a constrained place like a cradle. Prativindhya hurried to the corner of the chamber where a three-foot-high wooden horse was mounted on a frame of four wheels. After Draupadi securely placed Shatanika on the horse, Prativindhya obliged by taking the lead to engage the little brother. Smiling and shaking her head at the joy and bewilderment motherhood posed, Draupadi turned back to what she thought was the 'easier' part of her life—the life of a queen.

And the first intrigue of her queenly life awaited her around the corner.

The guard looked unsure when he sought permission to usher the ageing guest who wanted her audience in the absence of Yudhishtira. Draupadi waved her approval and realized the guard's confusion. The guest introduced himself as Satyaratha, a warlord from the borders of Videha, now under the control of Magadha.

What does a remote warlord have to do with us?

Draupadi offered him a seat and planned to arrange for his meals when grief erupted in his eyes and he placed his silken headgear on the ground, a yard away from her feet.

'No, Arya. You are of my father's age!' she stepped back in alarm.

'Maharani!' the voice broke at every syllable. 'Save my sons. They are hardly of eighteen springs.'

'What happened to them?'

'People will call me mad to say this. But I swear upon my ancestors and my virtuous wife, who is in the high heavens, that emperor Jarasandha took them away!'

'Why would he take them away? Pray, calm down and tell me everything,' Draupadi said.

'To sacrifice them in his gruesome ritual!' Satyaratha could not speak more. 'I tried to appeal to the kings of Panchala and Hastinapura…but in vain.'

Why would Father turn away an aggrieved father like him? And what had stopped Dhritarashtra from acting against it?

'They didn't believe that Jarasandha would engage in a ritual like *Nara Medha*. But I can bet my life, My Queen. He even has a goal! Of offering the lives of ten thousand princes and unmarried men of royal or noble blood.'

The prospect of any living king engaging in *Nara Medha* seemed distant. Even for a ruthless king like Jarasandha. Draupadi now realized why the rulers of Panchala and Hastinapura had not taken Satyaratha's words seriously. But there was something about the old man's claims that she could not dismiss.

Organizing a temporary residence for the weary guest, Draupadi began contemplating. Even Kunti noticed her distant demeanour during the afternoon meal the women shared. Upon Kunti's insistence, Draupadi told her about Satyaratha. Contrary to her expectation, Kunti's eyes spoke of a sad memory.

'He is ruthless, that king of Magadha. Ruthless enough to indulge in something like this!' Kunti sighed.

'My foster father, Bhoja of Kunti kingdom, also lost a son. That was when he adopted me,' Kunti recollected. Draupadi thought she saw a sense of bereavement shoot up in Kunti's eyes. It seemed unnatural to grieve for a foster brother who Kunti had never met.

Perhaps Kunti loved her foster father so much that she had made his grief hers.

'He suspected Jarasandha. But his own ministers and generals told him that it was far-fetched to blame Jarasandha when the province of Kunti had no enmity with Magadha. But I believed him. I had seen the evil that was Jarasandha far too closely.'

Kunti did not speak for long and Draupadi chose to not prompt her.

'Even Pandu had wanted to put an end to Jarasandha's sway and had undertaken great pains and campaigns to unite the Kshatriya world against that monster of Magadha!'

Draupadi frowned. Kunti was seldom herself when she spoke about her late husband's unfulfilled aspirations. She knew where this conversation would go.

'We shall take steps to ascertain the news and we will try helping Satyaratha, Mother Kunti,' she squeezed Kunti's shoulder.

The day's activities failed to put Draupadi at ease. The ageing chief from Videha would not have come to the banks of Yamuna to Indraprastha if he had no faith in the rising Pandava strength. That itself, Draupadi felt, was an opportunity worth seizing. But where would this lead? How could they pursue the case with Magadha? Could they, with their current strength, take on the vast armies of Jarasandha on the battlefield? That too, on the basis of some speculation? For some reason, she felt it was premature to discuss the same with Yudhishtira. There was only one person whom she could bare her heart to. Draupadi decided to send a messenger to Dwaraka.

∿

'Bored with the city and your household so soon?' the cheery voice almost startled Draupadi after her morning sun worship. 'You must be, if the issues of the rest of Bharatavarsha have started to bother you!'

She beamed at the familiar visitor.

'Someone had once exhorted me to consider the whole of Bharatavarsha as my home!' Her eyes threw him a challenge, bringing back the memory of one of their earliest meetings. Her smile turned tender the next moment. 'At times, I feel guilty to disturb you with my...ideas—what is the better word for it—vision.'

'It is true, Sakhi!' Krishna turned solemn. 'The spies at Mathura, as well as Jarasandha's own son, Sahadeva, confirm that the old king is engaging in gruesome rituals like *Nara Medha*.'

Draupadi stared at him, overwhelmed with the news.

How gruesome was the father if his own son was admitting to his wrongdoings?

She had seen the Prince of Magadha once or twice. Prince Sahadeva had not inherited any of his father's characteristics. Neither his physical robustness, nor his ambition. 'We can't sit here, doing nothing now, Krishna.' *Nara Medha* was an esoteric practice of the distant past, which had been banned by Brahmarishi Vishvamitra during the era of the famed King Harishchandra. Whether the ritual yielded the desired result or not, Jarasandha could not be ignored. A thought struck her. 'Why did you never think of ending Jarasandha's life, Krishna? I am aware that you met him more than once on the battlefield. You had even stopped brother Rama from killing him. Did you not?'

Krishna inhaled and nodded. 'You are also not ignorant of the sway that Jarasandha holds over the countless provinces of Bharata, Draupadi. And they vie with each other to win his blessings.'

'And his death will only cause a mad scramble amongst those minions to "inherit his dominion",' Draupadi nodded. 'And who knows what that will lead to? We cannot end him unless we have an alternative.'

An alternative that would be accepted unanimously across Bharatavarsha!

A maid announced that King Yudhishtira awaited them in the Yajnashala. Draupadi glanced at Krishna. The same thought had struck them both.

When they met Yudhishtira and his brothers who had just concluded their morning rituals, Draupadi was surprised to find out that even the king of Indraprastha had received a cryptic message from Magadha.

'It has to be my namesake,' Sahadeva remarked after a second examination of the scroll, and they saw Krishna nod.

Yudhishtira's eyes betrayed a desire to act. But his characteristic contemplation or what Bhima often termed as "needless hesitation" clouded the rest of his face.

'People like Satyaratha from distant confederacies have started to reach out to us. It is a sign of the growing faith that they place upon us, Eldest,' Sahadeva continued.

'We are talking about an opponent like Jarasandha,' Yudhishtira countered him. 'As much as I would like to see him defeated on the battlefield, we have to be prepared for a situation where we might not receive military assistance even from the closest of our allies. While Magadha, on the other hand, will command the assistance of all its allies, minions, and possibly, even hired assassins.'

Draupadi seconded his deliberation. 'Covert operation?' These words drew stares of varied expressions from each of her husbands. She thought Yudhishtira's eyes brightened for a moment before they settled back to their placid selves. Her gaze involuntarily turned to Krishna. She knew that the idea had its risks, the biggest being found out, which would expose them to a confrontation with Magadha on the battlefield as well as a loss of reputation among their dearest. But if everything went well, they would save the lives of countless innocent men being readied for the gruesome sacrifice! It was worth it.

Contrary to the expectations of his brothers, Yudhishtira responded with a nod. Draupadi leaned back in her seat, thoughtful. Executing her plan needed first-hand information about Jarasandha's strengths, weaknesses, and more than anything, the predictable facets of his personality.

'You have faced him on the battlefield time and again, cousin Krishna,' Yudhishtira prompted. 'Very few understand your wisdom behind relocating the Yadavas to Dwaraka. Even fewer see your thoughtfulness behind sparing his life! We rely on your experience and insight to proceed with this plan, Vasudeva.'

Krishna's intense gaze acknowledged Yudhishtira's request. 'Killing Jarasandha needs to be covert enough to minimize the damage, but fair enough to hold his allies back in a moral stalemate. Jarasandha has his indulgences. Wrestling is one of them. Death in a bout of wrestling is considered fair. Fair enough for the prince of Magadha to let us escape unhurt as well as ally with us in future.' Krishna arched his brows, seeking their reaction and pointedly looked at Bhima.

Not used to diplomatic conversations, Bhima leaned forward. 'When do we start for Magadha?'

Draupadi grinned. Always the first one to put his foot forward, Bhima was a perfect contrast to Yudhishtira's insightful hesitation.

Krishna, too, laughed and patted Bhima's shoulder in a mix of affection and admiration. Gazing at the fire burning at the Yajnavedi, the fire altar, he added, 'In addition to being covert and fair, the killing of Jarasandha should be accompanied by a vision to handle the power vacuum that his death will create.'

Feeling Krishna's meaningful gaze rest upon him, Yudhishtira reassessed the might of Magadha. 'Avanti, Chedi, Pundra, Vidarbha, perhaps even Kashi, and a considerable part of the southern provinces, have been loyal to Jarasandha. The princes of those kingdoms have gone out of their way to please him and "inherit" his sway.'

'All they need is an acceptable alternative, Eldest.'

Draupadi took the cue and placed her palm over Yudhishtira's. 'I know that you have resisted Mother Kunti's push to fulfil your late father Pandu's dream of uniting Bharatavarsha. Your deliberation is well-placed, Arya. But now it is time to assert your rightful position as the worthy descendant of the great emperor Bharata. Perform Rajasuya, My King.'

Yudhishtira felt the sparkle of ambition in her eyes. Rajasuya was a yajna that followed a successful military campaign in four directions. Performing Rajasuya would raise him to the status of an emperor—a samrat. It would fill him with new-found faith in himself, in his brothers, and above all, in the path that he had always walked on—the path of dharma.

Perform Rajasuya to unite the land as the empire of dharma.

Seventeen

Rajasuya

The lamps were lit, and the floral decoration was tailored to his taste. He had just returned to Indraprastha after Bhima had successfully eliminated Jarasandha. But a strange melancholy filled Arjuna's heart at the sight of the woman who had entered the household because of him. For whom he had to wait for four long years before his turn had finally come. Arjuna tried to drive the untimely gloom away, attempting to focus on the musical notes Draupadi played on her veena. But his mind kept asking the same nagging question.

Would this come to be?

Draupadi brought her rendition to an abrupt stop when she felt his hand upon hers. Her kohl-smeared eyes opened wide. 'Did the rhythm go wrong?' Finding him stare at her with no response, Draupadi's face fell.

'Rhythm eludes me whenever I change the pace!' she rued, her frustration showing.

Arjuna felt compelled to smile. 'Like you elude me whenever I dare to think you are mine.'

Hurt surfaced in her eyes though Draupadi tried to remain unaffected. Her marital life had begun with her garlanding Arjuna, going against almost every soul present in her swayamvara. But Kunti's bizarre demand had made her Yudhishtira's wife first. Arjuna had to wait for two long years for his time with her—something fate cruelly doubled, when he ran into her and Yudhishtira in an inappropriate moment. His stipulated year-long pilgrimage after that had ended with him marrying Subhadra. To be fair to Subhadra, Draupadi had insisted that they start their marital life together right then, and had chosen to spend the year designated for him with Nakula, and the following year with Sahadeva.

Now that the moment had finally come, Draupadi noticed that Arjuna was still lost in the misery hidden deep in the crevices of his heart. Steeling herself, she thought of ways to lighten his mind. 'Destiny delays somethings so that more can happen in the wake, Arjuna. A river joins the sea in its natural course. But when humankind delays its union by digging canals and building dams, the sea and the river pine for each other, only to realize that the wait was worth it, when they see the lush land and flourishing civilization that benefitted because of the wait. Isn't the wait worth it, Arjuna?'

Arjuna sighed, helping her keep the veena away. 'Do namesakes also come up with similar metaphors? Krishna told me exactly this when I poured my heart to him.'

'Did he?' Draupadi paused while pouring wine into two silver goblets.

Arjuna nodded, 'Krishna knows a side of me that none of my brothers, or even you, know. I dread to even remember what I felt then, Draupadi. You'd hate me if you ever came to know.'

'We all have darkness within, son of Kunti. It raises its hood when misery strikes. But wisdom lies in overcoming it with our stronger side.'

'Or as our friend in Dwaraka would say, own the "misery" and the factors causing it enough to celebrate the joy it gives another.' Draupadi was about to add her own bit to the philosophical discourse, but she stopped. 'Wait, don't tell me you too have this habit of thinking what Krishna would do or say at every nook and corner of life!'

'Guilty,' Arjuna nodded sheepishly. 'You do the same? By Mahadeva, we are doomed!'

'Own the doom and the one causing it!' Draupadi said aloud, emptying the wine down her throat, and laughed. He joined her. Before long, they were teasing each other like long-lost friends, childhood sweethearts, and a couple that had seen decades of life together. It continued until the last of the lamps blew out, and Arjuna, in a moment of passion, pulled her into a tight embrace. An embrace which neither felt strange nor new. A proximity which seemed to extend through many lives.

Women were not new to Arjuna. The seductive naga woman, Uloopi, who had gone to extreme lengths to please him just for a night's company, the coy but firmly grounded Chirtrangada of Manipur, Subhadra with her childlike adoration and spellbinding wisdom—he had experienced the company of many astounding women. But Draupadi still made him yearn for her. Her very entry into their lives had turned the fortunes of the sons of Pandu and Arjuna allowed himself the feeling of pride in knowing that he had played a key role in winning her hand. In the depths of his heart, she uniquely belonged to him. He was sure that he commanded a similar place in her heart too. Whether their conversation was on love, stately affairs, war strategies, or philosophy, he found his match in her.

Only in her.

An exciting phase had started while he stood on the threshold of the impending military campaign for Rajasuya, with his wife—Draupadi.

∿

The city seemed to have grown multiple times in size in the last couple of years. The city of Indraprastha. She remembered the day the city doors had been formally opened to the villagers, nagas, travellers, and other migrants from neighbouring provinces who had chosen to pursue their fortunes with the Pandavas. Draupadi's spirits soared seeing the hustle-bustle in the city from her balcony. Their own mansion had been transformed from a humble summer palace on a hillock to a grand complex of buildings. With the Rajasuya campaign gaining speed, more and more people sought luck, fortune, and refuge in the new and promising city. Now, Draupadi could not even see the ends of the city from her high mansion.

Military campaigns in all the four directions, each led by one of the four brothers of Yudhishtira, had resulted in this expansion. Arjuna, in his northern campaign, had brought under his sway the regions of Matsya, northern Kuru, Kimpurusha, Darada, Anga, Vanga, Pragjyotisha, and so on, while Sahadeva had overcome resistance from Avanthi, Mahishmati, Nishada and Kishkindha among others, and had also secured the friendship of Lanka in the far south. Nakula's share was the western expanse of Bharatavarsha, a mix of allies and subjugated vassals that included Kekayas, Madras, and Yadavas of Saurashtra, Trigartas and Yavanas. Bhima, having gone east, was expected to return any time, with victories scored against regions including Magadha, Kalinga, Dasarna, Vatsa, Chedi and Malla.

The sudden chatter of six hyperactive children startled Draupadi out of her reverie. Subhadra's indignant voice followed them. Draupadi could not help but smile at her plight. The children were a handful even with the slew of attendants around them.

'Believe me, Elder Sister! Being a queen is easier. Being a mother is the hardest part of our lives,' she halted in her steps, trying to stop little Abhimanyu from pulling at the toy cart that Shrutakirti held with all his might. 'Not queen! With brother Bhima's return, which is bound to happen soon, you will be the empress, samragni of the whole of Bharatavarsha!'

The younger woman's enthusiasm was contagious enough for Draupadi to grin indulgently. The grin faded as soon as she saw Sutasoma crush a new toy to pieces.

Like father, like son!

Chiding the child, she sat upon the carved stone couch covered with silk and cushions, motioning Subhadra to sit next to her. 'How are we going to bear the responsibility of this land, Subhadra? The sheer amount of trust placed upon us is overwhelming. If we ever let them down...'

'You will learn and figure it out soon, Elder Sister,' Subhadra assured her. 'And I shall learn from you, being the one who can afford the luxury of being in the shadows!' she teased. If there was something Draupadi loved immensely about Subhadra, it was the younger woman's unique manner of speaking the truth with the bubbling enthusiasm of a child. They had indeed come a long way together.

The footsteps approaching the chamber were hurried, making Draupadi turn around. 'Sahadeva?'

'Brother Bhima will return soon now, Draupadi,' he turned and nodded at Subhadra before two of the children scampered towards him.

'The military campaign for Rajasuya has been concluded

indeed!' Draupadi exclaimed. The pressure of planning each campaign while remaining abreast of administrative activities of the growing city, along with supporting Yudhishtira, had taken a toll on her sleep in all these years. It was hard to believe that it was finally concluded. She saw Sahadeva's beaming face.

'It has indeed been concluded, Samragni!'

∿

Poornahuti, the final offering to the gods, was performed. Draupadi held Yudhishtira's hand till the last of the offering of grains, precious stones, gold, and other homadravyas, were dropped into the all-consuming fire. In a surreal chain of events that followed, she found herself seated on the high throne, not just of Indraprastha, but of the whole of Bharata—the entire land united by one code of arya dharma. At that instant, her eyes swept the expanse of the sabha assembled for the purpose, searching for the one with whom she had actually dreamt of this. Her smile widened, remaining that way, till Yudhishtira gently patted her arm.

Dhaumya, the family priest of the Pandu household had signalled that it was time for the *agra puja*—the customary ritual of honouring a guru, a mentor or an ancestor that the yajamana—the host of the yajna—would perform in gratitude. Draupadi saw many pairs of eyes look at Bhishma, the unmarried patriarch of the Kuru family and the grand-uncle of the sons of both Pandu and Dhritarashtra. She recollected that all the five brothers had remembered him multiple times with great fondness over the last few years. As the princess of Panchala, she had formed a different opinion of the grand old man. She could respect the affection that her husbands had for Bhishma, but honouring him with *agra puja* seemed a bit too much. She saw Sahadeva requesting Yudhishtira's attention.

'Samrat,' Sahadeva started, briefly turning around to gain the attention of the other guests. 'It is a challenging task for us to choose one benefactor to confer upon him the honour of the *agra puja*. Among the distinguished guests, we have revered elders, some of who were responsible for saving our lives, guiding us through various intrigues and trusting our prowess when we had nothing else to prove.' His eyes briefly landed upon Bhishma, Bhagavan Veda Vyasa—the rishi whom the world revered and the biological father of Dhritarashtra and Pandu—Guru Drona, and Guru Kripa, the noble Vidura who had played a key role in saving the Pandavas from the fire, and finally, upon Drupada. 'However,' he turned back to face Yudhishtira, 'as much as we owe our utmost reverence to these venerable elders, we have amongst us, a person who stood by us, extending his invaluable insights while we embarked upon this daunting campaign of Rajasuya. It is not an exaggeration to say that this ambitious campaign of Rajasuya would have failed without his constant inspiration.'

Yudhishtira briefly glanced at Draupadi. Given the poise he had to assume for the occasion, he could not show more delight at the suggestion than what his eyes permitted. Draupadi could sense his joy when Sahadeva uttered the name.

'I propose, to you and this distinguished sabha, that Krishna Vasudeva be honoured with *agra puja*.'

Bhishma rose to his feet and walked up to Sahadeva, his majestic gait boasting of the vigour of men decades younger than him. Beaming widely, he patted Sahadeva and lauded the decision. Immediately after his applause, a loud cheer erupted among the Yadavas, followed by others who dearly loved Krishna. Joyful numbness took over Draupadi's limbs. Having just been crowned the empress of Bharata, she was yet to get used to the new position, but deep in her heart, she was Krishna's dearest sakhi, celebrating the honour of her friend. Dhaumya uttered Krishna's name along with other epithets, inviting him to grace the throne for the ritual.

Yudhishtira and Draupadi rose to assume their roles in the puja. However, Krishna's characteristic smile was absent. She concluded that it was out of surprise and grinned at him, taking the golden jar that contained water from the seven holy rivers.

The ritual continued for a while; each of the Pandavas and Draupadi were occupied in their own tasks. None of them saw a guest burn with rage at the decision. They missed seeing his friends restraining him from saying anything aloud. The chants gradually died down as the dissenting guest finally managed to make his presence felt—with a loud and obnoxious laughter.

Draupadi saw him, recognizing him as Shishupala, the king of Chedi! The groom who had initially been chosen for Princess Rukmini before she had broken out of the forceful engagement and eloped with Krishna.

She heard him call Yudhishtira an irreverent host who had insulted the venerable elders by offering the *agra puja* to someone as 'lowly' as Krishna.

Then, things deteriorated. She saw Nakula attempt to pacify Shishupala and restrain him from saying anything more. But to everyone's agony, it only infuriated the king of Chedi more. Bhima and Arjuna began to lose their temper. Arjuna warned Shishupala to respect the decorum of the grand hall where kings, princes and warlords from all corners of Bharata were present.

But Shishupala kept hurling insults, now at Krishna himself. A part of Draupadi wanted to grab one of the lamps placed on either side of the stairs leading to the high throne and smash

Shishupala's head. The only thing that bothered her more than his uncouth behaviour, was Krishna's silence.

One word, Krishna. One word, and this abomination will be shown his place.

Yudhishtira, she knew, was not in a position to speak his heart out, being the host, though Bhima was compensating for his elder brother's silence.

When the situation showed no sign of returning to normalcy, Bhishma tried to intervene and advised Shishupala to respect the host. Shishupala further shocked everyone by abusing Bhishma.

'Enough, son of Damaghosha and Shrutashrava!' the thundering voice was Krishna's. No one had ever seen this form of Krishna before. The boyish smile, the placid forehead and the unaffected eyes were no longer there. This Krishna looked like the god of death—the personification of rage—Rudra—demanding the destruction of the world. The guests, rishis, and the elders present in the sabha who were aware of Krishna's ever-pleasant demeanour were too shocked to react. The only person who dared to defy him was the foolish Shishupala whose past atrocities Krishna recounted to the whole sabha. Knowing about Shishupala's actions in the past, one of which included molesting the wife of a Yadava noble during her pilgrimage, Draupadi wondered why he had been invited to Indraprastha for the august finale of Rajasuya in the first place. It was then that she remembered that Shishupala's mother, Shrutashrava, and Kunti, the mother of Pandavas, were biological sisters. Kunti had been adopted by King Bhoja of Kunti kingdom later.

What an embarrassment of a cousin Shishupala was turning out to be!

The whizzing sound of the dazzling Sudarshana Chakra, a weapon that Krishna used in the rarest of occasions, brought her back to the sabha. Before anyone could react, Shishupala's head lay on the ground, away from its body. She stared at Krishna who stood rooted to the spot, still the embodiment of destruction. Having recollected the various atrocities that Shishupala had committed against the Yadavas in the past, the anger in Krishna's eyes was so intense that some of the rishis present started to pacify him, reminding him of his affectionate and protective side.

Yudhishtira looked like he had been struck by lightning. After a signal from Rishi Dhaumya, she inched closer to him. 'Samrat,' she squeezed Yudhishtira's arm, prompting him to conclude the ritual. He was displeased with the killing; she could sense that. But he loved Krishna too much to say anything, especially when Krishna was the recipient of the *agra puja*. But Yudhishtira looked like someone who had lost everything.

Not at all like the emperor he was.

Eighteen

Krishna's Farewell

It was late that night when Draupadi could retire to her bed, and when she finally did, not much time was left for the sun to rise. The daybreak started on a fatiguing note, given the way the Rajasuya had ended.

Empress of Bharata!

It still seemed surreal. She fondly remembered each of her husbands who had put in years of incessant hard work, even in trying times. She remembered and inwardly thanked the countless people, labourers, seers, soldiers, and merchants who had laboured with them to make this happen. If only Yudhishtira had managed to find some time to share this moment of realization with her. Even as an emperor, he laboured like an ordinary citizen. Disinterested in catching any sleep, Draupadi stared at the eastern sky, waiting for the rising red ball.

'Who can sleep when their dream is becoming a reality?'

Draupadi turned around, staring into the eyes that had dreamt of this along with her. Holding his arm, she led him back to the window, and they remained silent for a while. But the time came when he had to break the joyous silence of togetherness.

'Grant me leave, Samragni.'

Draupadi's eyes widened. 'So soon?' she mouthed and realized how selfish she had been to keep him away from his home all this while. But the instant pang of separation had managed to break through her eyes and blur her vision.

'Sakhi!'

She blinked the tears away, tightening her grip on his arm. 'It won't be the same without you, Krishna.'

'Where will I go, Draupadi? Wherever I go, I shall remain in the land under my Sakhi's rule.'

'I can "summon" you back any time, Vasudeva,' she smiled, assuming an air of mock authority. Softening as soon as she saw his tender smile, she whispered, 'My days as the queen of a principality flew by! And I am suddenly an empress with no prior experience of ruling vast empires.'

Krishna nodded and arched a single brow. 'To offer a conventional line of wisdom that is easier said than done, think of yourself not as the wife of an emperor, but as the mother of those who live on this land. Not as a wife, but as a mother.'

The glint of humour disappeared in his eyes when he uttered the last sentence. Looking at each other for a long time, letting the unexpressed words speak, they tore their gazes away from each other.

'Where are Rukmini and others?' she suddenly asked, springing into action. She owed them all a befitting farewell.

'Taking leave from other family members. They will be at your door soon,' Krishna replied, picking up a fruit that lay on the golden plate beside her bed. 'A whole day without food does make you hungry!' he said, seizing a knife to cut the fruit.

Draupadi had hardly realized that, like her, he, too, had gone hungry the whole night when she saw blood spurting out of his finger.

'By Mahadeva!' she gasped, tearing the softer edge of her upper garment to tie around the fresh wound.

'By Mahadeva, indeed! That was the garment in which you offered the *Poornahuti* in the yajna yesterday!'

Relieved when his bleeding stopped, Draupadi gradually settled down to face the day. 'You've been around at Indraprastha too long, Krishna. Now you must spend time with your wives so that they do not curse me for snatching their husband away!' she tried to laugh, but it was hard to swallow the emotions that churned in her.

⁓

Rukmini and the other wives of Krishna came to meet Draupadi, and in her usual lively manner, Draupadi took all the care to extend them a warm farewell along with the Pandavas, who were equally emotional at the impending separation from the one without whom they could not imagine a life.

But the time did come when the chariot, bearing the eagle flag, sped away from the ramparts of Indraprastha, taking a part of their lives with it.

Bidding farewell to the rest of the guests took up a large chunk of the day. Draupadi had not even had her meal. Not that she could not steal the time, but Krishna's departure had not left her with much appetite. Bhima, who would have been the first to coax her to eat, was caught up at the far end of the city, supervising the induction of new recruits to their imperial army. Yudhishtira, the new emperor, seemed to have skipped his meal as well, deep in discussion with the rishis who had graced the Rajasuya. Draupadi had decided to join him when a guard hurried in.

'Crown Prince of the Kurus, Duryodhana, seeks your audience, Samragni.'

Draupadi had been expecting Duryodhana, for the cousin of her husbands had been entrusted with accounting the tributes brought in by the allegiant kings. She had hoped to take over the treasury the following day. But sensing that the prince of Hastinapura might be in a hurry to leave, she bade the guard to usher him in.

Duryodhana. She had first seen him as a prisoner of her father, years ago, when he and his brothers had committed the folly of attacking Panchala. He had not seen her then, but she remembered the sullen adolescent pushing and kicking against the heavily built Panchala guards as they had held him. Draupadi bit her lip at the memory. She had also seen him at her own swayamvara. Handsome and promising, yet failing to deliver. It was later that she had learnt about his various plans to assassinate the sons of Pandu, including the fire at Varnavata.

Still, Yudhishtira had chosen to trust him with accounting the tributes. It was a decision that had been unanimously opposed by Bhima and Arjuna. But Yudhishtira strongly felt that trusting Duryodhana could mark a new beginning.

Draupadi had Duryodhana seated in the spacious quadrangle that extended in front of her mansion, overlooking the garden, with small lotus ponds and bushes of seasonal blossoms alternating along the path.

'Here are the accounts of what came from each of the vassal kings, princess of...pardon me, Samragni.'

Draupadi beamed at his abrupt change of address. 'You can call me sister-in-law, Duryodhana. You have been of immense help. I really can't thank you enough.' The nod of acknowledgement, Draupadi thought, came with a bout of hesitation. At that moment, she regretted dropping the formal protocol.

'Would you like me to accompany you to the imperial vaults and check on the treasures before you confirm everything, Sister-in-law?'

It presented a diplomatic challenge. The age-old convention regarding the accounting of wealth stated that even one's own shadow was not fit to be trusted when it came to matters of wealth. But choosing to verify the accounts would amount to showing mistrust, contrary to Yudhishtira's expectations. Thinking quickly on her feet, Draupadi chose not to sow the seeds of mistrust.

'Verifying the treasury after your meticulous accounting would amount to mocking the choice of the samrat, Yuvraj!' she smiled, bidding the royal treasurer to leave. The attendants brought refreshments and Draupadi asked about the well-being of the elders in Hastinapura who could not grace the occasion.

But before long, she sensed tension on Duryodhana's face. *Like something bothered him greatly.*

She was almost startled when Duryodhana slammed the goblet of drink on the parapet wall beside him.

'Pardon me, Samragni. I will take your leave now.' Without waiting for her reaction, he hurried down the flight of stairs leading to the garden.

'Wait, Yuvraj!' Draupadi called out, partly annoyed, partly surprised. Composing herself, she descended the stairs. 'I hope you are going to meet the emperor before you leave.'

'No, Samragni,' Duryodhana shook his head. 'Affairs await me at Hastinapura. Apologize to the Eldest on my behalf,' he said and walked away.

'Watch out!' Draupadi exclaimed. But it was too late.

The eldest son of King Dhritarashtra found himself waist-deep in one of the lotus ponds. The splash of water startled the gardener nearby who was attending to the adjoining row of blooming bushes. The shocked gardener tripped over the spade lying by his feet. His fall caused the female attendants to break into giggles.

Duryodhana looked up, annoyed. He saw Draupadi call the guards to help him out of the pond. The attendants were still giggling over the fallen gardener. Draupadi frowned at them, bidding them to bring dry clothes for Duryodhana. But the Kuru prince's temper was at its end. He pushed the guard who held him. That reminded Draupadi of the sullen Duryodhana of olden days. A chuckle escaped her lips. 'It seems that you will now *have to* stay!' she bid the guards to usher him back to the guest house.

The attendants were still caught in a helpless fit of giggles.

'Enough!' Draupadi snapped.

Duryodhana turned and hurried towards the guest house. None of them caught the change in his expression.

Nineteen

Yudhishtira's Fear

A gale blew through the windows, upsetting a couple of huge bronze lamps. Draupadi woke up, startled, realizing that she had dozed off while waiting for Yudhishtira to retire. It seemed like a few hours of the night had passed. The maids rushed in to secure the windows and light the lamps again. Draupadi rose in a hurry to secure the door that opened into the lavish balcony, overlooking the western expanse of the city. The familiar figure standing in solitude surprised her.

'Samrat! When did you arrive? Why did you not wake me up?'

Yudhishtira did not move until she bade the maids to leave and shook his arm gently. Distress loomed large in his eyes. He let her lead him to their bed. He saw her trying to fix her long hair, disrupted by the gale, and smiled through his melancholy.

'What ails the emperor of the land, My Lord?' she beamed when he caught her hair in a futile attempt to braid it.

Yudhishtira shook his head. It seemed insensitive to not share what he felt with her—his distress at the killing of Shishupala, his sorrow at the omens and warnings by the rishis.

It is only the beginning of a violent phase, you being the innocent cause.

The whole idea of Rajasuya seemed like a huge mistake. He knew that Draupadi did not take such predictions seriously. Perhaps her lighthearted remarks would set his mind at ease. But there was something in her mirth that he hated to disturb. 'I know what can put my emperor at ease!' Draupadi chirped, pointing at the game of chausar. Playing the game was the last thing he wanted, but he could not refuse when she tugged at his arm, determined to shake him out of his self-imposed melancholy. He felt a strange rebellion in his limbs when he took the dice in his hands and cast them.

Draupadi threw up her head in mock despair. 'Why doesn't this game like me at all?'

'The dice know that what belongs to me, belongs to you as well, Samragni!' Yudhishtira quipped. The dice always made him win. Every single time. Even against his own wishes.

'I don't seek a false victory,' she shook her head. 'Let us play another game. I just can't keep losing.' But the victories continued for Yudhishtira. 'There goes the last of my jewellery.' He could not help grinning at her dramatic show of despair at every loss.

All to keep him distracted from whatever she thought was worrying him.

He saw her pause amidst her struggle to unhook the ornate waistband and look at him. Helping her with the jewel, his heart leapt when her shapely waist showed, the flawless dusky skin a proud contrast against the yellow silk. Desire drove him to hold her by her waist. The sight of her gasping in anticipation made him pull her closer into his arms. He saw her eyes assume a mischievous glint when she withdrew abruptly. And he knew what would follow. Not letting her go away from him, he grabbed at her lower garment and pulled at the loose knot. The night claimed their bout of passion. Yudhishtira lost all track of time, until the bell, announcing the last quarter of the night, rang. He saw her smile through her half-asleep eyes and roll towards the other edge of the bed. Her loosened braid slid from his hands and moved towards the ground below when she turned the other way.

'Draupadi!' he hurried to her side of the bed, catching her tresses before the ends touched the ground. Draupadi woke up to see him stroke her hair and gently place her braid across her half-covered breasts.

'Never let them touch the ground, love,' he sighed, inhaling the fragrance of the herbs offered in the Rajasuya in her hair.

Draupadi encircled his neck with her arms. 'What had burdened you, Yudhishtira? I have a right to know.'

'Everything,' he said after a long moment of silence. 'The moments of this emperorship, the grandeur of the Rajasuya, everything threatens to claim its price. And I fear I might not be able to afford it!'

Abstract fears were not something that ever made sense to Draupadi. But Yudhishtira's concerns could not be taken lightly. 'Rajasuya did claim a lot, Samrat. I am aware of the debt we owe to the traders who financed the campaign. But as far as the accounts of the treasury show, we should be able to pay them off any moment now. In fact, let us arrange for a befitting ceremony to felicitate those who supported us at the soonest.'

Yudhishtira nodded, 'We cannot afford a war now. Even if we are attacked by anyone.'

'Attacked by who?' Draupadi frowned. 'Not that our neighbours, your cousins, dote on you. But even Hastinapura in its present state will not think of war, Samrat. In other directions, we are surrounded by our allies.' Yudhishtira breathed easy. A war with anyone seemed like a distant possibility and he knew it. Just hearing it from Draupadi seemed to ease his heart. 'Perhaps, it is just Shishupala's death,' he sighed.

'I knew it,' Draupadi's voice betrayed annoyance. 'You aren't very pleased with Krishna killing him. But who would tolerate that king of Chedi, Samrat?'

'Krishna is as dear to me as he is to you, Samragni,' Yudhishtira said. 'And his enemies are ours too!' Pain resurfaced in his eyes. 'But he made newer enemies by killing Shishupala. God forbid, if one of them attacks Dwaraka, it will be too late even to reach out and assist him.'

'It is tricky to interpret his moves, Yudhishtira,' Draupadi relaxed, pulling the soft rugs over her. 'I can't boast of understanding him fully. But thoughtlessness is definitely not his trait, Yudhi. But perhaps you are right. We would have been in a much better position to shield him if he had stayed a bit longer at Indraprastha.' It was her turn to worry for Krishna's safety.

The fatigue of the day finally claimed Yudhishtira, but something kept Draupadi up. Some unknown fear.

Part Three

The Empress

Twenty

The Game of Dice

'Attack on Dwaraka?' Draupadi and Yudhishtira exclaimed in unison.

The messenger nodded. 'Lord Vasudeva and his brother were away at Prabhasa, Samragni. Dantabaktra, who was posing as a regular pilgrim, attacked them there. It was a close fight, but Krishna managed to kill him. Before they could even recover, Dwaraka was caught unawares when the king of Salva launched a surprise attack.'

'Did Krishna and Balarama reach on time? What about the women of Dwaraka?' Yudhishtira asked.

The messenger had no clue about the safety of women at Dwaraka. But he knew his master well. 'I am sure there are contingencies, Samrat,' he assured a concerned Yudhishtira.

After the messenger left, neither Draupadi nor Yudhishtira spoke for a long time. The throne they sat on seemed like a burden before their helplessness.

'Samrat, we must do something,' she knew Yudhishtira's mind was already planning. 'Salva and Sindhu are allies. The king of Sindhu, Jayadrata, is married to our Dusshala, the daughter of Uncle Dhritarashtra.'

'Are you thinking of influencing Jayadrata to convince Salva to back off?' Draupadi exclaimed.

'Extending military help is the least we can do, Samragni,' Yudhishtira said. 'But the help will take months before they reach Dwaraka. Additionally, if Uncle Dhritarashtra can send one of his messengers from Hastinapura on the fastest horse with a convincing message to back off, it might work to our advantage.'

A multipronged effort was necessary. If Bhima or Arjuna came to know of this, Draupadi was sure they would rush to Dwaraka. She herself was dying to know about Krishna's safety.

Can't you keep yourself out of trouble, Sakha?

Yudhishtira summoned all his brothers to his private council room and was about to send for a messenger when the guard interrupted him. There was a visitor from Hastinapura. Uncle Vidura!

'I shall talk to Uncle Vidura, Draupadi.'

'And let me see if Subhadra is fine after hearing the news, Samrat,' Draupadi hastened towards the palace. Subhadra was shocked. But she was convinced about the alternate plan. 'My brother had foreseen the need for such an escape route when the city was still being constructed,' she sighed in relief.

Draupadi was still disturbed and it was beyond familial reasons. The news of this aggression by Salva was outrageous. It held the sovereignty of Yudhishtira and Indraprastha in contempt. If the forces from Indraprastha could not reach Dwaraka in time to help their dearest ally, what message would that send to the other allies as well as the kingdoms who had pledged their allegiance? She impatiently waited for Yudhishtira to return after convincing Vidura. Whatever diplomatic action he thought was required, military action had to accompany that.

Draupadi assessed that it would take about a fortnight for the contingent to set out to Dwaraka with the necessary preparations, assuming that the kingdoms in the route acceded free pass to them, which was not a problem.

She had reached the end of her patience by the time Yudhishtira concluded his meeting with Vidura and sought her. But far from assurance, Draupadi saw worry on his face. 'What did Uncle Vidura say, Samrat?'

'Uncle Vidura was not himself today,' Yudhishtira's frown deepened. 'Even after my repeated appeals, he insisted on conveying Uncle Dhritarashtra's invitation to us to attend the opening ceremony of Jayanta sabha and grace the occasion with a game of dice. He remained non-committal about Hastinapura's interference regarding Salva and Dwaraka.'

Draupadi found it equally perplexing. Even though she had not expected Hastinapura to readily support them, she had anticipated at least a favourable response. 'So, military action is all we can take right now.' 'I shall instruct the commander, Indrasena, to prepare a large contingent of the army to march westward,' Yudhishtira replied after some thought. 'The army shall march to Dwaraka in case our mission in Hastinapura fails. But something bothers me, Samragni. This king of Salva is one of the most inconspicuous kings of Bharatavarsha. He had remained neutral about his alliances, though I am aware of his tilt towards late Jarasandha and his erstwhile friends. How did he muster the courage and forces to attack Dwaraka?'

It was a pertinent question that had been troubling Draupadi too. 'So, there are others who are backing Salva,' she thought aloud and saw Yudhishtira nod. 'Probably someone close enough to him to supply the forces?'

'Gandhara, Sindhu, Madra, Kambhoja,' Yudhishtira listed

out the kingdoms on the western frontier. 'The princess of Madra is Krishna's bride and chances are less that they would harm the marital home of their own daughter. But the other three are related somehow or the other to Hastinapura!'

'Did Hastinapura know it? Or did it clandestinely support this attack too?' she saw a mix of anger and shock on Yudhishtira's usually calm face.

'I will have to confront Uncle Dhritarashtra about this, Draupadi.'

'You can order them as the emperor, Yudhishtira,' Draupadi replied.

'I could,' Yudhishtira nodded. 'Probably the situation and its urgency warrant it too. But the court of Hastinapura is full of venerable elders, Samragni. The hostility between us cousins notwithstanding, it was with the blessings of elders like Bhishma, Baahlika, Kripacharya and others that I ascended the throne of Indraprastha. Though not evident, I am sure that they played a key role in convincing Duryodhana against opposing our Rajasuya campaign. Ordering their king who, despite his failings, is still an elder, would be akin to insulting all of them.'

The situation seemed to get trickier by the moment. Draupadi felt like they were walking amidst treacherous thorns. 'Do we accept their invitation to the game then and use the opportunity to delicately confront Uncle Dhritarashtra?'

Yudhishtira took a deep breath. 'Uncle Vidura usually lets me in on the plans of Hastinapura and indirectly guides me to the next step. But today, he seemed inscrutable, and if I may add, defeated.'

'It is unlikely that your cousins will commit another mistake like the lac-house fire again. They would lose too much now,' Draupadi frowned.

'Highly unlikely,' Yudhishtira concurred, 'I shall leave for Hastinapura in another two days. Bhima shall personally look into readying the army contingent in my absence.'

'Like your brothers will let you, the emperor, go alone to Hastinapura when so much is under suspicion!' Draupadi protested. 'Nor can I stay back, Samrat. Subhadra can look after the children for a couple of days.'

Yudhishtira was about to shake his head but something in her eyes made him feel otherwise.

Like he would be better off with her beside him at Hastinapura.

Twenty-one

Court Scene I

Hastinapura

The messenger's voice interrupted her troubled nap. Draupadi sat up on the couch. On seeing the male intruder, otherwise not allowed into the inner chambers, she glared at him. He was trembling, as if dreading saying whatever he had come to convey. Draupadi softened and nodded at him.

'You…you have been called to the sabha…Devi,' he immediately lowered his glance.

Draupadi did not mind honouring Dhritarashtra's wish of seeing her in the sabha. But asking a guard to call her, a samragni, seemed odd.

'Did the game conclude?' she asked, remembering the game of dice that was supposed to take place.

Swallowing hard, the messenger opened his mouth, 'Emperor Yudhishtira…wagered and…lost you.'

It took a full moment for her to digest the news.

Lost me?

With some effort, Draupadi managed to remain calm. 'Who

is calling me to the sabha?'

'The crown prince…Duryodhana, in the name of King Dhritarashtra, Devi.' His eyes begged her to not ask him any more questions.

Draupadi rose, showing neither hurry nor anger. 'What did the emperor lose in the game?'

The guard mumbled, 'Everything, Devi. His treasury, his army, kingdom, empire, brothers, weapons, himself…and you.'

The reality now hit her.

She was being summoned as a wagered win. Possibly as a slave?

Instinctively, Draupadi's hand felt for the dagger placed by the side of her couch. She loosened her grip, realizing the futility. If valour could save the day, the Pandavas would not have let it come to this. Desperation and poise rivalled each other within her. And rage she did not know who to direct upon. The wily host or her gullible husbands? Steadying her shaking lips, she drew herself to her full height.

'Pratikami,' she addressed the guard, 'do hasten back to the sabha and ask the king of Hastinapura. Did the emperor lose himself first, or me? If he lost himself first, wagering me would not have sanction, according to the rules that govern the game of dice.' She saw him stare at her. Admiration replaced his shock for a short moment before his eyes narrowed in pity. She hated seeing that. 'Hurry back and pose my question to the court of Hastinapura. I would like to know what the elders think.'

The guard left and Draupadi collapsed on the couch, trying to get a grip over herself. Wagering riches and jewellery was one thing. But wagering a principality played with the hopes of the people of that land. The question here was of an empire. The empire that was built on their vision, sweat, and blood—

right from the late King Pandu to the lowest foot soldier in the Pandava army.

Upon the unthinkable, he wagered and lost his own brothers and himself? And her?

As futile as it seemed now to invoke the rules of the game, Draupadi thought fast. The betrayed woman and queen within her made the task even harder. But something made her feel responsible. For the empire, for the hopes of countless people. At one instant, her hands shook so much that she had to curl her fists hard.

Like a part of her wanted to strangle Yudhishtira. Who, by the name of Mahadeva, had given him the right to do this?

She began to ponder over the order of the losses, assuming the guard had recollected them correctly. The game should have stopped the moment he lost the last of his jewellery. But Yudhishtira was not used to losing in a game. Losing the treasury would have driven him to desperation. They had, only a day before, discussed the prospects of financing and sending a portion of their army to Dwaraka to help Krishna. The treasury was crucial. Wagering the army to win it back must have been the next step in desperation and she could see how things had spiralled to this dire situation.

She hated him. She hated his trait that had brought him to that situation!

Krishna!

The cry within sounded distraught.

What would he advise me to do in this situation?

'Mother of this empire!' Krishna had quipped cheerfully when they had last spoken to each other. A tear trickled down her cheek at the memory of him tenderly brushing her cheek. She had hardly a year's experience as the empress of Bharata.

But she had been a mother for long enough to realize what she had to do. Determination replaced everything else and she rose to take measured steps towards the sabha. She walked past the dark corridors, undaunted. She was not the 'lost wife' anymore. She was the mother. And a mother left no stone unturned when it came to save her children—her subjects, her empire.

The flabbergasted guard met her midway. 'Devi...they said you should come to the sabha...to find the answer to your question.'

Draupadi walked ahead, 'Who else is there in the sabha? Is Queen Gandhari present?'

The silence told her that the guard was clueless. She was sure that news of this magnitude would not be hidden from Queen Gandhari.

If she could somehow stall the proceedings till then and influence Gandhari to impress upon the king...

Telling the guard to hurry forward and announce her arrival, she began to delve into the nuances of statecraft she had learnt under the able tutelage of Acharya Upayaja. 'Be with me in spirit, Acharya. Guide me to save the day.'

Entering the vast corridor outside the sabha, Draupadi made her way towards the ornamental mezzanine that usually served for seating the women of the royal family. It was then that she felt a hand reach out to pull her by her arm.

'Dushasana!' she snapped, thwarting his grip.

The look on the face of the younger Kaurava prince when he blocked her was like that of a hungry hyena. 'Acting smart for a slave, aren't you?'

'What did you dare call me...?' the retort was hardly out of her lips when he caught her hand again. When Draupadi resisted, his other hand caught her long hair.

'Let go! Dushasana, you uncouth... Let go!' The pain almost made her shriek. But pride stopped her from doing so. Before she knew, Draupadi had slipped on the stairs that descended into the sabha. But Dushasana's grip on her hair did not loosen. Despite her resistance, he managed to drag her. 'Shame on you, lowly jackal!' her nails dug into his palms, but his brute strength prevailed.

Her feet hit the sharp edges of the stairs. In an attempt to hold on to an empty seat, her hands were wounded.

Were the courtiers of Hastinapura simply watching her ordeal? It can't be!

Draupadi was not in a position to look at anyone present in the sabha, her long tresses blocking half her view and the force of his grip rendering her unable to turn the other way. Draupadi panted for breath, trying to rise, when she felt something. The monster had placed his foot upon her back, pinning her down.

Grunting like a cornered leopard, Draupadi mustered her strength and finally shook him off her. Raising her head, her eyes fell upon the silk cloth, embroidered for the game of dice, and then on the pair of white dice. Her eyes blazed red when they fell upon the five familiar figures, sitting rooted to the spot. She was about to address them—no, order them—to kill the foul-mouthed Dushasana on the spot. However, no words escaped her when she saw their downcast pale faces. She doubted if they would ever look into her eyes. For their own good, she hoped they would not. Turning her gaze towards the blind King Dhritarashtra, she rose like a cobra.

'King of Hastinapura! Is it "customary" in your "illustrious" Kuru sabha to drag women by their hair?' a haunting tenor echoed from her. Not waiting to hear the King's response, she turned to glare at the others in the court. 'Am I in the same land which believes that gods turn wrathful when the honour of a woman is violated? Or was I dragged into a land devoid of all the principles that a civilization imbibes and follows?' The elders—Grandsire Bhishma, Kripa, Drona, Uncle Vidura, the grand old man Baahlika—everyone turned his gaze away from her. Draupadi's gaze stopped at one man. The first one who had dared to meet her gaze.

Either he had no conscience or...

'The woman who serves five husbands, what "honour" does she deserve in any civilized land, Draupadi?' If she knew a way of controlling the elements, Draupadi would have burnt anyone who said those words. But the sheer satisfaction that the man showed in uttering the insult told her how low his conscience had stooped.

'Vasusena Karna!' a lone voice came from the other side. 'Uncivil rhetoric does not speak of civilization either!' He was one of the younger Kuru princes, a person unlikely to defy his own brothers.

At least someone has a spine in this court of imbeciles!

The young prince stepped forward to face King Dhritarashtra. 'Father, being the king of Hastinapura, you bear upon your shoulders the burden of keeping up the ethos of our ancestors. The Princess of Panchala has indeed posed a valid question. The eldest Pandava had no rights to wager her after losing himself.'

Karna turned to his side, laughing dismissively, 'Prince Vikarna, one does not expect a boy like you to know the nuances of a game like this. But the courtesy of not defying your own elders is the least that is expected of you!'

'Besides,' Shakuni, the maternal uncle of Duryodhana and the mastermind behind the dice game, interjected, 'Yudhishtira himself sits in silence without a protest. Do you, Vikarna, need a greater proof that Draupadi was won in a lawful wager?'

Vikarna scoffed, 'None who acknowledges the legacy that we strive to uphold would stand back, doing nothing at this sheer injustice.'

A murmur broke among the courtiers. Draupadi chose to not look at Yudhishtira or any of his brothers. She sensed a movement, and it seemed like one of them was about to break the ominous silence and teach them a lesson, but he was held back by another. But at the moment, none of that mattered. She was here to protect her dreams and what she had spent years working for. The chances of her succeeding seemed bleak but she could not give up!

'Besides,' Vikarna continued, 'when the princess of Panchala is the wife of all the five brothers, the eldest Pandava has no right to wager her in the first place!'

Duryodhana finally cleared his throat to speak. Not missing an opportunity to cast a gleeful glance at Draupadi, he turned to Vikarna. 'The game is a fair one, Vikarna. But to satisfy you and probably…' his glance hovered over Draupadi again, betraying his forbidden longing, and then passed on to the five brothers. 'Ask the younger brothers of Yudhishtira themselves. If they can defy their eldest, even if one of them can defy Yudhishtira, he is free to go along with *his* wife!'

Draupadi glared at him when the truth struck her. It was this unity that they were aiming to damage. The survival against deadly intrigues, the meteoric rise of Indraprastha, the unrivalled expansion—all of that had happened due to the unity of the five brothers. The unity that Kunti had nurtured and preserved, the unity that she, Draupadi, had furthered, sacrificing the joys of a simple marital life to endure the complicated relationships a polyandrous wedlock presented.

At that instant, her gaze turned to the Pandavas. The contrast was distinct. One pair of eyes was still downcast and four pairs of eyes were showing readiness to defy him at her signal. Draupadi had to make an effort to steady herself.

The fight remained.

To their horror, she shook her head, raising a forbidding finger—being as discreet as she could be. Moments of quiet followed. Nerve-racking pain threatened to overtake her limbs, but Draupadi held on.

Duryodhana stared at the four brothers of Yudhishtira and shrugged, 'Looks like your husbands have spoken... I mean, by not speaking.' He guffawed and continued, 'Draupadi, any more "questions"?'

'What would nuance mean to those who take pleasure in bending principles and subverting the tenets of kshatra dharma?' Draupadi scoffed.

'Enough, slave!' Karna interjected. 'The court has wasted enough time deliberating over her pointless question! Dushasana, drag her here and throw her at the feet of her new lords.'

Twenty-two

Court Scene II

The shock on the faces of the elders was palpable. Dushasana was about to reach out to grab Draupadi again, but he was held back.

'Lord of Kurus! Pray, stop this tragedy! Would you want your progeny to remember you as the one who let his daughter-in-law be molested in the sabha, under your rule?' Vidura, Dhritarashtra's younger brother and his prime minister, urged him. He tried to hold back Dushasana. But the Kuru prince shook him away with ease.

'Molested? You amuse me, Uncle,' Duryodhana chuckled. 'But to allay your fears, let me give this "daughter-in-law" a chance to redeem her honour. She is free to desert her husbands and choose anyone present in this court as her new husband. She would be freed this very moment.'

At that instant, Draupadi saw Karna step forward. The involuntary rise of hope in his eyes made her want to laugh aloud. She did, but at Duryodhana's idea of justice. 'Fie on you, Duryodhana! In fact, I pity you! Unable to better my husbands when their valour is unleashed, you have resorted to this unjust game of dice. You dishonour me even by thinking that I would choose one of the spineless souls in your court as my husband. Given the cowards that you all are…,' her eyes pointedly blazed on Karna, 'you don't even deserve to stand by my side, forget getting my hand!'

Duryodhana threw his head up. 'As my dear friend rightly said, enough time of this sabha has been wasted in addressing pointless questions. Dushasana, bring her to me.' He added, baring his left thigh, 'Let her take her place, here!'

'Mark my words, Duryodhana!' Bhima sprang up, shaking off whoever had restrained him until now. 'You gloat over my condition today and dishonour my queen. But think of the day,' his own frame shaking with rage, Bhima paused as he glowered at Duryodhana's brothers, 'when I shall smash your thighs to a pulp and drink the blood of your brother who dared to drag Draupadi by her hair! None, I repeat, none of your other brothers will remain alive by then to come to your aid.'

An eerie silence filled the court. But Dushasana only laughed. Shoving Vidura out of his way, he pulled Draupadi by her arm.

'Wait, why is the slave still wearing silks that only queens and noblewomen wear?' Karna bellowed. 'Pull those garments off her body and bring her here.'

'Karna!' Arjuna's voice broke. 'All your life, you have ached to compete with me in archery. I promise you, that wish will be granted. That day, your mother will weep over your corpse! The corpse with a missing head that my arrow will claim!'

'Stay away!' Draupadi thundered at Dushasana who advanced despite the spine-chilling oaths taken by Bhima and Arjuna. 'This is a sabha blinded not only by lust and vileness, but also by foolishness of the worst kind.' Turning to the elders, she added, 'Are you all unaware of the combined might of Panchala and the other allies that the house of Pandu enjoys?

Are you under the delusion that they will care about the "rules" of this damned game when it will come to avenging this assault on their daughter and queen?'

Her threat had a mixed effect on the onlookers, but not much on Dushasana who caught hold of her upper garment.

'Grandsire Bhishma! Acharya Kripa, Acharya Drona!' she called out to the elders. 'You stand on the threshold of eternal infamy...' her voice faded, seeing the helplessness that had overcome Bhishma's face.

She remembered the love and pride she had seen in his eyes on the day of the crowning of Yudhishtira. She remembered the awe and fear that his name had struck among the formidable warriors of Bharata. Helplessness did not belong to that name. Draupadi's eyes narrowed in pity as her grip over her garment loosened. The knot began to give way.

Vikarna, the lone dissenter of this ignominy among the Kaurava brothers, had left the court. Vidura, the only voice that spoke sense, was not being heeded by anyone. King Dhritarashtra sat rooted to his spot.

'May you remain in history as the ones who shamed the house of illustrious Bharata. Lusty jackals, it is not my body that you stare at! It is your doom! The doom of your house! The doom of your lineage! The doom of your peace!'

The garment gave way and Draupadi collapsed because of the impact. A strange sense of abandon overtook her. Modesty was the last thing she cared for. The day awaited this doomed land when royal families and commoners would tear each other apart, like her garment had been torn apart. Now there seemed no way to stop it.

Perhaps, that was for good!

At that instant, another garment miraculously landed over

her shoulders. It covered her just as her torn garment slipped off her body. Draupadi felt faint even as those present in the court stared, spellbound at the phenomenon.

Krishna! You're with me indeed.

Steadying herself, she glared at Dhritarashtra who had not uttered a word. Meanwhile, Vidura put himself between her and Dushasana.

'Let it be, Uncle Vidura,' Draupadi said. 'Let those asking for their own destruction have their wish granted. Let their women…'

'Dushasana, you are playing with fire!' a female voice rang behind her. 'Duryodhana, son, have you decided to write your own doom?'

Queen Gandhari. You are too late.

The blindfolded queen stumbled twice or thrice in her hurry to reach Draupadi. When her steps faltered for the fourth time, Draupadi herself rushed to support her.

'My sons have taken leave of their wisdom, senses, and everything that keeps a man sane, Princess of Panchala. Forgive them! I beg you, forgive them!' Gandhari attempted to kneel at Draupadi's feet but was stopped midway by Draupadi. The next moment, the queen of Hastinapura turned to face the throne. 'Lord of Kurus, save our sons. Undo the wrong done to Draupadi. Otherwise, I fear we will live to see our own progeny die. We will live to see people celebrate their deaths and berate us!'

Dhritarashtra stirred like a statue which had come back to life. 'Daughter of Drupada, it is unfortunate that you have been wronged this way.' Dhritarashtra's voice shook with guilt.

Draupadi's contemptuous glance intensified.

'Ask for a boon, my child! Ask for anything that I can

do to undo at least some of the damage done this day in this unfortunate sabha!'

Gandhari's hand pressed upon her shoulder. Draupadi knew she could ask for Duryodhana and Dushasana to be put to death. But that would still not achieve anything.

'Release Yudhishtira from the bond of slavery, king of Hastinapura! No one should dare call my firstborn, Prativindhya, the progeny of a slave.'

'As you wish!' Dhritarashtra uttered in a hurry. 'But this can't be all. Ask for something more, my child.'

Draupadi gathered her thoughts. Asking favours from the blind king seemed insulting after what she had faced. But her work was only partly done. 'Release Bhima, Arjuna and the twins along with their weapons.' Dhritarashtra nodded readily, 'That is the least I can do, Draupadi. But this is still not enough. Ask for something more.'

Draupadi laughed, 'I stepped into my marital home where my prosperity was only the valour of my husbands, king of Hastinapura. Besides, a woman with a free and valiant husband need not demean him by asking boons from someone else!'

Dhritarashtra tried to offer more. But Draupadi turned away. Further proceedings and settlements were of little interest to her. 'Uncle Vidura, take me to your home,' she requested a tearful Vidura, who readily escorted her out of the sabha. There were praises from the very mouths that had jeered her ordeal. But Draupadi did not stop to hear anything else. She had fought like a tigress. She had enabled her husbands to fight against the wrong that had been done.

Twenty-three

Nakula and Draupadi

The sounds of the night died down one by one. The noises from the city, footsteps of the maids from the corridor, and even the chirping of night birds died down. But ominous sounds echoed in her ears. Draupadi did not attempt to sleep. Visions of what had happened in the sabha replayed mercilessly in her mind. 'How could it happen?' she questioned repeatedly. Her soul felt shattered into pieces, each of them pulling her in a different direction. Justice? Revenge? Wrong? Right? Each thought dragged her through an arduous journey to an uncertain future. A burdened future. It was past midnight by the time sanity prevailed.

When she heard footsteps, she remained stoically seated, waiting for him to enter.

'Nakula.'

He approached her only after she called out to him. She silently stared into his strained eyes that clouded his otherwise handsome face.

'Why, Draupadi?' The two words seemed to drain him of all his strength. Draupadi stirred, seeing him collapse to the ground. 'There was a second game of dice, upon King Dhritarashtra's wish', he narrated. She let out a sigh. 'The loser had to go on an exile for a period of twelve years followed by a year of living incognito, the kind of incognito in which the detection of their identities would result in a repeat of the exile.'

'When do we have to leave?'

Something about her unaffectedness made him shudder. 'As soon as possible,' he said. 'Not for the exile, but out of the unfair world of Kurus.'

For the first time since he had entered the room, Nakula saw a movement on her face, even if it was a small frown.

'You did not answer my question, Draupadi. Why did you stop us from…protecting…' Nakula struggled for words. '…from fighting…for the last bit of honour that we could have guarded.'

'What would have happened if I had not done so?'

Nakula thought he saw her smile, though reproachfully. But only for a fleeting moment. 'My own conscience would not have burned me the way it does now,' he said. Her eyes narrowed, unimpressed.

'You would have rebelled. They would have ordered one of your own brothers to fight you. The unity would have broken…'

'For the sake of Rudra, let it break!'

'Dare say that again, Nakula!' her eyes turned crimson.

'Draupadi! Pray, stop binding us together and leave this undeserving wedlock,' Nakula said, in agony.

Undeserving wedlock! Indeed!

Draupadi's fists curled. She had not cast herself into the vortex of a polyandrous life to see this day. She had not subjected herself to live with a different brother every year, just to see them break this way. She could not let the labour of years go waste at the first stroke of bad luck.

'What will you do if I leave you all, Nakula?' her tone got harsher.

Nakula did not respond for a long moment and then sighed, throwing up his head. 'Perhaps I might find courage to go my way,' he saw her brows arch in further reproach. 'Don't take me for an ungrateful son, Draupadi. I shall take care of Mother Kunti with greater care than those three would ever do.'

Draupadi turned away, dismissing the plea in his eyes, and rose to her feet. Her heart threatened to crumble. 'You are free to leave, Nakula. I shall not bind you to your brothers.' Her limbs grew limp. But she held on—to speak the most painful words he had heard in his life. 'Do leave if you happen to concur with "noble" Karna's opinion of my character.'

Nakula's face turned pale. Ever since she had entered his life, he had worshipped her. She knew that too well to throw this hurtful allegation at him! His fingers curled around the sharp edge of his dagger in a vain bid to redirect the pain elsewhere. But the blood that oozed out did nothing to assuage his numb heart. 'You know me, Draupadi.'

'I hope I do.'

Nakula said, 'Tell me what to do.'

Draupadi turned towards the door. 'We all leave together for the exile.'

∫

The rishis, headed by Dhaumya, had stayed up to chant hymns invoking the gods to protect them during the period of their exile. Draupadi stared at the humble ceremonial fire set up at the western outskirts of Kurujangala province of the kingdom. To her right was the beginning of Kamyaka forest. Draupadi stepped out to the portico of the rest house that the people of Kurujangala had lovingly provided them. Throughout the day, she had heard women of the province curse the Kaurava cousins, some of them asking her to stay with them in disguise, promising to protect her and her family with their own lives. She had thanked them and convinced the people to leave. But they had to wait for the Panchalas and Yadavas before entering the forests.

Her thoughts were interrupted by Shrutakarma's murmur. She hastened to calm the child.

They did not deserve this. But who did?

Draupadi took a hand fan and started fanning the five children. It was after a while that her firstborn reached out to her, placing his hand in her lap.

'Get some sleep, little one.'

'How many days till Uncle Dhrishtadyumna comes?' Prativindhya asked.

'They should be here in a day or two,' Draupadi stroked his hair. Her eyelids closed in a bid to hold back tears. 'Take care of your brothers at Panchala, Prativindhya.'

'May I stay with you, Mother?'

Draupadi looked into his pleading eyes. Her sons had never been separated from her, even for the short visits to their maternal grandfather's home. The prospect of not seeing them for thirteen long years broke her heart. She shook her head.

'Great princes from history, Lava, Kusha, the sons of Sri Rama, and our own ancestor Bharata, were born and brought up in the forests. Why can't we stay with you?' he persisted.

Prativindhya had inherited the trait of quoting historical instances from his father. Draupadi hoped that this was all he had inherited from Yudhishtira. 'They were brought up under the protection of rishis in ashrams, son,' she explained, 'moreover, they did not have enemies in their pursuit. You, on the other hand, need to protect your brothers, and till you become capable, you need to stay at your grandfather's home.'

She could feel Prativindhya's silent rebellion in the way he clutched at her garments. She could also feel the obedient son in him quelling the rebellion within him.

Just like his father!

'When I see you again, I will be of twenty-five springs,' his voice broke in the end. But Prativindhya hid his face in her lap, determined to not break down.

'I know. And you will make me proud, son,' she hoped that he would sleep soon. But whatever kept her awake kept him up too. Even the rishis completed their rituals and went to sleep. Draupadi could not move from her children's side. Something about them helped her sanity prevail. Checking her emotions, she continued to fan Prativindhya until the boy held her hand again.

'Are you angry with Father?'

Draupadi's hands froze. Anger had indeed managed to take root in her heart. A part of her wanted to vent it out. The rest of her questioned the very purpose.

Does it even matter if she was angry or not?

She found herself shaking her head. 'Anger gives no solution in trying times, son.'

'Have you forgiven him?'

She shook her head again. She had not spoken a word to Yudhishtira since the fateful day. Even with the other brothers, her communication had remained limited. Would she let one bad day ruin the tender bonds that she had nurtured? She brushed the boy's cheeks. 'I shall, when I deem him worthy of it.'

The boy realized that this was all he would get from

his mother and resigned himself to sleep. Draupadi felt a shadow appear behind her. As if the person had overheard the conversation. But then, the shadow receded. Turning her head, she found Yudhishtira stare into the darkness, towards the city— the kingdom he had ruled so benevolently. Countless citizens had gathered in his support after the incident.

How could he have gambled it all away—dealt the land they had all carved with their blood and sweat such a cruel blow? How had he dared to play with their emotions?

But still, they seemed to love him!

Draupadi leaned against the pillar, resigned to staying up the whole night. Perhaps there would be a day when he would unburden himself to her and she would do the same with him. But now was not the time. The distance would remain. For how long, she could not say. The only person to whom she could bare her heart was caught in a battle. She ached for his return.

Twenty-four

Meeting in the Forest

A fortnight had passed since the Pandavas had fashioned a residence for themselves in the wilderness of Kamyaka. The citizens of Kurujangala still visited them every day. They sought Yudhishtira's judgement to resolve the issues they faced. Rishis and Brahmins, too, lingered, and feeding them had become a challenge. Draupadi arranged for food with the help of some women. But the continuous stream of visitors had begun to test their patience. The will to maintain the façade of unity had started to wither. Draupadi feared an unpleasant confrontation to break out anytime, given Bhima's silent seething.

One day, Draupadi saw a stream of new visitors headed towards their residence. When the dust settled, the sight of the eagle banner made her heart leap.

He was safe.

Draupadi kept aside the stone on which she was sharpening Arjuna's arrows. She needed to speak to Krishna privately. Not because they had things they wanted to hide from the world, but because she felt the five brothers would not be able to face themselves if they had an inkling of what raged in her heart. Without a word, she hurried inside the hut. Even before the commotion of the Yadava visitors, she felt the presence behind her.

He had not even bothered to exchange pleasantries with his own cousins!

Before she knew, Draupadi felt a warm stream of moisture down her cheek.

'Sakhi!'

Grief threatened to break the dam she had built all these days. 'Hold me, Krishna!'

He turned her to him and she cried against his chest. His arms barely managed to steady her frame, which was shivering with her anguished sobs. 'Pray, calm down, Draupadi. Your tears could claim lives!'

She let Krishna wipe her tears. It was only then that she saw what her tears had done to him. They had turned his dusky skin crimson. Withdrawing from his comforting arms, she shared an understanding glance.

They could not give up!

'Thirteen years is a long time. Long enough for loyalties to change. Not just loyalties, but also the narrative of what is right and wrong. The narrative of what is dharma.'

'It is a challenge that cannot be undermined,' Draupadi agreed, wiping the last drop of tear from her eyes. 'The future generations will even wonder why we stuck to the five brothers after the thoughtless gamble.' In Krishna's sharp gaze, she saw her own will manifest. 'They told me I could choose another husband. They said I would cease being a "slave" even if one of my husbands rebelled against Yudhishtira.'

'Not everything is lost, Sakhi!' the curve on his lips suggested there was hope.

Hope against hope!

'Steel yourself against the twisted interpretations of dharma that Duryodhana will propagate with the help of his minions. They will try their best to weaken the support we have gathered. At the end of this trying period, all we will have is the stubborn persistence of staying united. Faith in nothing but our own selves and our commitment to dharma.'

'The game of dice was a grave error of judgement, Krishna. An error that made a mockery of everyone who supported us,' Draupadi stared into the expanse outside the window. 'But that does not take away the core merit of the five brothers. I say this not as their wife, but as someone who considers the whole of this land as her home.' She saw Krishna look at her with admiration that she had seldom seen him exhibit. 'I see the reason behind Yudhishtira insisting on completing this period of exile. It is not his blind adherence to the conditions of the game. But his readiness to face the consequences of his own choices.' Draupadi moved towards the lone wooden seat and collapsed on it. 'Our choices. Whether or not the population of Bharata understands the same.'

'Thirteen years, as I said, is a long time, Sakhi,' Krishna leaned against the hand rest of the seat and stroked her hair. 'Time long enough to prepare ourselves for whatever will face us at the end of it!'

'One thing puzzles me, Krishna,' Draupadi sighed. 'Where did we go wrong? No amount of preparation will suffice if we fail to learn from our mistakes. Yudhishtira knew that the game would not be fair. He said so repeatedly before we left for Hastinapura. But we thought it would only cost us a principality or two in the worst case. None of us ever expected that it would result in...'

'Underestimating the enemy,' Krishna explained, his tone

turning solemn. 'Rajasuya was the kind of victory that graces us once in a lifetime, Draupadi. As an emperor, he could have initiated the change in the codes that undermine dharma. The delay in consolidating that victory has taken its toll.'

'Complacency!' Draupadi threw her head up. 'If only we had realized that dealing with victory was as crucial as dealing with threats! Of course, thirteen years is a long time!' After a long moment of silence, she placed her hand in his outstretched hand and rose to her feet.

'Sticking together when time tears you apart is what makes a true winner, Draupadi,' Krishna's gaze turned towards the door, outside which he knew the five brothers waited to talk to him. None of them had dared to interrupt the conversation between dear friends.

It was time to reunite to face what lay ahead.

'Let them know you are with them, Sakhi. Not just in silent actions, but also in setting the direction. Their strength will get a new lease of life when they know that you are with them in your heart despite what has happened.'

Draupadi nodded. Krishna turned to exit the hut and she caught his arm. 'Grant me another wish, Sakha!' she smiled, seeing his assent. 'I shall send the message to Panchala myself. Let my sons grow under your care at Dwaraka. At Panchala, they will be guided by my father and brothers, who will only drive them to vengeance. The boys deserve better.'

Twenty-five

Journey to the Himalayas

L ife at Dvaitavana had not been the same after Arjuna's departure. He had been the embodiment of poise who would moderate heated discussions. He had been the peacemaker between Yudhishtira and Bhima, who in the early phase of the exile, had been difficult with his temper. After Arjuna left for his tapasya, Draupadi had attempted to moderate once or twice but had ended up exhibiting her own emotions, further infuriating Bhima. The strain between her and Yudhishtira had continued for days. After the coldness showed little sign of dissipating, the rishis suggested they go on a pilgrimage and join Arjuna at the peak of the snow-capped mountains that lay on the northeastern borders of Bharata. It was an idea that they had unanimously agreed to—a rare occurrence after the fateful game.

Trekking from the forests of Dvaitavana, they halted in the familiar wilderness of Kamyaka. Being acquainted with the forest and the rishis, their stay here continued for years. When Rishi Lomasa arrived, they travelled towards the northern hills. Draupadi found her own spirits lifting on the northbound travel. The dropping temperature was a welcome sign and so was the delightful topography that almost made them forget that they were serving a period of exile. The ever-meditative Sahadeva would spend hours staring at the sky. Nakula would gather bits of information about the fauna and flora of each place. Yudhishtira would seek information from other travellers about the mysterious Yaksha tribe that was believed to control the mountainous region.

Often she was left in the company of Bhima, which she greatly enjoyed. In her presence, the giant would vent the suppressed agony the atrocities of the sons of Dhritarashtra caused him, and she would listen patiently. This often caused new troubles as Bhima went to unreasonable lengths to please her.

Once, the enticing sight of a valley in full blossom made Draupadi long for a walk in the terrain. She bit her lip as soon as she had voiced her wish. 'Bhima, let it be.' She shook her head.

'Come on, don't dash my hopes to the ground this way, Draupadi!' he persisted till she gave in.

'Just promise to not repeat the Saugandhika incident where you disappeared for days to search for a flower,' she shrugged and walked with him after Bhima had promised that they would return before sunset.

'I know your love for blossoms,' Bhima smiled his most tender smile. 'Even at Indraprastha, you would spend more hours supervising the gardens, than your mansion. Even at the risk of the gardeners dreading your presence!' he guffawed at his own joke before the stab of realization of what they had lost hit him. He looked at Draupadi who was already interested in a strange-looking creeper blooming with long flowers. She was commenting on the contrasting effect the creeper would have when planted against a row of Kadamba plants. Unwilling to break her reverie, Bhima walked towards the end of the cliff.

Draupadi paused, sensing him walk away. Her lips pursed at

the thought of their serene bliss disturbed by bitter memories. Forgetting the day at the Kuru sabha was not possible. Mechanically gathering the seeds from the creeper, which she hoped would germinate in the warmer temperatures near the foothills, she proceeded to explore the lower row of bushes. It was then that she sensed the treacherous camouflage. As she was swept off the ground, Draupadi could not see the abductor who sprang upon her from nowhere. Before she could alert Bhima, his rough hand closed upon her mouth. Her legs kicked the air, frantically trying to make some noise that would reach Bhima's ears. Even though her hands were free, it was futile trying to overpower the brute. Draupadi, by now, was sure it was a rakshasa—a cannibal! Mahadeva knew whether he intended to feast upon her, or worse, force himself on her. She tried to hold on to anything that would impede his speed. Bhima was bound to notice her silence and absence and look for her soon. She only had to delay the progress of the rakshasa. Draupadi attempted to hold on to a branch, but the cannibal was too strong for her grip. A part of the branch broke and remained in her hands. Draupadi tried beating his legs with it. But the attempts were in vain. Finally, she gave up and dug her nails in his leg instead, causing him to move his hand from her mouth.

'Bhima!'

The rakshasa grunted in anger, tightening his hold over her, realizing her trick.

'Bhima!'

She managed to scream before he gagged her again. But Bhima seemed too far to hear her. The rakshasa gained speed after that. She, too, was exhausted by now.

'Leave her, Jata!' A voice came from the path ahead of them. The rakshasa stopped in his tracks. 'I said, leave her!'

The voice was familiar. Draupadi saw a figure emerge on the slope covered with wild plants. The voice sounded a lot less menacing, almost protective. The rakshasa—Jata, as the other man called him—continued to advance.

'I shall not say it again!' The voice was much closer. As he landed right before Jata and compelled him to leave Draupadi alone, she saw his eyes widen.

'Samragni?'

'Ghatotkacha!' she mouthed, remembering the son of Bhima by Hidimba, the woman chieftain of the rakshasas. He had even attended the Rajasuya. In the couple of years that had followed, Ghatotkacha seemed to have grown into an able-bodied rakshasa. Draupadi saw them pounce on each other. The style of fighting differed a lot from what she had seen in the urban parts of Bharata. The moves spoke of brute force but she could sense their remarkable ability to take advantage of the topography. None of them gave the other a moment to breathe easy. Nor did any of them show signs of fatigue. Resilience seemed to be a quality ingrained into their minds and bodies. It was terrifying to watch. But it was fascinating too. It was only after she saw them engaged in a deadlock that she remembered to call out to Bhima again.

Jata's desperation seemed to grow upon the thought that his opponent could receive more help. The young Ghatotkacha, she could gauge, was a strategic fighter too. She could guess that his mother had possessed the presence of mind to train her son under experienced wrestling teachers from urban Bharata as well. It showed in the way Ghatotkacha retained his breath even when Jata's started to falter.

But where on earth was Bhima?

Draupadi began to get worried.

Was he too caught up with some other rakshasa lurking in the wilderness?

Draupadi's eyes quickly surveyed the rugged route downhill, and then, she turned her gaze back to the bout. Ghatotkacha managed to land a powerful blow on Jata's head that sent the latter sprawling down the slope. He hit against another boulder. Neither Draupadi, nor Ghatotkacha, saw him move for a while. Draupadi exhaled and looked for Bhima who had disappeared. It was unlike him to not respond to her call.

'Ghatotkacha!' she exclaimed, stopping him in the middle of his greeting. 'I am worried for Bhima. We came together till there!' she pointed in the direction of the cliff and narrated how Jata had tried to whisk her away.

Ghatotkacha's lips parted in concern. It was not like Bhima to succumb to anything without a good fight and it required more than an average rakshasa to defeat Bhima. Ghatotkacha surveyed the valley for other possible exits. Nothing seemed out of place.

Draupadi saw what Ghatotkacha had missed. She sensed the shadow from a distance and whirled around just in time to see Jata sneaking behind them after recovering from his fall.

'Watch out!' she cried, on seeing Jata's club, ready to hit Ghatotkacha.

The lad ducked before he turned around but Jata screamed and fell down before his club could deliver its intended blow. Draupadi and Ghatotkacha saw a grinning Bhima behind him!

∿

The second layer of wolfskin had become a necessity in this altitude. Draupadi opened her eyes to see Nakula massaging her cold feet and Sahadeva trying to protect the fire from the winds.

She had heard of the beauty of the snow-capped mountains and had always cherished a dream to visit the Himalayan valleys. But with the increasing height, the topography seemed to turn more hostile. She tried to sit up and felt her head spin.

'Don't get up so soon, Samragni. Rest a while more,' Yudhishtira patted her from behind.

Succumbing to physical fatigue and helplessness was a first in her life. Much against her own wishes, Draupadi fell back, resting her head in his lap. Yudhishtira proceeded to massage her head, and she was in no position to protest. 'Don't we have more distance to cover today, Samrat?' she managed to ask.

It seemed to her that Yudhishtira's voice too had considerably weakened. 'We have, Samragni. But Ghatotkacha offered to carry you for the rest of the journey. We have some more time to rest before he returns with a hunt.'

Bless Ghatotkacha! But how mortifying was it to be carried like this!

Draupadi groaned in disgust. She heard Nakula chuckle sadly.

'If it makes you feel any better, even the three of us need help if we want to proceed any further. Of course, Bhima being the exception,' Nakula muttered.

'Did our empire extend till here?' Draupadi wondered. As per her knowledge, Arjuna, in his northward campaign during the Rajasuya, had brought under the empire the territories of Kimpurusha, Yaksha and Gandharva. Nakula nodded. Draupadi's respect for the soldiers who had accompanied Arjuna rose, and she began thinking about the perils they might have encountered while fighting against the better-positioned local armies. How had their sacrifices been squandered away over a stupid game? Warm tears washed down her cold cheeks. Suddenly, the insults she had faced from Karna, Duryodhana and Dushasana seemed smaller than what an average soldier in the army of Indraprastha would have felt at the news of the loss of the empire. Why did Arjuna, who was well-aware of the sweat and blood of the soldiers, not stop Yudhishtira? She had no answers, and she knew even Yudhishtira had none. This journey to the Himalayas seemed meaningful now.

Never should a soldier's sacrifice go unnoticed, much less, squandered away in the name of meaningless diplomacy.

Bhima and Ghatotkacha, along with his followers, returned with the hunt for the day. Following them were eminent rishis, known for their extensive travelling and experiences. Draupadi sensed Yudhishtira move and sat up to welcome the guests. While the meal was cooked, they would have a story to listen to! The story turned much more interesting when one of the rishis informed them about Arjuna's current whereabouts and his return journey. The fatigue of the arduous trek was forgotten when tales about Arjuna's encounters with the divine beings were recounted by the rishis, the highlight being his possession coveting of the Pashupatastra that had belonged to Lord Shiva himself!

Draupadi's mood changed on hearing about Arjuna's return. It was almost like how it had been when he had returned from his military campaign for the Rajasuya. Kunti had been right. None among the five brothers could be himself when one of them was not around.

Twenty-six

Duryodhana's Ghoshayatra

The return to Dvaitavana was more pleasant than the onward journey. Draupadi felt that Arjun's return had lifted the spirits of the other four too. It showed in all aspects of their daily life, right from their appetite to their enthusiasm about hunting, discussing statecraft, and weapons. She expressed it to Yudhishtira once and could not decipher the wry smile on his lips. Before she could ask him the reason, the rishis came to visit and welcome them back to Dvaitavana.

The rishis engaged them by narrating tales of heroic kings and queens, and of the learned rishis of yore. The tales came with messages of inspiration that lifted the spirits of the five brothers in the trying times. Some of the rishis and travelling Brahmins often brought valuable information about what was happening in the various Mahajanapadas, especially in Hastinapura.

Before they had embarked on the northward journey, Yudhishtira had kept himself abreast of the information with a keen interest. Duryodhana, in the early days of the Pandavas' exile, had indeed gone to extreme lengths to keep the citizens and other vassal kings happy.

But in recent years, while the citizens found little change

in their lives, trouble had started brewing amongst the various kingdoms of Bharatavarsha. The royal family of Kekayas had broken up, with hostilities rising amongst paternal cousins—a situation the Pandavas could relate to. The kingdoms of Matsya and Trigarta were in constant tussle, at times, even stooping to the level of raiding the borders and stealing each other's cattle. The rulers of the central kingdoms of Avanti and Vidarbha maintained a diplomatic demeanour, but the travellers told Yudhishtira that signals of economic dominion were surfacing, and it was a matter of time before the ambience turned hostile. The onus of resolving these tussles often fell upon Dhritarashtra who sat on the throne of the empire. However, he often left the decisions to his eldest son and Duryodhana's skill of resolving hostilities was not popular.

That day, the travelling rishis told them something that made Yudhishtira sit up.

'The crown prince of Hastinapura aches for a break. The news of your arrival at the forests of Dvaitavana has reached Duryodhana, Samrat. To humour him and keep him away from the issues of governance for a while, Shakuni and Karna have impressed upon him the need to organize a pleasure trip to Dvaitavana. The royal retinue is set to arrive here accompanied by a thousand attendants, cooks, soldiers, entertainers, servants, and pleasure girls,' the rishi tried to summarize what he knew.

Sensing the hostility in the faces of Arjuna and Bhima, Yudhishtira concluded the conversation swiftly and bade the rishis farewell after a brief meal. The evening passed in an uncomfortable silence, with each of them attempting to distract themselves.

Draupadi observed Yudhishtira's restrained anger. It surfaced once or twice in his eyes. But the eldest Pandava knew how to suppress it. At times, even at his own cost. Draupadi felt compelled to ask him about it when she saw Yudhishtira awake, long after the rest of his brothers had gone to sleep.

'I know why Duryodhana has suddenly set out to interact with cattle rearers on the bordering regions. It's a pretext,' Yudhishtira's tone assumed an uncharacteristic acerbity.

'The real intention of this Ghoshayatra is to flaunt what they have in front of us so that he can escape from his own inadequacy in governing this empire,' Draupadi replied, mirroring his unaffectedness. 'Worry not, Samrat. Neither the flaunting, nor the ostentation they are going to exhibit, is going to disturb me now,' she paused. Both of them knew that Duryodhana would not be foolish enough to get into a confrontation with them. With Arjuna's newly-acquired astras and Bhima's strength, they did not stand a chance, especially when they came accompanied by their servants and courtesans. Nevertheless, she added, 'I shall make sure that all the weapons are sharpened and ready for use.'

Yudhishtira caught Draupadi's arm when she turned to enter the hut. 'It is going to hurt, Draupadi.'

'Not me, Yudhishtira. Neither should it hurt you.'

The Kaurava retinue did arrive in a few days' time. The Pandavas saw architects arrive at the other side of the lake, a few days in advance, to set up an elaborate encampment. The cooks and servants followed to arrange for food, drink and other necessities for the royal couple. Draupadi tried to ignore the noises that often disturbed her night's sleep. To her relief and Yudhishtira's, Bhima set out to hunt in the other direction. They often underestimated the giant's perceptibility.

The rishis, however, continued to visit Yudhishtira and life continued like before. One day, a young rishi expressed his displeasure at the way the lake was being polluted by the retinue of Hastinapura, with remains of food, meat, and even discarded garments and containers. The fauna that used to visit the lake for drinking, had stopped coming to the vicinity in fear.

'It is blatant flouting of dharma, Samrat!' the rishi exclaimed. 'Dvaitavana is host to human inhabitants like us. What kind of a guest dishonours his host and violates the sanctity of the premises this way?

The very kind of guest who dishonours and tries to violate his own guests!

The five brothers understood the young rishi's impassioned expression of love for the forest and its creatures. Before any of his brothers lost his restraint, Yudhishtira thought of an action that would pacify the rishis as well as keep their minds off the intruders. He proposed performing Rajarishi Yajna, a fortnightly ritual performed in the honour of the beings present in the forest. The rishis lauded his initiative and readily helped him with the arrangements. With Draupadi by his side, Yudhishtira performed the yajna, invoking the various beings of the forest and thanking them for their safe and peaceful stay in the premises, and the enriching experiences of Vanavasa—a phase they had feared would be much more arduous.

To his relief, the day passed uneventfully with all of them immersed in the ritual. To his surprise, the noise from the encampment at the other side of the lake also stopped. After sunset was the time for singers and entertainers to perform and entertain the Kuru princes, and the soldiers would join in, blowing trumpets and beating drums. But for some reason, an uncharacteristic silence prevailed upon the encampment, as if the inhabitants had suddenly vacated the camps. Upon Draupadi's suggestion, he sent two young rishis to cross the lake and find out the reason. Before long, the rishis returned, and to Draupadi's surprise, they brought Princess Bhanumati—the princess of Kalinga and the wife of Duryodhana—with them.

For a moment, Draupadi's eyes narrowed, remembering the fateful day.

The very princess who had not spoken a word in her defence.

Shaking her thoughts away, Draupadi stepped forward. A closer look at Bhanumati raised her concern. The wife of the Kuru crown prince had not bothered to wear her jewellery and even her braid was undone. Draupadi walked up to Bhanumati, noticing the redness in her eyes, and held her arms with tenderness. Bhanumati broke into hysterical sobs and collapsed on the ground.

'Princess Bhanumati!' Draupadi exclaimed in genuine concern and tried to raise the distraught woman. But Bhanumati clung to her feet. The sound of her wails made Yudhishtira and his brothers hurry closer. Yudhishtira looked for Duryodhana or any of the Kaurava brothers and found none. He looked at the rishis, confused.

'The Kuru crown prince angered the Gandharvas who were also camped at the far end of the lake, Samrat,' one of them replied. 'The Gandharva lord was outraged, and overpowered the prince, binding him and taking him away.'

'Arise, Bhanumati,' Draupadi said, and led her inside the hermitage while Yudhishtira moved towards the deserted camp to probe for more details.

Bhanumati's tears continued. 'Believe me, Draupadi. I warned him against this Ghoshayatra. My heart was against intruding on these enigmatic forests with unwelcomed pomposity. But my words fell upon deaf ears.'

'What happened to Du...Dushasana? Was he captured by the Gandharvas too?' Draupadi enquired, fighting a flood of emotions. Something about Bhanumati's state reminded her of her own lonely battle on the day of the dice game. She saw Bhanumati nod, a new wave of pain in her eyes.

'And Karna? He must have fought off the Gandharvas?' Draupadi enquired. 'Karna was too drunk to even take proper aim at them!' Bhanumati wailed. 'Mahadeva knows where he fled in a bid to save his own life!'

Draupadi moved away, allowing Bhanumati to vent her grief. Bhanumati sprang to her feet and caught her arms. 'Your husbands can save him. Only they can secure Duryodhana's release!' Seeing Draupadi's lips part, she went down on her knees again.

'Pray, arise, Bhanumati!' Draupadi said.

It was surreal, the slew of emotions that overwhelmed her. Bhanumati's grief melted her heart. The wife of the enemy who had dragged her into the court and had tried to disrobe her, now knelt at her feet, begging her to save that enemy. The very enemy who had come all the way to Dvaitavana to gloat over her misery and that of her husbands. Draupadi extricated herself from Bhanumati's grip and stepped out of the hermitage. She saw Bhima argue with Yudhishtira.

'The brute who insulted our queen had the nerve to intrude our peace, Eldest. I desisted from teaching him a lesson. But then, he had to sow seeds of enmity with the Gandharvas and insult their women as well. Who are we to interfere, Samrat? Even if we try, what can we tell those who fought only to guard the honour of their women?'

She saw Arjuna and the twins in a similar mood. 'If you insist, we shall accompany Princess Bhanumati to the outskirts of Kurujangala and make sure that the patrol guards of the kingdom escort her back to Hastinapura safely.'

Draupadi exhaled, as if an invisible burden was lifted off her shoulders. Bhima and Arjuna were overcome with rage, but neither of them had the heart to gloat over Bhanumati's misery. She waited to see Yudhishtira's response.

'Let the Kuru household not look broken in front of a stranger, dear Bhima. We owe it, not to Duryodhana, but to those ancestors who brought glory to our lineage,' Yudhishtira reasoned.

'Bah! To keep up their honour, we go and secure the release of the one who sent that hard-earned goodwill down the river?' Bhima turned away.

Draupadi had seen him rile and rant at Yudhishtira's obstinate restraint. But this was the first time she saw him disobeying the eldest Pandava. As absurd as the idea of saving Duryodhana seemed, there was something wrong about Bhima's mutiny. Draupadi went forward and held Bhima's arm. 'Listen to him, Bhima. Secure Duryodhana's release.'

Bhima glared at her in disbelief and walked away.

Draupadi stopped Yudhishtira from following him and went herself. She saw Bhima trying to immerse himself in watering the plants she had sown, but in vain. He saw her and paused, slamming the pot of water aside.

'Bhima…'

'Enough, Draupadi,' he snapped. 'Looks like even you have forgotten what happened on that fateful day.' He looked into Draupadi's eyes, conveying his struggle of the past years. 'I know what I saw in your eyes when that…coward Dushasana…kicked you in the sabha. It haunts me and it will haunt me long after I kill all those brothers with my bare hands.'

'It is exactly what I don't want, Bhima,' Draupadi replied calmly, placing her hand on Bhima's shoulder. Suppressed rage made his muscle flex and squirm under her hand. 'We cannot allow the wounds of that day to fester within us.' Bhima saw her eyes narrow. 'Overcome those Gandharvas. Let your cousins know whom they will face after our exile. Go, Bhima.'

'Naiveté was never your nature, Draupadi,' Bhima shook his head. 'Like they will give a damn about favours we grant them today.'

'They shall not remember, Bhima. But morally, as well as strategically, we stand at crossroads. If we turn Bhanumati away in this state, we are being callous and petty. Mother Kunti did not give birth to such men. I did not marry such men.'

Bhima threw up his head. But for all his frustration, he gave in and mutely picked up his club. Draupadi held his hand tenderly. 'This is not just a moral stance, Bhima. This will be an act that shall stay in the memories of many.' Remembering the days at Indraprastha, her eyes assumed a nostalgic look. 'Remember when our Krishna killed the king of Chedi at the Rajasuya, Bhima? You cited the incident many times, saying that is how one needs to deal with enemies who heap insults at us. But Krishna killed him only after a series of wrongs. Some wrongs so heinous that we wonder why he waited in the first place.' Her husbands knew she had a soft corner for Krishna. And she knew how they loved him. She continued, 'Shishupala, the erstwhile king of Chedi, was his cousin. Your cousin too. Krishna waited his crimes out to a point where even Shishupala's mother, his aunt, could not blame him for killing her son.'

Bhima sighed, knowing what came next. 'You will now ask me what Krishna would have done in our place today. He would have charmed those Gandharvas into releasing Duryodhana. Like he charmed his brother Rama from killing that Jarasandha. Remember that I had to finish his job!'

Draupadi beamed through her own flood of mixed memories. 'I do not urge you to be Krishna, Bhima. Your brothers are what they are because you are what you are. But this is something which only you and Arjuna can do.'

Draupadi's face withered in painful speculation. 'Who knows what will happen after the period of exile? It shall not harm us to help our enemy in need once. So that he knows. So that Bhanumati and the rest of the world know who the Pandavas are.'

Twenty-seven

Jayadrata

Bhima and Arjuna left in pursuit of the Gandharvas. With great difficulty, Draupadi convinced Bhanumati to have her meal before they retired to bed. Yudhishtira decided to keep watch for the first quarter of the night, convincing Nakula and Sahadeva to catch some sleep. He looked at Draupadi with gratitude when she came to share his watch, leaving Bhanumati safely inside the hermitage.

'How is the princess of Kashi?'

'Still in shock, but she managed to sleep,' Draupadi replied, putting more firewood into the yajnavedi. When it wasn't the time of a yajna, the flame served as a night light in their courtyard.

'Will she be able to bear it when Duryodhana dies?'

Draupadi's hands froze at the calm yet firm determination in those words. She looked at him.

'Can I count upon you consoling her the same way, when the day comes, Draupadi?'

It took her some time to find the words to speak. 'Are you… Samrat, are you implying the certainty of war?' She looked at Yudhishtira closely. He didn't react. Remembering their past arguments where Draupadi had favoured immediate action against Duryodhana while Yudhishtira had always advocated restraint, this seemed new to her.

'Princess Bhanumati might not be this compliant that day when she knows that your husband killed hers. But still, the onus of her future lies with us, Samragni,' Yudhishtira's voice had assumed a prophetic tone. Something about it seemed odd. He did not seem like the Yudhishtira she knew. Draupadi shook him by the shoulder, hoping to snap him out of whatever it was. But Yudhishtira remained unmoved. 'What disturbs *you* about Duryodhana's death, Draupadi?'

Draupadi had to think. It was one thing to wish for Duryodhana's downfall. But it was another thing to envisage a war that would claim much more. If the cost of re-establishing dharma was war, then Draupadi knew they had to pay it. It was just that the certainty with which Yudhishtira spoke of it seemed unnerving. The fact that the peace-seeking Yudhishtira not just desired but was predicting the destruction of his enemy was something different. It threatened a whole shift in the balance that she was guarding. If Bhima or Arjuna came to know about their brother's readiness for war, even gods would not be able to restrain them. Draupadi remained thoughtful till Yudhishtira gently held her palm.

'I knew that my pacifist attitude bothered my brothers. I am also aware that the ordeal you had to bear that fateful day was due to the same, Draupadi. But I never thought this would bother you,' he smiled.

Draupadi shook her head, 'Arya, I would be equally unnerved if Bhima started to favour peace at the cost of all that we have lost.'

Yudhishtira raised a finger, 'Now is when I need to confess, Draupadi. Perhaps, I should have done this earlier. Ambition to reunite the land of Bharatavarsha was sown in my heart by my late father Pandu. His fateful death left us at the mercy of our uncle. Our uncle's desire was to see us face everything, from ridicule to multiple attempts at assassination. I have tried to fight my desires ever since. But I could only suppress them, never overcome them. Ambition kept rising within me. But my attempts to control that ambition cost me my wife and brothers, their self-respect, and dragged the empire to another vortex of power struggles.

'But as long as the desire to fulfil my father's dream remains within me, it would be foolish to try and prove the lack of ambition to this world. It is high time I owned my desires, Draupadi. When we lay back the claim to what is rightfully ours, we shall stop at nothing. We shall go to any lengths in undoing the damage done till now.'

He saw Draupadi look at him without batting an eyelid. 'Are you with me, Draupadi?'

Only the last question seemed to bring about a movement in her eyes. Her brows arched in surprise and amusement. 'What makes you think otherwise, Yudhishtira?'

'Even if ambition has taken root within me, I need you to share it. Without you as an integral part of any initiative, I will stumble. I also need you to inspire the other four. They wish for a war. But there might come a time when they might waver. Breaking apart in such circumstances would be disastrous on multiple levels.'

The image of the burning flame in her eyes was her only response. 'Let the twins sleep, Yudhishtira. Tell me more about war.'

The night passed in grave discussions between them—about allies, their own motivations, strengths and weaknesses, various pitfalls they would encounter, the worst-case possibilities, and more. They continued until the predawn hours, till they heard the rishis from the neighbouring hermitages wake up. More noises could be heard from the northern side of the lake. Draupadi sprang to her feet on hearing Bhima and Arjuna's voices.

Arjuna entered the courtyard first, accompanied by a stranger—tall, sun-tanned, yet radiant with pronounced features. 'Chitrasena, the lord of Gandharvas. He insisted that he would release Duryodhana only in your presence,' Arjuna introduced him to Yudhishtira and Draupadi.

Yudhishtira nodded and glanced over Arjuna's shoulder. He found Bhima standing with a group of Gandharvas, each wearing a different expression, ranging from glee to annoyance. He found Duryodhana encircled by them, still bound and roped. 'Welcome to our abode, Lord Chitrasena. I cannot express my gratitude for your agreeing to release our cousin, Duryodhana.'

Chitrasena, who had remained stern until then, found Yudhishtira's smile too infectious to not smile back. 'I had heard about you too much to turn down your request, Samrat Yudhishtira.' He walked to a seat and greeted Draupadi. After being seated, he called out to his followers who brought Duryodhana inside. 'But, eldest of the Pandavas, do you even know what your "dear" cousin was doing on the banks of Dvaitavana? Are you aware of his flouting the code of this serene forest and violating nature after intruding with his noisy and pompous retinue?'

Seeing Yudhishtira tackle the question with the best of his diplomatic skills, Draupadi kept herself out of the conversation and glanced at Duryodhana who was wounded and bruised. Battered with defeat and dishonour, his face had lost all emotions. She then turned to see Bhanumati, still asleep. It would be heartbreaking for the princess of Kashi to see her husband in this state. When she turned back, she saw Yudhishtira tell Bhima to free Duryodhana.

'It was too close this time, but don't repeat this folly again, dear brother,' Yudhishtira smiled at Duryodhana.

With the twins returning with more firewood, Draupadi busied herself with preparing food for the Gandharva guests. She saw Duryodhana leave immediately without a word of gratitude. The Kuru crown prince did not even wait for a pleasantly surprised Bhanumati to get ready and accompany him. Draupadi shrugged to herself, and asked a couple of servants from Hastinapura to stay back to escort Bhanumati safely to the Kuru capital.

The Gandharvas left after the meal on a cordial note. She observed Bhima's glee continue over the day, at times peaking when Nakula or Sahadeva joined him in his amusement. There was a moment when even Yudhishtira gave in. It reminded her of their days at Indraprastha before the preparations for the Rajasuya had started.

As a family.

At least till the next intrigue faced them.

After this, the days passed uneventfully for some time. Draupadi sensed the anticipation of war gradually rise among her husbands. It was exhilarating as well as terrifying. Especially when she imagined the full might of the land of Bharata, divided and pitted against each other.

On days when the five brothers left to hunt or fetch water and wood, she would ponder over the impending war. On one such day, she was so preoccupied with the multiple possibilities, that she realized the presence of a royal host in front of their hermitage only when the king entered the ashram. He looked familiar.

177

Where had she seen him?

Draupadi narrowed her eyes and called out to Rishi Dhaumya, who had come to live beside their hermitage as soon as they had returned to Dvaitavana. Rishi Dhaumya received the king and looked unsure when he came to Draupadi to convey the news. 'He is Jayadrata, the king of Sindhu, Samragni. The husband of Princess Dusshala, Duryodhana's sister.'

Another Ghoshayatra?

Draupadi frowned, looking at the army that accompanied Jayadrata. Unsure about the sudden arrival, she saw the king of Sindhu waiting at the entrance of the ashram. Stepping out of the hermitage, she welcomed Jayadrata cordially.

Jayadrata stared at her before he found words to respond to her pleasantries. He marvelled at her dusky skin, resisting age with all its vigour. He looked at her arms, strong and supple. 'Queen Draupadi,' he acknowledged her at last, his gaze coming to a halt at her eyes. 'A forest is not the place for the likes of you!' The words were spoken even before he could get a grip of what had come over him.

Draupadi looked up, her eyes narrowing at the crass remark. She had only extended a welcome to him because of the Pandavas' affection for Dusshala. 'The valiant sons of Pandu will be back soon, king of Sindhu. They will be eager to know about the well-being of sister Dusshala.' She led him to the stone seats that had been erected in the courtyard, and proceeded towards the hermitage. 'Let me guide your army towards the lake so that they can refresh themselves.'

To her relief, Rishi Dhaumya was at the entrance of the ashram. A look at his face told her he sensed trouble too. She thought about asking him to send some young rishis in search of the five brothers. But she was stopped. Draupadi turned around when Jayadrata held her hand.

'Jayadrata!'

'I was on my way to Hastinapura, My Queen. But your stunning beauty changed my mind. Come away with me before your husbands return...' Before he could continue, Jayadrata felt a stinging pain on his cheek. Draupadi shoved him out of her way and hurried towards the hermitage. Jayadrata's gaze followed her. She was moving towards the dagger she had been sharpening! He chased her, just managing to grab her by her arms before she could reach for the weapon. He pulled her towards him. She tried to wrestle out of his grip, but Jayadrata had blocked her way.

'King of Sindhu!' Rishi Dhaumya thundered, grabbing his staff. 'Stop this folly or death by the hands of the Pandavas awaits you!' Hurrying to Draupadi's side, the rishi tried to help her to her feet. But Jayadrata's sword swished across the air, dangerously close to his neck.

Draupadi thought fast. With his army by his side, it was humanly impossible for Rishi Dhaumya or herself to stop Jayadrata. 'Rishi Dhaumya! Rush to the five brothers!' she urged the shocked Dhaumya. 'Pray, leave!' She dearly hoped that the Sindhu army would not stand in his way.

Jayadrata laughed at her instructions. Pulling her along the pathway, despite her resistance, he jeered at Rishi Dhaumya. 'Pray, rush and fetch those husbands of hers! They shall swoop down on me and protect her like they did at the sabha in Hastinapura!'

Draupadi swished at the rebuke, like a cobra would at the arrival of an intruder upon its anthill. The Pandavas would surely fight and overcome this rapacious brute within no time. But his army of over a hundred cavalry and many more foot soldiers had to be taken care of!

'Bhima! Arjuna!' Draupadi screamed at the top of her voice. Jayadrata, unable to drag her anymore, lifted her over his shoulder and took her to his chariot. 'Foolish army of a foolhardy king!' she shouted at the cavalry. 'My Arjuna, with his newly-acquired astras, my Bhima, with years of hardened muscle who overcame fearsome rakshasas with his bare hands, will come for your king. They will come for you!' she thundered, simultaneously trying to hold back Jayadrata from cracking the whip. 'Run for your lives and save yourselves from being beheaded by the archer who faced the Mahadeva himself in a single bout! Worse, if you fall under the wrath of Bhima, even your own wives will not be able to make out your disfigured faces dangling on your corpses! Desert this rat and run for your lives!'

A frustrated Jayadrata slapped her hard across the face. Not giving him the pleasure of seeing her pain, Draupadi bit her own lip until she bled.

Her repeated warnings worked and the armies began to scatter. Jayadrata ordered them to regroup. Some of the cavalry tried to goad the foot soldiers to fall in line. But Jayadrata could not stop his army from splitting and fighting with each other.

'Foolish woman!' he spat, shoving Draupadi. 'Don't you see your misfortune if you continue with those good-for-nothing imbeciles?'

Draupadi sneered through her pain. 'My misfortune is much lesser than poor Dusshala's! For my husbands do not lust after women against their consent! My fragile sister-in-law is better off widowed, than as a wife to a brute like you! My husbands shall see to it!'

Jayadrata ignored her warning. He finally managed to get some of his men in line and cracked the whip, 'Towards Hastinapura! Let me see how far her husbands come for her!'

Draupadi kicked at his groins.

Stunned at the pain, Jayadrata held her cheeks with his left hand, digging his nails into her face. He was about to force his lips on hers when an arrow whizzed between them and took down the banner of his chariot.

Twenty-eight

Farewell to Dvaitavana

The resounding twang that followed sent the army into another round of confusion. Jayadrata turned around in shock. But he found no one. Such a precise aim had to be Arjuna's. Before he could spot the archer, Jayadrata heard a horseman shriek in pain and fall from his horse, with an arrow through his back. Another did not even have the chance to scream as the next arrow beheaded him. The rest of the army that surrounded Jayadrata scattered when the third life was claimed.

A roar was heard behind them—a battle cry that froze the blood in everyone's veins. Bhima! Draupadi laughed, unaffected by the bruises on her body and the blood trickling across her face. Something about her laughter terrified Jayadrata more than the arrows and the roar. He let go of Draupadi and jumped out of the chariot. In a bid to escape undetected, Jayadrata mounted one of the horses and tried to gallop away.

Only after his exit, Draupadi felt her bruises burn and ache. The dust that rose around her because of the confused horses galloping hither and thither did not allow her much visibility of what happened next. She held on to the flag post till she saw the Pandavas rush to her, each wearing an expression of worry and anger. Draupadi pointed in the direction she had seen Jayadrata escape. Nakula and Sahadeva helped her out of the chariot when she discovered that she had sprained her leg in the tussle with Jayadrata. As she clutched her leg, she heard Bhima curse aloud and set out in Jayadrata's pursuit. Arjuna and the twins followed him, leaving Yudhishtira and Rishi Dhaumya to take her back to the ashram.

Yudhishtira did not speak until they had reached the porch, where he seated her. Lifting her face, he saw welts of Jayadrata's fingers, and fetched water to clean the blood on her face. 'They will bring him back and throw him at your feet, Draupadi!'

Draupadi nodded, saying nothing. Every encounter like this reminded her of the fateful game. Her eyes lashed out though she kept her tongue in check. She knew Yudhishtira could hear the unspoken. She could feel it when he began to pace across the path, sighing.

'We have less than a year before the term of Agnatavasa starts,' he spoke after applying another round of medication. Agnatavasa was the year of living incognito, which they were to spend in disguise. 'To avoid the risk of our plans being overheard, we might have to move away from here, Draupadi. At least then we would be free of unwanted visitors, though newer intrigues might await us.' He reached out to massage her sprained leg, but Draupadi withdrew. He knew he deserved the silent chastisement, though at times it broke his heart.

'Let us prepare to leave soon, Samrat,' she spoke at last. 'We need to appropriately honour the rishis, other forest-dwellers, Gandharvas, and whoever shared these troubled times with us and helped us in our stay at Dvaitavana. How about a yajna in their honour?'

Aware of her attempts to distract herself from the assault,

Yudhishtira nodded. A thought entered his mind, pushing him into another bout of silence, until Draupadi patted his knee. He looked up, asking if she needed anything.

Draupadi shook her head, 'Something troubles you, Samrat.'

Yudhishtira sighed, 'I have heard the rishis mention time and again that our buddhi, or intellect, is driven by our own karma, our past actions.' Brushing his hair along his temples, he added, 'Was the game of dice a result of the burning of the Khandava forest?'

It was Draupadi's turn to fall into deep thought. It was not as if this thought had not troubled her in the past. She had battled the dilemma with varied arguments, turning her own mind into a philosophical battlefield. 'Yudhishtira, the burning of the Khandava forest was necessary to protect those whose safety was our responsibility. The forest was sheltering those who threatened not only our rightful sovereignty, but also killed the villagers and nagas, their own brethren, for being friendly with us. Burning of the forest rendered those criminals homeless. Wasn't that crucial to control the heinous crimes?'

Yudhishtira remained unmoved. 'There were animals, birds and a whole ecology that was destroyed. Today, we find ourselves dependent on the ecological balance of Dvaitavana. We are indebted to all the animate and inanimate beings of this forest, who have made way for us to live here all these years. Can we then deny that we are facing the consequences of the same?'

Draupadi frowned. 'I have faced this troubling thought many times before, Samrat. But even if what you say is true, would it be right to pursue action while being personally responsible or live doing nothing against the crimes?' The force of her statement drew a spark of admiration in Yudhishtira's eyes. Draupadi backed away, realizing something. 'Was this discussion a ploy to make me forget my pain?'

'Did it work?' Yudhishtira beamed, trying to escape her annoyed nudge. 'Draupadi, inaction is the first step towards meek surrender to the forces of adharma. In our fight for dharma, we might falter, take wrong decisions, and pay for it, but we shall emerge stronger. The forces that threaten dharma should always know that we will continue to fight. And we will fight to prevail.'

Draupadi looked at him and reflected on how the same statement, said about fourteen years ago, would have made her fall in love with him all over again. But the past decade had been full of too many tough lessons. She had learnt to guard herself before trusting even her own husbands who, she knew, would die or kill for her.

'Allow me to tend to it,' he pleaded when she nursed her swollen cheek. Draupadi relented.

Not long after, they were informed by Rishi Dhaumya that Jayadrata had been caught by Bhima, Arjuna and the twins. Rising to their feet, Draupadi and Yudhishtira saw Jayadrata's state and realized that Bhima had indeed unleashed himself upon him. With his face disfigured, and body covered with mud and blood, Jayadrata found himself cast at Draupadi's feet.

When he tried to lift his head, Bhima's foot landed on his neck, forcing Jayadrata down again. Jayadrata almost lost consciousness, but Arjuna managed to pull Bhima away.

'It is Dusshala's husband!' Draupadi heard Arjuna hiss.

'Draupadi! He is *your* slave today! You can seal his fate,' Bhima bellowed.

Jayadrata murmured something before he fainted. Moving away from Jayadrata's prostrate form, Draupadi saw Yudhishtira nod at her, leaving the decision to her. In his attempt to abduct her, the king of Sindhu had wronged not only her, but also his own wife, Dusshala. She saw Bhima silently urging her to pronounce death upon Jayadrata. Such men deserved to die before they repeated the same crime with another woman. But death, Draupadi mulled, was irreversible. Killing Jayadrata, and leaving Dusshala bereaved, would also hurt her mother, Gandhari. Draupadi could not forget how the queen of Hastinapura had influenced the blind King Dhritarashtra to annul the first game of dice. Somewhere, she felt grateful for Gandhari, and could not bring herself to pronounce widowhood upon the old queen's daughter.

It was indeed a great clash of priorities.

Why did women like Gandhari and Dusshala stick by men like this one?

Grace won over anger. 'Let Dusshala not be widowed.' The words came out of her lips, though she was aware of her own disappointment at letting Jayadrata go.

Bhima whirled around and left.

Like he spoke that part of her mind which dearly wanted Jayadrata dead.

As she expected, she saw Yudhishtira's facial muscles relax at her decision. The brothers loved their sister Dusshala too much. She saw Arjuna drag Jayadrata away from the ashram.

'Through the rishis, we should let Dusshala as well as Mother Gandhari know what Jayadrata was up to here. They have a right to know,' Draupadi declared to the other three. The twins nodded and left to find a rishi travelling northward.

There was still something that bothered her.

Like it had been a mistake to let Jayadrata go.

'What if there comes a day I regret letting him go?' she thought aloud.

Yudhishtira looked in the direction in which Bhima had left. 'Fate can play dreadful games, Draupadi. But rest assured, if there comes such a day, the regret will not be yours alone.'

Nodding with an understanding glance, Draupadi let him tend to her other bruises. They had a lot to plan for the next eighteen months. They could not afford to let anything go wrong.

Twenty-nine

Yaksha Prashna

The Brahmin looked distraught when he reached out to the five brothers. Draupadi heard him share his woes.

'There aren't a lot of sources of Arani sticks in this part of the forest, Maharathi!' His voice broke twice as he spoke. 'Years of my sadhana are at stake now. A deer ran off with the only sticks I had to produce the ceremonial fire.'

Life at Kamyaka had been an eventful one, each encounter throwing up its own unique lesson. Staying in the wilderness did not deter the Brahmin from performing his duties. Draupadi smiled at him kindly, offering him the refreshment she could manage. Yudhishtira watched him drink the buttermilk and assured him that his lost Arani sticks would be retrieved. Draupadi sensed the remaining four Pandavas look at him in disbelief.

'The deer must not have gone far from water sources,' she remarked. 'If we can plot the route it took and follow the same, we might track it.' She saw Bhima shrug and Arjuna take up his weapon. Work of any kind kept them from brooding and she readily co-operated with Yudhishtira in keeping them busy. 'We would all like some deer meat too!' she heard Bhima, and noticed him looking at her, as if searching for a smile. But her lips remained non-committal.

The four brothers left in search of the miscreant deer, a task that seemed unrealistic. But from the multitude of experiences they had been through during their exile, Draupadi could sense that it would be an eventful day. Every intrigue they had overcome in the past had added something to their lives. But contrary to her expectations, the first half of the day passed without any of the brothers returning.

The Brahmin returned a couple of times to enquire, only to return disappointed. Draupadi saw Yudhishtira's restlessness mount. With only an hour left for sunset, he picked up his spear to join the search.

'Let me come with you, Samrat.'

Yudhishtira shook his head. 'I doubt it is just the elusive deer, Draupadi. I fear some mishap.'

'All the more reason for me to accompany you, Arya,' she insisted and followed him, picking up her own dagger.

He tried to dissuade her. But when he finally agreed, Draupadi thought she saw relief flicker in his eyes. He also picked up the sack of medicines and rags that served for any emergency. After a gruelling hour of search, Draupadi felt a sense of foreboding. This part of the forest was unexplored and the darkness only added to their worry. Yudhishtira stopped to light a flame when her foot hit something soft and cold. Draupadi almost shrieked. The touch felt familiar.

'Arjuna!'

Arjuna's hands felt colder than usual, his radiant form almost blue.

He had been poisoned!

'He is conscious! Arjuna, open your eyes. It is us!'

Yudhishtira rushed to where she had collapsed, holding Arjuna.

Where were the others?

Draupadi could hardly move, and stared at Yudhishtira as he disappeared into the darkness. Moments later, she heard him shout, taking Bhima's name.

'Twins too!'

A faint chirping of birds greeted Draupadi's ears.

Water!

She followed the sound and reached the banks of a desolate lake. A lake of its size should have attracted a variety of birds and other creatures to its water. But the surrounding seemed unnaturally deserted.

'The lake is poisoned!' a husky voice came from nowhere. Draupadi did not show alarm and took out her dagger.

'They did not pay heed to my words of wisdom!' This time the voice seemed much closer.

And much more menacing.

'Show yourself, you coward!' she thundered. It was hard to believe that the four valiant brothers had fallen for the tricks of this elusive being. If it was true, she knew that she and Yudhishtira did not stand much of a chance. Still, the enemy, whoever it was, would not have them without a fight.

A hand suddenly clutched her arm.

'Stay behind, Draupadi!' Yudhishtira had heard the voice too.

She shook her head.

'We are together in this!'

'For the sake of any sense left in this world, this is not the time for those ideals!' he cried. The voice responded this time with spine-chilling laughter.

'Not a day to exhibit wisdom, I guess!'

Then, they saw him.

Perched on one of the low-lying branches of an enormous dead tree, he looked like a starved creature.

Skin covering bones. Like an apparition had possessed a semi-decomposed corpse.

Anyone in that state would have been long dead.

'The world has lost itself in pursuit of meaningless objects. Nobody cares for the wisdom of what lies beyond this life!' His words were almost melancholic. Had it not been for his poisoned brothers, Yudhishtira would have stepped forward to comfort the being.

'I told them that the water of this lake was only meant to be drunk by those with great wisdom. They did not listen to me!'

'You poisoned them!' Yudhishtira hissed. Draupadi held his arm before he could advance further.

'I have the antidote!' the creature smiled.

'Who are you?' Yudhishtira's question was a little louder than a whisper.

'I am a yaksha, human! You have no power over me!' he sang rhythmically. 'And your brothers will be dead in no time if they are not given the antidote!'

'Yudhishtira, let us carry them away. The rishis we know will give us the medication they need,' Draupadi whispered.

'They will be long dead by then. I told them that the water was meant only for knowledgeable ones, and not arrogant fools like them!'

Draupadi felt Yudhishtira's hand over her cheek. 'Beloved, if something untoward happens to me, escape and live to fight another day.'

'Samrat!'

Yudhishtira approached the creature. 'You seem to value

knowledge and wisdom, Yaksha. What kind of wisdom drives you to let innocents die? If my brothers succumb to the poison, your claim of valuing knowledge will be proved a farce! You will be reduced to a murderer who violated the rule of nature in the frenzy of pursuit.'

The yaksha laughed again. Draupadi hurried to check on Bhima. The twins showed signs of succumbing to the poison. Bhima was nearly unconscious. Only Arjuna's limbs showed life as he fought the poison with his best efforts. Draupadi shook each of them in a bid to keep them conscious. 'It is either all of us or none, sons of Kunti!'

She frantically looked in the direction of Yudhishtira.

'Test my knowledge, Yaksha. But on the condition that you will hand me over the antidote if I pass your "test"!' Yudhishtira calmly negotiated.

'But if you fail, you will lose your life too!' the Yaksha croaked gleefully.

To Draupadi's horror, Yudhishtira nodded.

A gamble again?

She saw Yudhishtira glance at her and mouth his frantic instruction. 'Leave!'

With four of her husbands fighting death, Draupadi could not but defy. Caught in a hostile patch of the forest, she knew that being together was their best bet.

Even when facing death.

Checking on each of the prostrate figures, she almost screamed when she felt Nakula's pulse. Sahadeva was in no better condition. Bhima was still breathing, though close to fainting. Arjuna was the only one who alternated between consciousness and fainting. He uttered words of warning but the sheer lack of coherence in his speech was terrifying. The creature, whatever it was, seemed to be a dangerous combination of supernatural elements and frenzied anger. Who else would poison an entire lake in this jungle if not a cold-blooded apparition? Looking up, Draupadi saw Yudhishtira negotiate with it, answering questions with a clarity that astounded her.

Alternating between listening to the conversations between them, which she would have greatly appreciated had it taken place in an ashram amongst learned rishis, and hustling to keep Arjuna and Bhima conscious, Draupadi could only pray for the twins. She had always felt fiercely protective of them. Even the thought of losing them filled her with despair.

Suddenly, Yudhishtira rushed back and knelt by Nakula's side.

'Has the yaksha given you the antidote?' she called out. But caught up in his own distress, he did not respond.

'Yudhishtira!'

'I have the antidote to save just one person!' he replied without turning.

Why Nakula when Arjuna had better chances of surviving?

The question remained within the confines of her mind, realizing how agonizing it was to make this choice. That very moment, Draupadi felt her own limbs fail her. As if the poison had affected her too. It was only when Yudhishtira clasped her shoulder that she felt conscious again. Her gaze immediately shifted to the other four.

'Samrat?'

'They will live!' he replied, reading the unspoken question in her eyes. But before she could ask him what had happened, he hurried to support Arjuna who was trying to rise up.

Choosing not to press him for the moment, she helped Sahadeva to his feet. Bhima was alert enough to help Nakula.

None of the four spoke much and went to sleep early.

Draupadi was fatigued but fought to stay awake and ask Yudhishtira about what had happened. When the latter returned after a brief conversation with Rishi Dhaumya, she could not contain herself.

'What happened at the lake, Samrat?'

Yudhishtira looked hesitant.

Holding his hand tenderly, she smiled, 'Mahadeva knows what you did there, but you did well, Samrat.'

Perhaps it was the first time after the game of dice that he had felt her admiration for him return. He eagerly held her hand close to his, but decided to not push further.

'You will not believe me if I told you what happened, Draupadi. I am still having a hard time believing it myself!'

The pride and joy that showed on his face was something she had not seen even during the final moments of the Rajasuya. 'Tell me, Yudhishtira.'

'Would you believe me if I said I met the God of Dharma himself?' Yudhishtira clutched her arms, his response startling her.

Draupadi smiled at the sudden rush of enthusiasm in his voice. 'If we can believe Arjuna about his encounters with gods like Shiva and Indra, why won't we believe you, Yudhi?'

'You know that we, the five brothers, are not the biological progeny of King Pandu. You might have also heard who our fathers are, Samragni.' After a brief pause, he added, 'I thought the ability to meet the celestial beings was limited to my mother. Turns out…turns out we are fortunate too.'

'That fearsome creature who poisoned the lake was the Lord of Dharma? And the Lord of Death himself?' Draupadi exclaimed.

'He had come to test me.'

'With that list of bizarre questions? I had heard a part of the conversation...'

'Perhaps he wanted to test my ability to gather myself when everyone I love was in danger. Especially when we are in this state because of the choices I made.'

'What did he tell you when I was...in that daze, after you tried reviving Nakula?'

'He asked me why I chose him of all the brothers, when choosing Arjuna or Bhima would have been, in his words, a "better" choice considering the circumstances.'

'Because he is the son of the princess of Madra and you wanted to be fair to your late stepmother?' Draupadi smiled.

Yudhishtira beamed, staring into space, until she asked the uncomfortable question.

'How will Bhima or Arjuna react when they get to know this, Yudhishtira?'

The indulgent smile on his lips became more pronounced. 'I don't know what they will say, but had I chosen them instead of either of the twins, Bhima would have cursed me till the end of my life and Arjuna would have been miserable for the rest of his life, blaming himself for not keeping our mother's word to Princess Madri. Why do you ask, Draupadi?'

Draupadi considered telling him about her conversation with Nakula right after the game but decided against it. Nakula's thought of separating from him had obviously been an impulsive reaction. All Draupadi needed to know was if she had done the right thing by dissuading him, despite her own agony at that time. She now knew she had.

'The period of Agnatavasa starts in about a month, Samragni,' he said after a long time, settling to lie down on the hard floor.

'To begin with, we might need to stop calling each other samrat and samragni, just in case...' Draupadi paused, hearing his breath even out into a gentle snore. She was indeed glad that their time in the forest had come to an end.

But a new phase awaited them, promising more intrigue and excitement.

Thirty

Agnatavasa

'That is quite a collection!' Nakula exclaimed, pointing at the basket of blossoms that Draupadi was carrying when she returned from the river.

'The woman who claims that she was the *sairandhri*, the hairdresser, to Empress Draupadi, has got to show what she is capable of!' Draupadi smiled, inviting him to help her braid her hair. Being the one who was the most conscious when it came to appearance, among the five brothers, Nakula readily agreed. The last five months had been hectic and full of activity. They had spent days deciding where they could spend their year of living incognito and in which disguises. Panchala and Dwaraka had been ruled out, keeping in view that those were the obvious places that would be scrutinized by Duryodhana's spies. After a good deal of deliberation, Yudhishtira had suggested the kingdom of Matsya. Ruled by King Virata, the kingdom had been a loyal ally to the Kurus during the times of their father, Pandu. Even during the campaign of the Rajasuya, King Virata had extended a lot of co-operation. The Rajasuya being the only event where they had met him face to face, there was lesser risk of him recognizing the Pandavas or their queen.

Then, there was the question of the roles each of them would play, to stay undetected. Nakula first suggested that they could adopt the role of commoners and mingle with the citizens. Sahadeva too agreed with the suggestion citing that it was crucial for them to stay abreast of what the commoners and travellers thought of the royalty and about the happenings at Hastinapura. But for strategic reasons, Yudhishtira strongly opined that some of them should stay close to the royal family and if possible influence them to stay favourable to the Pandavas after the period of exile. These discussions often led to someone's heart breaking at the turn of events. Each worried about how the other would face the hardships and hazards involved in the professions they chose.

Draupadi noticed that each of them tried to look at the year as an opportunity to indulge in their passions—Nakula opting to join the royal stables, Sahadeva choosing to mingle with the commoners as a cowherd, and Bhima choosing to be a cook as well as a trainer to the aspiring wrestlers under the patronage of the king. To their dismay, Yudhishtira opted to pose as an astrologer-turned-mendicant, by the name Kanka Bhattaraka. It was one thing to live the life of an ascetic in the forests, but living in a role subservient to a king, who was much inferior in valour as well as wisdom, was distressing.

Like a herd of elephants forced to pass through the throat of a mosquito!

Draupadi sighed, immers herself into the task of collecting herbs, flowers and other ingredients, and fashioning herself some tools that a sairandhri of a superior grade should have. Turning the other way when Nakula helped her with an exquisite style of braid, she caught sight of Bhima and Yudhishtira examining themselves for one last time before leaving for Matsya.

Swallowing the lump in her throat when Bhima's gaze met hers, Draupadi tried to smile at his unspoken inquiry. Yudhishtira looked at her new form. Regret shadowed his face. Something she had seen numerous times in the past twelve years. But this time, she walked up to him and squeezed his arm, 'Pray, don't worry about me, Samrat. The five invincible Gandharvas, Jaya, Jayesha, Vijaya, Jayatsena and Jayatbala—my husbands—will ensure my safety throughout this year,' she beamed. The five names had been chosen by the brothers for discrete communication during the year.

'It is almost time! Where is Arjuna?' Sahadeva halted midway. 'Arjuna?' he mouthed, staring into the smiling eyes of his brother, now dressed as a eunuch.

'Brihannala, the dance teacher,' Arjuna corrected, mimicking the body language of the third gender to perfection. Considering the shocked expressions around him, he smiled, 'Someone needs to stay in the palace, close to Draupadi, as she claims her husbands will ensure her safety.'

'Actually,' Bhima retorted, 'Draupadi, you keep a watch on him! Posing as a eunuch among the women of the palace, you know what I mean!' he guffawed, drawing smiles from the rest.

Yudhishtira's smile faded seeing Draupadi and Arjuna exchange meaningful glances, and he chided himself for entertaining the thought. It was not the first time he had felt that the intimacy Draupadi had with Arjuna was more than what she had with others, including himself. But he could not bring himself to ask Draupadi directly, given what she had gone through because of him. Shaking his head, the eldest Pandava brought his attention to the task in hand.

'Now we need to reach the outskirts and conceal our

weapons while Draupadi seeks the audience of Queen Sudeshna of Matsya.'

He led the way.

◡

The temple of Ambika, a much-revered Shakti Peeth, situated in Matsya, was in its usual morning bustle. The ageing priest had gathered flowers from the sellers and was returning to the garbhagriha when his eyes fell upon an old woman accompanied by her granddaughter. They were regular visitors to the temple. The old man melted seeing the woman break down in front of the goddess.

'How long will you grieve like this, sister?'

'Till the goddess secures justice to my daughter who died under her very watch!' the old woman retorted, her indignation directed at the deity in the garbhagriha.

The priest sighed, brushing the hair of the little girl with pity. 'It was not said in vain that one should avoid any association with royalty. I pray to the goddess every day to secure justice for your daughter.'

'My child was brutally raped and murdered within the walls of the palace, I can swear!'

'Shh, sister! Why do you want to invite more trouble upon yourself?' the priest tried to pacify her. 'Strange are the ways of the goddess. She tests her children. But rest assured, she will punish the monsters who prey upon defenceless women this way!' he paused, sensing a movement. 'The question is when. Only she knows,' he whispered, turning to see who the visitor was.

The woman was the epitome of grace and majesty even in her humble fabric and simple jewellery of various beads and rosary strings. The old priest looked at her approach them with a warm smile after bowing to the goddess.

A goddess herself!

'I am Malini from Indraprastha,' she introduced herself, folding her hands together. 'I was told that the queen comes here to worship the goddess. I seek her audience and compassion.'

The priest informed her that Queen Sudeshna was expected soon. The temple was usually emptied for the royal family to carry out their worship. But today, the priest decided to make an exception for this strange woman. He carried out his rituals, and eventually, the queen came. He saw Malini approach the queen and request her to hire her as a sairandhri.

The old woman who was a mute spectator almost intervened when the priest blocked her. Sudeshna was too happy to hire her as the previous sairandhri had died months ago.

Let her not face the same fate that my daughter did!

The prayer in the old woman's eyes was clear. Before long, Sudeshna left the temple, taking the newly-appointed sairandhri with her to the palace.

Following the queen, Malini discretely exchanged glances with four men who had positioned themselves at various points on the street leading to the palace.

Agnatavasa had begun.

Thirty-one

Matsya

Princess Uttara hummed the composition she was learning from the new dance teacher she adored. Tapping her feet to the rhythm playing in her mind, she felt the sairandhri's expert hands braid her hair. She could even hear the female guards at the door of her chamber gasp in admiration. She frowned, thinking of what the dance teacher had remarked on her hairstyle.

'Malini…' she called out to her mother's favourite hairdresser and hesitated. She knew too little about braiding and grooming to say anything. But then, the opinion of her dance teacher could not be dismissed that easily. 'Acharya Brihannala seems dissatisfied with my hairdo,' she added, turning to assess Malini's reaction. 'The braid always seems to loosen in between the dance sessions. And…'

'That eunuch needs to learn some grace, Princess Uttara,' Malini shot back. 'I always thought dancers learn grace with time and practice. But your teacher seems to be a sad exception.' Malini suppressed a grin. 'Let me throw a challenge, princess,' she beamed. 'Ask Brihannala to braid your hair as well as I do. I shall teach you to dance better than she ever can.'

Uttara sighed, 'I cannot help thinking, sairandhri, that if Brihannala was a man, you both would make a great couple!' In her banter, Uttara did not notice Malini's hands freeze for a moment before the hairdresser recovered and went about addressing the finer aspects of grooming. 'Don't you feel so, Malini? Mahadeva made a grave mistake by making Brihannala a eunuch. As a man, he would have stolen and broken hearts!'

Malini wordlessly adorned the last string of flowers in Uttara's hair and then turned the princess around to supervise her work. 'Well, what can I say, Princess? I am a mere sairandhri to dare disagree with her mistress.'

Uttara's face fell. 'Those words hurt, Malini. I share things with you I don't share with my own mother.'

Malini could not help beam tenderly at the indignant fifteen-year-old. Princess Uttara was indeed delightful.

Almost like a daughter she never had.

'You know that I am married to the five great Gandharvas, each vying with the other in their physique and valour,' her words assumed a tinge of pride. 'How can I even consider a eunuch like Brihannala as a prospective husband?'

Uttara clutched her arm. 'Believe me, Malini! Pray, come with me to the Nartanashala today and watch her do the Shiva Tandava. I swear, even Lord Mahadeva would not look as handsome as Brihannala does. Witness her finesse and then deny my claim. She is more masculine than any man!' Uttara did not stop there. 'She is a warrior too! She also drove Arjuna's chariot on many occasions and is his close friend. Though I am sure you know this, having worked as a close attendant to Queen Draupadi herself.'

A polite cough interrupted them. Uttara grinned at the colourfully dressed Brihannala. 'Come in, Acharya Brihannala!

I am vouching for your Shiva Tandava to impress Malini.'

Brihannala cleared her tone again. 'Apparently, impressing your sairandhri is something that was beyond even her five husbands, Princess Uttara.' The eunuch winked suggestively, earning an immediate frown from Malini. But Brihannala did not miss the momentary curve on Malini's lips.

'The charioteer and friend of the great Arjuna does not consider a lowly sairandhri worth impressing, Princess Uttara.' Turning at the dance teacher with mock anger, Malini raised a finger, 'I also hear that our little princess is tiring with your dance practice, Natyacharya. Perhaps you need a reminder that the Nartanashala is not a battlefield.'

Uttara rose and began inspecting her hair in the small artificial pool constructed in the centre of her chamber. The princess of Matsya was too lost in admiring herself to notice Malini and Brihannala exchange more than just looks behind her. The next moment, something else drew her attention. Uttara straightened, hearing the guards scuttle before falling into line. Her smile faded. Not even King Virata, her father, inspired that kind of fear among the palace employees. The one causing the fear among her guards could only be...

A voice boomed along the adjoining corridor. 'Where is my favourite niece? Why don't I see her welcoming her dear uncle?' The footsteps were a telling indication of the visitor's exuberance.

Uttara stared at the door and at the sight of the burly visitor, dressed in the finest silks and intricately crafted jewellery. She smiled widely, 'Uncle Keechaka!' She ran into the muscular arms of the commander-in-chief of the Matsya army.

Malini and Brihannala looked at each other. None of them had missed seeing the flicker of fear in Uttara's eyes before she had received her uncle. Involuntarily, their eyes fell upon the sky through the window, trying to gauge the position of the moon and the stars.

'About five fortnights more,' Arjuna whispered.

But Draupadi's face told him that she was already busy planning something.

‿

'When the war with the Trigartas comes upon us, my heart breaks because my husband who is in the army has to leave for the front. But when it concludes, I am overcome with fear, because along with my husband, Commander Keechaka returns!' The palace maid broke down in the middle of the spacious chamber where the first rung of Queen Sudeshna's companions lived. Her friends tried to console her.

'What happens when Keechaka returns?' Malini looked up at the group of women. She immediately bit her tongue for forgetting to use a reverent salutation for the commander, but the palace maid was too aghast to notice.

'What happens? Malini, haven't you seen him?'

Malini shook her head, deliberately omitting the fact that she had heard Keechaka barge into Princess Uttara's room.

'Do yourself a favour, don't let him see you,' another palace maid advised her. 'Or better, apply something on your face that looks like a skin affliction or something and make yourself look unattractive. You are new here, Malini. Understand why we are advising you to do so.'

The maid who had started the whole conversation broke into sobs. Malini could not stop herself from trying to comfort the distraught woman. She did not need any more indication of what had happened. 'Sister, why do you tolerate his advances? Why don't you let the king of Matsya know what his dear brother-in-law and commander is doing to the women under his protection?'

The other woman shook her head. 'Do you think the king does not know what he is up to?' Angrily brushing her tears aside, she gazed at Malini. 'And do you know what happened to the erstwhile sairandhri who dared to resist his advances? Her mutilated body was found near the cremation ground outside the city.'

Malini did not speak much except for some comforting words. Even those made her feel restless. Granted, she was passing through hard times. But that did not mean that she closed her eyes to the predicament of those who worked with her. It did not mean that she helplessly fell into line, trying to look unattractive. Even the idea made her tongue go bitter. She might be a sairandhri today, but her spirit was still that of the empress she had been.

The maids gasped when they saw her decked up with flowers and beads the next day. They shrugged, knowing that they had done their job of warning her. Beyond that, her safety was not their concern. Though to them, it looked like the queen's favourite sairandhri was doing her best to attract the unwanted attention of the lusty commander. Had she not said that she had five husbands, and that too, Gandharvas? Malini noticed even Queen Sudeshna regard her with wide eyes that day. 'By Rudra, Malini! How on earth are your husbands able to stay away from the beauty that you are?'

Malini smiled and said nothing. But after a moment or so, she clutched her stomach in mock pain. 'The food, Maharani. I could not sleep a wink because of the ache in my stomach!'

The kind Sudeshna was too overcome with concern to notice her pretence. 'That is worrisome, sairandhri! I shall immediately send a warning to the head cook, Ballava.'

Malini nodded, gulping the water that the queen offered her. 'Pray, specifically tell him that the sairandhri of the queen herself had to spend a sleepless night!'

Sudeshna nodded and immediately sent a maid to the royal kitchen. Draupadi sighed with satisfaction. The clue of her sleepless night, would, she knew, be enough to warn the head cook of the palace. Her Bhima would never fail her. 'Malini, if you want to take the day off and rest, it is fine.'

What a contrast between the brother and sister of the same blood!

Malini nodded gratefully. 'Maharani, the day of my husbands' return is drawing closer. I would request an audience with the king's personal adviser, Kanka Bhattaraka. I heard that he is peerless in astrology and can grace anyone with an accurate prediction.'

Sudeshna nodded. 'Fine, once you are rested, seek Kanka Bhattaraka in the afternoon. Feel free to tell him that I recommended his expertise to you.'

Malini bowed thankfully and left. She still had to meet Brihannala before she left to meet Kanka Bhattaraka.

∫

Kanka Bhattaraka had not expected Malini's arrival. Her expression told him the situation was grave. He sent his attendants away from the room. 'Astrological predictions and remedies are highly confidential,' he told the guards. 'Overhearing someone else's details might anger the gods as well as the planets. Make sure that nobody overhears what I tell Malini, for their own good.'

The instruction was enough to ensure privacy. 'What is the matter, Draupadi?' Yudhishtira leaned forward, still putting up the act of opening a bundle of tala leaves.

Draupadi told him about Keechaka, being as discreet as she could. 'If the king is being a clandestine supporter to his brother-in-law's overtures, we should take matters into our own hands, Samrat!'

'The king is helpless, Draupadi,' Yudhishtira pointed out.

'If you heard the predicament of the maids, and the story of the woman who was in my place before, you would act, Samrat.'

He knew that Draupadi would not be satisfied with anything less than Keechaka's death. But the circumstances were too tricky to carry out even a covert killing. Keechaka's palace was more heavily guarded than the king's. Even the enemies of Matsya knew that it was the commander who was the de facto ruler of Matsya.

'I shall lure him and bring him out of his "fortress" to somewhere more convenient,' Draupadi leaned forward.

'It is more complicated than that. Anything done in the shadows also has the danger of being noticed and reported to Duryodhana in Hastinapura,' Yudhishtira pondered. An idea struck him. It could work. He looked at Draupadi and then shook his head. 'No, not that way.'

'Not which way?' Draupadi persisted, moving closer. 'Your strategy cannot go wrong, Yudhishtira.'

'It has to be known in the open that Keechaka lusted after you despite your warning about the Gandharvas protecting you. The killing, only then, would be attributed to the Gandharvas. Any other covert operation that causes his death is sure to raise alarms everywhere,' Yudhishtira paused after every sentence and that made Draupadi feel even more restless. He felt her hand upon his knee, convincing him to be more specific about her role in the plan.

Yudhishtira cringed at the idea that had struck him. 'If you can make him lust after you and try bringing it to the notice of the king, in the presence of all the courtiers, it is sure to send the message to everyone that Keechaka played with fire, inviting the wrath of celestial beings. Later, he can be tricked into coming to a convenient location, and his death soon after will come as no surprise, Draupadi. There is still some risk in outing yourself as the wife of five husbands. But…'

'This sounds promising, Yudhishtira,' Draupadi rose. 'Even with the risk associated, I am sure by the time our enemies figure it out, the year would have passed.' She turned to leave but stopped when Yudhishtira caught her arm.

'The court…I mean…are you sure you want to do this, Draupadi?'

An unaffected smile and a nod were her only responses. Gently removing his hand from hers, Draupadi left the room.

Thirty-two

Keechaka

As expected, the guards blocked her way. Malini stood her ground. 'I have the queen's permission.' She dismissed the guard with an air of authority. Glancing at the empty entrance, she raised her pitch. 'Don't you know that, as a sairandhri, I have the permission to check on all the gardens of the royal family and fetch the seasonal blossoms that will please Queen Sudeshna? Your commander cannot be immune to the queen's orders.' Malini tried forcing her way in and was promptly shoved out by the other guard. She raised a hue and cry. It continued until she saw an intimidating figure emerge from the grand entrance.

'What's the matter, you fools?' Keechaka thundered. 'Can't a tired commander get some quiet...' he paused, seeing the beautiful woman. 'Who are you?' His gaze lingered on her lithe form, highlighted by a thoughtful combination of bead jewellery.

'Malini, the sairandhri of Queen Sudeshna.'

The words were melodious, matching the grace of her curves. Keechaka had to think his words carefully. 'You could have easily said you were a damsel from the heavens and I would have believed you!' he quipped, coming closer, unmindful of the guards.

Malini smiled, 'Had I been a celestial damsel, would I be arguing with your guards instead of magically appearing in your garden and plucking the choicest flowers?'

Keechaka dismissed the guards and attempted to hold her by her waist. Malini skilfully moved away, towards a creeper that caught her eye. Keechaka had not even noticed the presence of a blooming creeper in his own garden. 'I do see that you have an eye for true beauty!' he chuckled, covering the distance between them. 'A quality you share with me.'

Malini bowed again at the flattery and went about plucking the blossoms. Keechaka kept staring at her. He had seen professional seductresses, well below thirty springs of age, and even their bodily charm had not kept him satisfied for long. The woman who claimed to be his sister's sairandhri was much older. But she was the epitome of charm, probably the only woman who had dared to tread into his gardens. He had to continue the conversation. 'Share the truth with me, woman. A ravishing beauty like you would not be working as a mere sairandhri without a reason.'

Malini paused and looked at him. He was, as she had expected, drunk with lust. But his observation was so close to the truth. She frowned. 'Many women, forced by circumstances to live away from their husbands, have taken up this profession, Lord Commander. I, Malini, the wife of five powerful Gandharvas by names, Jaya, Jayesha, Vijaya, Jayatsena and Jayadbala, am no different from them.'

Keechaka now overtook her and blocked her way. 'You mean to say, those are the names of the unfortunate beings who don't value the boon that is your beauty?'

Malini looked at her basket, half-filled with the seasonal blossoms from Keechaka's garden. 'This unfortunate phase of

211

separation is not their fault, Lord Commander. My husbands love me with all their hearts,' she smiled and walked towards the exit, leaving him stupefied.

Why would she smile and encourage conversation with him if she was that loyal to her husbands?

Keechaka shrugged. Like any woman endowed with beauty, she possibly sought more attention. Possibly, she preferred some initiative. He saw her cross the gates and walk towards the queen's mansion. Keechaka rushed after her and caught Malini's arm, unmindful of the stares of the other palace folk.

To his surprise, Malini pushed him away like he was a poisonous reptile. 'Lord Commander!' she thundered, stunning the onlookers, and strode towards the queen's mansion.

Keechaka, though stunned by her abrupt spurning, was angrier that she had done so in the presence of lowly palace guards and maids. He had to show her who was in control. Grunting, he pursued and caught her again, this time, in a rougher and firmer grip. 'Playing with me, aren't you?'

Malini glared at him, considering the changes that Keechaka had undergone from the time she had met him. Drunk with power, arrogance and lust, the commander had even lost the idea of what his behaviour did to his own image. Left to his whims, he would force himself upon any woman of Matsya, irrespective of her consent!

'Stay away, Keechaka!' she warned in a level tone.

Keechaka smirked at her words. 'You amuse me, sairandhri. Are you this wild even in bed? Wait, why don't I see for myself?'

The basket of flowers fell from her hands at the tussle that followed. Keechaka was proving more than a handful. His brute strength was difficult to overcome. But she had to lead him towards the court before he could do anything worse. The stupefied onlookers, Malini gathered, would not lift a finger in her defence.

Goddess Ambika, the guardian of Virata! Lord Surya, the eternal witness! Don't remain mere onlookers!

With an extraordinary effort, Malini shoved Keechaka away from her and rushed towards the court. Alerting the soldiers and guards on the way, she knew, was a futile exercise, but she continued to do so, as Yudhishtira wished everyone to be aware of Keechaka's overtures.

After being nearly caught by him twice, Malini managed to reach the entrance of the court. 'King of Matsya! Pray, save my honour!' she screamed when Keechaka finally caught up with her. The courtiers sat, their limbs frozen at the very sight of the commander. 'Are the women who serve the royal family doomed to succumb to the lusty overtures of this brute?'

Even though she had not expected the old King Virata to rise to the occasion and stand up to Keechaka, his lack of reaction dismayed her. The eerie resemblance to the ghastly assault by Dushasana at Hastinapura made her blood boil. She stared at Kanka Bhattaraka. His face was pale. But his eyes were full of concentration. His fists, though, remained curled. The situation had indeed turned riskier. But they knew they had to charge ahead!

Keechaka laughed, this time, the contempt in his tone overriding his lust. 'I pity you, sairandhri, if you put your hopes on this puppet to protect your "honour".'

He looked at the face of each courtier, meeting their gaze as they averted theirs. Keechaka laughed again. 'Be wise, sairandhri, this sabha of eunuchs cannot save you from me even if I take you here, right now!' He tried to pull her into an embrace.

'Lord Commander Keechaka!' Kanka spoke in a challenging

tone that even surprised Malini. 'I was examining your horoscope sometime back. Forcing yourself upon a married woman would cause your untimely death—I saw! Back away for your own good!'

Keechaka looked at him, partly amused. It had to be some new entrant in the court who had dared to raise his voice against the powerful commander. Kanka's appearance told him the man did not even deserve a reply.

The old king finally found his voice, after multiple attempts to clear his throat. 'Commander Keechaka, is there a dearth of willing pleasure girls in the palace that you need to demean yourself by lusting after a sairandhri?' The sheer weakness in his voice made Malini feel angrier with him.

The reminder of his stature seemed to work on Keechaka. He let go of Malini and pushed her to the ground. 'Let it be a lesson to you, impudent woman. None, I repeat, none in Virata will be able to save you from my wrath. Come to terms with this and surrender to me before sunset tomorrow. Or else...' He towered upon her, despite her angry glare. With a dismissive smirk, he strode out of the court.

Malini looked at the old king. 'Imbeciles of Virata! Forcing unwilling women is inviting the wrath of the gods! The days of your commander are numbered! The invincible Gandharvas will come for his blood!'

Only Yudhishtira caught the tinge of sarcasm in Draupadi's tone when she uttered the word 'invincible'. He saw her rise and leave the court, leaving everyone shocked and aghast.

∿

'Why did your husbands not protect you?' It was an innocent question, especially coming from the palace maids. But it hurt her. It hurt her despite the fact the she was playing to a script. Malini did not reply and turned to the other side of the bed. She badly wanted to lash out and say that Keechaka would be dead shortly. But something stopped her from defending the 'five Gandharvas'.

Let their actions speak from now on, not my words.

Malini refused to eat, despite their words of consolation.

'Send back the food to the royal kitchen!' she thundered at the maid who came to serve their food. 'And tell that cook that Malini will eat only after that lusty commander bites dust! He need not bother cooking food for me till then!'

The fatigue of the day could not bring her the much-needed sleep. The more difficult part of the plan remained. Malini knew she had to gather herself and show utmost strength to face the next day.

Waking up before anyone else the next day, after an elaborate bath, she dressed herself with care. She had a charade to play and did not want to give the other women an opportunity to drown her in unwanted advice.

Helping Princess Uttara was a mellow affair. The princess of Matsya, for reasons Malini could only guess, remained quiet. An occasional tear or two fell from her eyes when she looked at Malini, full of unspoken emotions. After completing Uttara's grooming, Malini turned to leave, only to have Uttara grab her arm. 'Malini, I shall help you escape out of Matsya unnoticed. Don't stay here anymore. Pray, leave as soon as you can.'

Malini brushed Uttara's curls, wearing an inscrutable smile, and shook her head.

'My previous sairandhri. I loved her like an elder sister,' Uttara continued, breaking into a sob or two. 'I don't want to lose you.'

215

Malini wordlessly gathered her in her arms.

You will not lose me, little one. Nor will you lose anyone else dear to you because of that monster!

Determined, she extricated herself from Uttara's hands and left for the queen's mansion. She saw Sudeshna sitting on the couch, staring at nothing in particular. Sudeshna looked at her and cringed. 'Malini, I relieve you of all your services. Leave Matsya now. If you delay, things will get out of my hands.'

Malini looked at the queen. The darkness under Sudeshna's eyes told her that the queen had not slept even a wink the last night. 'Maharani, how can you have the heart to abandon me after months of faithful service?'

Sudeshna rose to her feet like one possessed. 'You can't question the queen, sairandhri. Either leave Matsya and save yourself or fetch me wine from my brother Keechaka's mansion. Keechaka protects the borders of Matsya from our enemies. I have to think about the safety of my subjects over that of one woman.'

Though overcome with pity for the queen, Malini laughed within at her strange priorities.

How can Matsya maintain the façade of being 'safe' from the enemy's hands when its very commander preyed upon the modesty of non-consenting women?

With a smile that displayed a mixture of contempt and pity, Malini grabbed the jar of wine.

'Malini!'

Draupadi did not look back. She did not want Sudeshna to display more helplessness or break down. She had no use for empty sympathy either. It was time for action. Action that would evaporate the fear the women of Matsya faced. Tracing her footsteps back to Keechaka's den, she thought of Goddess

Ambika again. The guards did not stop her this time. In their eyes, she saw a mixture of fear and pity—none of which were of any use in front of the internal danger their kingdom faced.

Entering the grand hall of the mansion, she found Keechaka sprawled on a lavish couch, relishing the service of slave girls who applied sandalwood paste on him. Malini's grip tightened on the bronze jar when she announced herself.

Keechaka had expected her arrival, but not this early. With a hurried wave of his hand, he dismissed the slave girls and rose from the couch. But something about her piercing gaze intrigued him.

'Welcome, Malini. I see that the sunrise dispelled your delusion,' he smirked, approaching her. But Malini surprised him by not rushing out of his reach. He stared at her as she walked up to the main throne and seated herself, betraying no fear.

'For a commander of a vast army, I expected better discretion from you, Keechaka. And you...' she sighed, prolonging the pause and enjoying the cluelessness in his eyes, 'turned out to be such a disappointment.' Leaning majestically against the lavish backrest, she raised her brows. 'Have you ever encountered a Gandharva? I bet not,' she spoke, giving him no chance to reply. 'If they want to keep a watch on you, the sun himself becomes their spy. And you did not think twice before challenging them in open daylight!'

Keechaka frowned and sat on the couch again. 'You intrigue me, Malini. Do you mean to say you don't want your husbands to know about my seeking you out?' When he saw the graceful tilt of her head which he interpreted for a nod, Keechaka laughed carelessly. 'You underestimate me, Malini. Your Gandharvas will not be able to harm me.'

Malini shrugged. 'That will be proven only upon an

encounter with one or more of my husbands. Keechaka, even if I risk trusting your valour, what is the proof that you...' she brought her brows together suggestively, 'can delight me like they did?'

Keechaka beamed, compelled to rise to his feet and approach her. 'You have crossed all possible limits and committed all the transgressions that the commander of Matsya can brook. Still...' he walked behind the throne and leaned forward, trying to inhale the fragrance of the flowers woven in her hair, 'something about you makes me feel you are worth this trouble. So, when would you like me to show you how I can delight you?' he added in a lower tone.

Malini remained unmoved for a long moment, playing with one of the strings of seasonal blossoms. 'As I said, the sun is the ally of Gandharvas. But the moon,' she smiled, turning towards Keechaka, 'is a friend of lovers!' Rising to her feet, almost startling Keechaka, she backed away.

'This full moon, at the Nartanashala. It is always empty at night.'

Thirty-three

Killing of Keechaka

The dancing hall of Virata was built most aesthetically. Draupadi entered the richly carved threshold soon after the guards had left. The number of night guards was minimal, considering the premises were generally empty after sunset. Keeping a close watch on them for a week had proved useful for Draupadi in spotting a convenient interval to slip in. The lamps were on the brink of dying out. Entering the main hall, Draupadi blew out the last lamp. The moonlight still shone through the multiple windows.

Surveying the hall, Draupadi felt a hand on her shoulder.

'Bhima!'

'Will he come?' the gruffness could be heard in his voice even when he whispered.

'Unless the mention of the five Gandharvas scared him too much...' Draupadi chuckled, 'he should be here by the second quarter.'

It was an excruciating wait. The risks taken were too high to fail. Draupadi sensed Bhima's restlessness increase. She wondered about the repercussions of Keechaka's death. It would possibly encourage Trigartas, the sworn enemies of Matsya, to attack. It might also ring alarm bells in Hastinapura, for killing Keechaka could not be the handiwork of a common man. The Gandharva cover would perhaps delay the speculation but it would not stop the Kauravas from making their own investigations. With just four fortnights left, they had decided that it would work to their advantage.

A whiff of fragrance interrupted her thoughts. Keechaka! The commander had indeed taken care to groom himself with generous amounts of sandalwood paste. Draupadi clutched Bhima's arm when they heard the footsteps. The irregular gaps between the footsteps and the words of endearment that accompanied indicated how drunk Keechaka was. Exchanging a glance with Bhima, Draupadi slipped behind the pillars, taking her position in one of the darker corridors. She saw Keechaka mistake Bhima for her. The commander must have drank lots of wine! Bhima's anger got better of him and he launched himself on Keechaka who surprisingly turned out to be a tough opponent even in his drunk state. The tussle got more and more violent with time. Draupadi lost count of how many times she rushed to the outer corridors to check if the noise alerted the two night guards. Thankfully, the Nartanashala was made to drown sounds and it worked well for them. Yudhishtira had chosen the right venue!

It was almost towards the end of the third quarter of the night that Draupadi sensed Bhima get a definitive upper hand over Keechaka. She rushed to the hall to hear Keechaka mutter his dying words, 'It...you...you can't be.... You are Bhima, the Pandava!' After two unsuccessful attempts to say more, Keechaka fell quiet forever.

Draupadi threw her hands around Bhima. They had rid Matsya of this lusty monster. They owed the city that had sheltered them this much. Then she helped Bhima leave and screamed as much as she could to draw the attention of the night guards.

The two guards, who were used to uneventful nights, had dozed off and took some time to respond. When they came in, they were followed by multiple men. Draupadi recognized them as Keechaka's brothers!

'He forced himself on me, despite my warnings!' she exclaimed. 'The Gandharvas spare none!'

Keechaka's brothers were overcome more with anger than with grief. One of them dragged her towards the corpse of Keechaka. 'Now they shall regret killing our brother!'

Another came menacingly close. 'Let us burn this witch along with him. Let us see if those Gandharva cowards have the guts to face all of us together!'

The fatigue of the night had caught up with Draupadi, and it was futile resisting all of them by herself. Besides, she could not afford to blow their cover. Offering little resistance when they bound her to the cart where they placed Keechaka's corpse, Draupadi thought fast.

'Valiant Gandharvas!' she cried as soon as she caught sight of the royal stable they passed by. 'The brothers of this monster Keechaka, besides having no remorse for the sins of their brother, seek to burn me with him. Jaya, Jayesha, Vijaya, Jayatsena, Jayadbala! Show these lowly mortals what the result of forcing themselves on a woman is!'

She paused, seeing movement at the entrance of the royal stables. Nakula! No, she could not let him expose himself to the city!

'Turn the burial ground into a battlefield, my husbands! Let your valour speak tonight! Let no man of Matsya lust after an unwilling woman hereafter!'

The last bit of warning exhausted her strength and Draupadi fainted. She could hear the brothers of Keechaka jeer at her call. They would pay for it soon, or so she hoped, closing her eyes. While alternating between consciousness and the lack thereof, she felt heat surround her. She was on the pyre! The logs had begun to catch the flame.

The jeering continued till the sound of a conch rented the air, quietening them all. Draupadi sat up, recognizing the notes. This conch had been acquired during the conquest of the Rajasuya and she herself had named it.

Anantavijaya! Yudhishtira!

A cry of confusion spread among the brothers of Keechaka. Draupadi could not see through the thickening smoke. But one of the cries, she was sure, was a death cry. The first of them had fallen. Another roar penetrated their ears from the southern side of the burial ground. As if the God of Death had personally come to claim their lives. Though weakness consumed her physically, Draupadi smiled, exhilarated at the way Bhima found ways to work the enemy out even before he was visible.

Before she closed her eyes again, she felt the flaming logs being moved away from where she lay. Before she could nod, assuring Sahadeva that she was all right, she saw one of the remaining brothers of Keechaka raise his spear to drive into Sahadeva's back.

'Watch out!' she sighed, seeing Sahadeva duck just in time.

The skirmish continued until dawn. The brothers of Keechaka, she knew, were no match to the Pandavas. Soon, she felt the ropes that bound her removed. The world again began to go dark, but Draupadi did not fight this time.

∫

When she gained consciousness, she found herself alone, in the temple of Ambika. The sun had risen. She saw the priest look at her dishevelled state and rush to bring water. The news of Keechaka's death had begun to break among the citizens. It was no secret that she was the cause. The two women who arrived early to worship the goddess involuntarily came up to her and knelt before her. The unshed tears in their eyes told her how grateful they felt. Not just Keechaka, but his brothers too, had made the lives of the common people of Matsya miserable.

'Goddess Ambika sent you to us, answering our prayers!' a girl in her teens held her arms and broke down.

'Pray, don't suffocate her. She needs rest!' the priest tried to control the swelling crowd. 'I have sent a word to the palace, Devi. Someone will be here soon to take you back,' he assured her. Cheering slogans with the name of Malini and her Gandharva protectors began to get louder.

Before long, they saw a palanquin halt at the entrance of the temple. A couple of maids rushed to her side, making no attempt to hide their joy and relief at Keechaka's death. She had almost forgotten that she still had four fortnights to live as Malini, the sairandhri.

'Can we also see your husbands and thank them, Devi?' an older woman asked, handing her some water.

Malini tried to rise to her feet and felt Brihannala support her. The dance teacher had accompanied the palanquin from the palace.

'Two months to go. And they shall reveal themselves before we all leave Matsya for good,' she told the woman whose eyes betrayed fear again. The fear that surfaced in every face around.

'No, stay with us,' the woman pleaded.

Malini sighed. 'Citizens of Matsya, stop depending on

223

invisible protectors. Every citizen of the kingdom who let the oppressors run riot is at fault. When they cast their lusty glance upon your daughters, sisters and wives, you advised them to "dress in modesty", to "cover their beauty", so that it would not "provoke" the molesting hands. But it only got worse. Then, your women withdrew to their homes, ceding more space to Keechaka and his monstrous brothers. Events spiralled to such a state that you were just thankful that none of them broke into your homes and forced themselves upon your women. But you had lost it, my brothers and sisters. You had lost the ground that was rightfully yours to those whose rightful place was either the prison or the cremation ground.' Her fatigue was visible in the way Malini sought Brihannala's support to remain standing. But her words found their mark in every heart around her. 'The fault lies not in the beauty of your women, but in the sheer contempt that your erstwhile commander had for the consent of women. Let his death and that of his brothers remain a lesson to this land. You will not need the intervention of celestial vigilantes,' she smiled and proceeded to exit the temple. The grateful crowd followed her till the palanquin moved off.

The Pandavas and their queen had indeed repaid the city of Matsya for sheltering them during the year of incognito living.

∿

Three fortnights passed uneventfully after Keechaka's death. Draupadi resumed her work as the sairandhri after a brief break. Sudeshna was understandably upset and requested her to leave Virata. When Draupadi told her that she would not stay beyond two months, the queen of Matsya had no courage to pressurize her. Draupadi had expected the queen to become aloof after the incident. But she was pleasantly surprised by Uttara's increased admiration and affection.

The first time Uttara saw her after Keechaka's death, she embraced her tearfully. Draupadi knew that the princess of Matsya was not an admirer of her uncle, but the girl's relief at Keechaka's death was touching. Uttara had truly felt the sorrows of the women who had suffered because of Keechaka. In the subsequent weeks they grew closer, talking about the various happenings at Bharata; Brihannala joined them at times.

Uttara often forgot herself, lost in narration or while expressing her fearless views. Else she would have noticed them share tender glances. Arjuna and Draupadi shared the feeling that Princess Uttara gave them what they had missed for long.

Being parents!

The last week of living incognito seemed to stretch forever. Each of the Pandavas felt restlessness overcome them. Draupadi, to her surprise, felt a strange sense of foreboding. Yudhishtira's prophecy of war when they were at Dvaitavana kept ringing in her ears. At times, she woke up from her sleep to the sound of battle drums and blaring trumpets blowing in her dreams. Life had indeed become a challenge. They would emerge out of one intrigue only to find another waiting around the corner.

True to her fears, Draupadi found Uttara and Sudeshna consumed by fear one morning. Sudeshna turned away when she entered, as if blaming Draupadi for whatever bothered them.

'Susarma of Trigarta launched a surprise attack, raiding our cattle in the southern borders,' Uttara explained. 'Father is leaving for the battlefront.'

'They have taken advantage of Keechaka's death,' Sudeshna spoke. 'Even the gentle Kanka Bhattaraka has been forced to take up weapons.'

Malini exited wordlessly, not caring for the protocol, and

hurried towards Kanka's residence. She reached just in time to see him at the threshold.

'Samrat!'

Yudhishtira looked at her tenderly and ushered her inside, where she found Bhima, Nakula and Sahadeva. The sight of the low-quality weapons given to them broke her heart.

'The weaklings of Trigarta don't require my favourite gada!' Bhima laughed, reading her thoughts, and patted her back.

It did little to ease the constriction in her heart. The five brothers were going to face a battle as common soldiers under the command of a king who was nothing in front of them when it came to valour and wisdom.

But she saw the point in staying undetected; it would be hard for Bhima to not be himself once he was unleashed in a battle.

'The citizens of Matsya are already grateful to the "Gandharvas" for getting rid of Keechaka and his brothers. Sons of Kunti, give them another reason to support you when they come to know who you are. Vanquish Susarma and return victorious.'

Yudhishtira came forward and brushed her hair, 'Guard the palace and the women of the Virata family in our absence, Samragni. Arjuna shall stay back with you, in case of any unforeseen need.' Lowering his tone, Yudhishtira added, 'I see birds of northern regions fly this way, which is uncharacteristic. Something might be brewing up north.'

Knowing that she could not afford an elaborate ritual of bidding them farewell to the battlefront, Draupadi applied the tilak on their foreheads and left for the palace, thinking about Yudhishtira's parting words.

The day passed restlessly for the women in Matsya and everyone thronged to the temple of Goddess Ambika, praying for the safe return of their menfolk. The night was also a sleepless one for most of the women, including Queen Sudeshna. It was in the early hours of the morning that the first messenger came carrying the news that Virata had gained upper hand over Susarma.

'It is not that Matsya is vulnerable just because Uncle Keechaka died,' Uttara remarked. Draupadi smiled to herself and Sudeshna was too relieved to react.

But the women had hardly the time to celebrate the news fully when the young Prince Bhuminjaya rushed in, his face flushed with anger. The queen and the princess rose in concern when they saw strange men follow him into the inner apartments, flouting all protocols.

Upon Sudeshna's chiding, they apologized. 'We are the cowherds who guard the cattle on the northern front, Maharani!' They introduced themselves in a hurry. 'The Kuru host descended upon us when we were grazing the cows and are headed towards the borders!'

Draupadi found it hard to believe.

The Kuru host had descended upon a neighbouring kingdom to steal cattle?

'We never had any rivalry with them. What made them resort to this new low?' Sudeshna exclaimed.

Uttara rolled her eyes. 'Mother, did you say "new low"? I thought they had breached all limits of lowliness when they had assaulted Empress Draupadi over that stupid dice game.'

'I wish we had the luxury of worrying about Empress Draupadi! The Kurus have turned into lowly robbers now who want to steal our cattle! In our arid lands, we barely grow enough food for our sustenance. The cattle are our only means to prosperity!' Sudeshna was on the brink of going hysterical when Bhuminjaya held her close.

'Worry not, Mother. I shall face them all and win our cattle back,' he promised Sudeshna. 'Ask my teachers if you wish, Mother. I never miss an aim. My teachers tell me that I shall, one day, become a great archer like Arjuna, the Pandava! In fact, today I shall end the worries of all the Pandavas too!'

Draupadi smiled to herself, touched at the young prince's enthusiasm. Shooting arrows at stationery targets was one thing and fighting a superior force like the Kuru army was another. But the young Bhuminjaya was unaware of the key difference. The situation needed Arjuna's intervention. Bhuminjaya's sudden sigh interrupted her thoughts.

'Father left me to protect the kingdom in his absence, but he never thought I would need a charioteer!' The prince exclaimed and sulked, tapping his spear against the floor.

A look at Sudeshna's face told her the queen was still lost in the memory of her dead brother. Princess Uttara refused to take the momentary disappointment and asked the handful of guards left in the palace if they could drive her brother's chariot in the war. But to her dismay, they expressed their inability to do the same.

'Princess Uttara, how have you forgotten your beloved Natyacharya?' Draupadi suggested.

Uttara turned around, eyes wide. 'Acharya Brihannala! One can't get a better charioteer in the whole of Bharata!'

Seeing the sceptical faces of her mother and brother, she leapt to her feet. 'Don't commit the mistake of dismissing Brihannala as a mere eunuch, brother Bhuminjaya. My teacher drove the chariot of none other than your hero Arjuna himself.' Taking Bhuminjaya's silence for acceptance, Uttara hopped towards the Nartanashala.

Knowing that Arjuna would not say no to his disciple, Draupadi slipped away from the main palace hall. Arjuna would seek her before leaving for the battlefield. It did not take long for Arjuna to find her in the garden of Sudeshna's palace. Draupadi tenderly held his arms, examining the armour and the quality of the metal. She had dreamt of the day she would see her husbands leave to face the Kurus on the battlefield. But this was not how she had wanted it. He would also be the single warrior against the entire host of Kuru warriors unaided by his brothers. However, it did not seem to bother him.

'Aren't there a few hours left before the term of Agnatavasa ends?' she asked, seeing the movement of the sun.

He brushed her hair with the same tenderness. 'Vijayadashami, the day of victory, is not far away, Draupadi.' Pausing to draw her attention further, he added in a low voice, 'Princess Uttara asked us to gift her the garments of the Kuru warriors to drape around her dolls. She might be unwittingly seeking to avenge her future mother-in-law.'

The statement drew a smile on Draupadi's face. 'Make her wish come true, Arjuna.'

She knew that his other name was Vijaya and the name would not go in vain.

Part Four

War

Thirty-four

Peace at What Cost?

The precious months of celebration flew by, filled with a slew of reunions. Reuniting with her son Abhimanyu and other sons of the Pandavas and their mothers almost made Draupadi forget the ordeals that had followed the fateful game. The celebrations increased as the day of Abhimanyu's wedding with Uttara drew closer.

Draupadi knew they had reached their peak when she saw a familiar chariot with the eagle banner approach their temporary residence at Upaplavya, a city gifted to them by King Virata on the occasion of the wedding. The formalities of meetings between the families of Pandavas and Yadavas seemed to stretch painfully. It was different when Krishna came alone. But today, the elders of the extended Yadu family arrived to grace the wedding of the son of their beloved daughter, Subhadra. Suppressing her impatience, Draupadi welcomed the guests. Unlike the times at Dvaitavana, the residence at Upaplavya, situated at the borders of Matsya, was spacious enough to host the royalty and nobility who visited them.

Seeing Krishna surrounded by her own husbands as well as the princes of Panchala and other allies, Draupadi decided to wait until he broke free of them, which happened only in the late afternoon. Words were not necessary to express what each had gone through. She could imagine Krishna's state. The Yadavas had divided into factions, one of them supporting the Pandavas, and the other supporting the Kauravas. Krishna's own son, Samba, had wedded Duryodhana's daughter, Lakshana, complicating the dynamics within his own family.

'The descendants of Kurus even managed to break the Yadava confederacy into two!' Draupadi remarked, her face reflecting the anguish that Krishna had suppressed within himself.

'People make their choices, Sakhi,' he beamed. He had distanced himself from these squabbles. 'At times, a conflict proves greatly useful in serving one's own interests. At times, it gives people the excuse to claim their own stakes and fight their own conflicts from the shadows.'

'Your father, the king of Panchala, offered to send his priest as the emissary to Hastinapura after the wedding of Abhimanyu,' Krishna informed her.

Draupadi laughed. 'Like an emissary would make a difference, Krishna! Had they been receptive to diplomacy, they would not have attacked Matsya like a gang of robbers to smoke us out of our disguise. And my father is not a fool to not have assessed that,' she pointed out. 'The emissary must be a ruse. This priest is going to collect information about the preparations in the Kuru capital and convey it back to us.'

Krishna's fists curled for a moment. 'It looks like it has come to the worst. Doesn't it?'

'At times, we have to give up the present to secure something for the future,' Draupadi sighed, staring into space. 'If it turns into a final confrontation, I have a favour to ask of you, Sakha. Don't fight on the battlefield.'

'Why so, Sakhi?' Krishna's eyes were devoid of all emotions.

Draupadi leaned back against the pile of cushions behind her and gazed at the high ceiling. 'You will fight to end it all and that will lead to a terror the world is not prepared to see. That is not the Krishna I want to see.' Training her eyes back to meet his, she felt her heart miss a bit at what she saw in his eyes. A glimpse of the terror he would unleash if he took up a weapon.

'Instead, let us all divide our responsibilities!' she briefly assumed the air of the empress that he used to tease her about in their younger days and then turned solemn. 'Fatiguing as it is, I have remained the driving force behind the five brothers, and you, the guiding force. We both know they are great as doers. They excel in execution. Let them fight it to the end. I dread disturbing this balance between us, Sakha!'

Krishna's eyes betrayed admiration—at the fondness she had displayed, even while taking the toughest decision, manoeuvring through the delicate knots of relationships, polity, and something that risked extinction in the present circumstances—dharma. Then his eyes turned grave. Graver than she had ever seen them before. 'War, if and when it comes to that, needs us to subject our willpower to the worst of tests, Sakhi.' Lowering his tone, he added, 'Yudhishtira is not yet ready for that!'

Draupadi nodded and wrung her hands. 'He gets caught in resisting the inevitable.' She then reminded him about the multiple times during their exile when Yudhishtira himself had warned her of a violent war that would unleash horror. She smiled and saw Krishna smile too.

He had thought of a way out!

♪

The wedding of Abhimanyu and Uttara was an event that brought together every family that cared for the five brothers under one roof. It was a much-awaited celebration, and brought great cheer. Though sceptical of the future, the bride and groom began to work on their own relationship. The fact that the elders were too preoccupied with the political uncertainty gave them the time and space to adapt to each other.

As predicted, Drupada's priest carried out the diplomatic mission and returned with the message that the sons of Dhritarashtra were rejecting the Pandavas' claim to the empire. Some of the reasons cited were flimsy and inaccurate, like their accusation that Arjuna had come out of incognito before the term of exile. However, multiple astrologers who knew calculations of time had dismissed this allegation.

It boiled down to each side canvassing the length and breadth of Bharatavarsha, trying to raise forces that they hoped would intimidate the other side. For many kings who were obliged to one of the two sides due to marital bonds, it was a fairly simple decision to make. But a grave dilemma was faced by those kings who were related to both sides. Yudhishtira resolved to reach out to every ally. After all, they had been ready to surround Hastinapura and raze it to the ground thirteen years ago.

'Thirteen years is a long time. We might not have the support of even half of them,' Nakula had voiced his apprehension then. His fears had come true and the support to the sons of Dhritarashtra had increased with time. Some with marital alliance, some with military campaigns, some with diplomatic outreach, Hastinapura had managed to garner a steady support for itself. However, the loyal allies of the sons of Pandu had also stayed on. The five brothers travelled again to all corners of Bharatavarsha, at times facing bizarre and twisted narratives of what had taken place in the Jayanta Sabha.

The most ridiculous one that Draupadi heard was from a warlord of the southern provinces who had changed his loyalties citing his respect for women and disappointment with Yudhishtira as the latter had gambled away his wife as if she was his property. It didn't make sense that he had then sided with those who had dragged her by her hair to the sabha, had called her characterless, ordered her disrobing, and had wanted her to sit naked upon their laps. She had been a witness to how her husbands had behaved with the wife of the enemy when she had been defenceless—the argument did not make sense.

'Don't even bother convincing the imbecile!' she hissed at an equally perplexed Sahadeva. 'Those who change loyalties with twisted arguments of dharma and then pretend to take the moral high ground aren't worth fighting by our side. Remember to kill him on the very first day and tell him that it is the punishment for daring to side with those barbarians, taking my name as an excuse!'

'He is not worth fighting by our side. And he is not even worth your anger, Draupadi,' Sahadeva smiled, brushing her cheeks that had flushed in rage.

'They are the pseudo guardians of morality, Sahadeva. These low lives behave like flag bearers of morality while no aspect of that gets inside their hard skulls. The earth is better off without them!'

'By Goddess Gauri, I haven't seen you ever curse Duryodhana the way you are lashing out at the nameless bloke, Elder Sister,' Subhadra held Draupadi's shaking arm.

'They are using my name and the ordeal I faced as an excuse to side with my enemy against me, Subhadra! How vicious can one get?'

237

'More like sold out,' Subhadra shrugged, 'possibly to some gold thrown by Duryodhana. As you said, such "flag bearers" of—what was that—"respect for women" actually end up harming our kind if trusted.' Eager to change the topic, she turned to Sahadeva. 'Isn't Arjuna expected soon?'

'He should have returned from Dwaraka by now,' Sahadeva thought aloud and walked up to the spacious western balcony, expecting to see his brother return.

'Subhadra, I thought you would have liked to accompany Arjuna to Dwaraka,' Draupadi asked.

Subhadra's face twisted in anguish. 'I have been there for thirteen long years, Elder Sister,' she started, suppressing her tears. 'They have been ungrateful to my brother. How will they remember me, his sister! Anyway, I sent a message that I shall step into Dwaraka only after seeing my husband destroy the enemy. They will understand and side with him if they want to please me.'

Neither Draupadi nor Sahadeva said anything, each of them trying to imagine how Subhadra must have battled the intrigues at her own natal home. It was easier to battle an enemy.

How could a woman take it when her own family turned against her?

A guard broke their silence. Arjuna had returned. With Krishna and his dear mentee, Satyaki, followed by a division of Satyaki's private army, which by no means was small in size or valour. Draupadi sighed with relief.

Later during the day, she heard Yudhishtira express surprise at Krishna's sudden decision to not wield a weapon during the war.

'Did he not promise you that day, that each of your tears would claim a life?'

'That was his way of warning me to not shed more tears,

Yudhishtira,' Draupadi replied with a nod. She decided against disclosing her discussion with Krishna.

'Possibly because a large contingent of the Yadava warriors have also joined Duryodhana under the leadership of Kritavarma,' Yudhishtira was still trying to reason. 'Krishna had once risked everything—his life, his reputation—to save them all from the wrath of Jarasandha. How can he lift a weapon against the ones he saved?' he asked Draupadi, who listened, betraying no emotions. 'It would be unfair of us to even expect him to do that, Draupadi. How did I turn this selfish?'

The lines of trouble lingered on Yudhishtira's forehead even after the conversation veered to other issues, mainly pertaining to the logistics of war. Strategizing for a battle was something in which Yudhishtira indulged with all his heart and soul, something that retained Draupadi's awe even after over two decades of their wedding. But this time, Yudhishtira kept returning to the topic of Krishna's abstinence from fighting.

'That is why Krishna attempted to secure a peaceful resolution one last time, Samragni.'

'Did he?' Draupadi asked. This was new to her.

'He did! A last attempt to save his people on both sides. The least I can do is make his task easier by offering a compromise! Draupadi, we transformed a land that was barren and wild into a magnificent province and built what became the capital of all of Bharata. We don't require an empire. We can do with a confederacy of five principalities!'

Draupadi looked up, shock rendering her speechless for a long moment.

Was this the same Yudhishtira who had once asked her to prepare for the worst, with a chilling certainty?

'Did you say compromise, Samrat?'

But by that time, Yudhishtira was already on his feet. 'Five principalities would do. Let the four of them enjoy autonomy without being under the obligation to do as I bid. Everyone's suffered enough,' he left the room without seeking her approval—one of the rare times.

'What in the name of all gods was that?' she exclaimed and looked at Sahadeva who had been a mute listener to their conversation all this time.

Sahadeva had nothing to say either.

'Tell me I dreamt it all! Tell me it is some apparition impersonating Yudhishtira!'

'Draupadi, calm down,' he held her arm in a bid to comfort her. But it was beyond him. All he could do was follow Yudhishtira and try undoing any damage his eldest would wreak again in the name of some meaningless compromise.

⁂

It was a painful couple of weeks for Draupadi. When the war stood at their threshold, with a number of loyal allies ready to offer their kingdoms, wealth and even lives to see Yudhishtira reinstated as the emperor again, the eldest Pandava had resorted to some self-deprecating compromise in the name of 'statesmanship'!

Complicating the situation further, Krishna had gone to Hastinapura, carrying that pointless message.

As if anyone in that court of barbarians and imbeciles would know to respect the stance! Men can be so disappointing.

More than six weeks after Krishna had left Upaplavya, the messengers came, conveying that Krishna's return journey had 'failed' to secure peace. What he had to endure at the sabha at Hastinapura was beyond disturbing.

'Brutes! Monsters!' Yudhishtira snapped. He dismissed the messenger after he informed him that Krishna would reach Upaplavya by dawn. 'If war is what they want, they will get it. And they will not live to even regret it, Draupadi!'

Draupadi stared at the sudden transformation and chose to not say anything. She was already resigned to the fact that her best friend was at times beyond her understanding. But it looked like her husband of two decades was the same! For the rest of the evening, she saw Yudhishtira strategize with his brothers and brothers-in-law in a fury that even surprised them.

'We need to see where the sun rises tomorrow. I bet it must be in the west!' Bhima remarked, suppressing a mischievous chuckle. He could hardly conceal his jubilation at Yudhishtira's transformation. 'So, it took a Krishna and another heap of insults upon him for the eldest to set his heart upon war!'

Krishna had talked about Yudhishtira's heart not being in the war. Now that had changed! In her mind's eye, she saw the two sides face each other in the battlefield.

She had been told that Kurukshetra would be the venue.

241

Thirty-five

Night Before the War

The camps at Kurukshetra swarmed with soldiers, charioteers, caretakers, doctors, attendants, and animals. Horses, mules, elephants and even bullocks, used to pull the carts of supplies, made each camp swell in size. It seemed as if a huge portion of life on earth had assembled there.

To kill or die in the name of dharma!

Draupadi felt a shiver down her spine when she imagined the first clash between these two seas of armies. It would not be an exaggeration to say that the earth might quake! A loud round of cheer from the foot soldiers in the camp startled her. The principal warriors of the Pandava camp had returned from the final meeting where the code had been decided. It was a wise decision to choose Drishtadyumna as the commander-in-chief. Known for his ruthlessness on the battlefield, Drishtadyumna, unlike his brothers-in-law, was not related to anyone on the other side. Nostalgic sentiments or emotions were not something that would slow him down.

She walked through the ranks of soldiers, noting their upbeat mood. They were talking about enjoying the night to the fullest for no one knew if they would see another night. Draupadi felt her bosom tighten.

If she felt this way, what would the five brothers feel on the following day when they saw half of their relatives waiting to kill them or die by their hands?

With Yudhishtira calling her to lead the ceremonial worship offered to Goddess Durga to seek her blessings for victory, she brushed her tears away and hurried to where they waited for her. Desire for victory, revenge, fame, recognition, and justice surfaced on the faces of each of the warriors in the camp.

> Grant us contentment. Grant us strength. Grant us intelligence.
> Grant us courage to fight on when the enemy gains.
> Grant us compassion when we better the enemy.
> Above all, grant us the unsullied heart and endless vigour.
> May we prove worthy of Your blessing to be victorious.
> May we fight for dharma, to uphold all that is fair and just!

Those who had the ability to compose sung their hymns to the Goddess, praising the Supreme Feminine who took on the demonic elements that once threatened the life and order of balance in the world. She was a manifestation of their cumulative energies, endeavours, and ambitions. She was what sustained them. She was what drove them. She was everything—the daughter, the beloved, the mother. She was the desire, the means, and the end. She would drink the blood of the monsters who threatened everything she had sworn to protect.

The stories of ancient legends, described with embellishments of devotional exaggeration, never failed to hold the listeners in awe. With Her blessings, they would go to battle the next day.

∿

NIGHT BEFORE THE WAR

Draupadi walked over to the tents where her brothers and sons slept and checked if they had kept their weapons within their reach, lest the need arose. To her disappointment, most of them had not. Draupadi conveyed her displeasure to Prativindhya who was the only alert warrior by that time, despite an overdose of wine.

'Pray, calm down, Mother!' Prativindhya protested. 'Like you expect the soldiers on the other side to break in here in the dead of the night and attack us. That would be flouting the code of war the very day it was made!'

'Like you expect them to follow any codes! After what they did...' Draupadi paused mid-sentence, not wanting to remind him of the bitter memory all over again.

'We shall not let you down, Mother. Please get some sleep now, I beg you,' Prativindhya pleaded.

Draupadi saw him collapse on the bed and kept his dagger by his side. It seemed like a huge mistake to have let the children mingle with the Panchala princes. When Prativindhya had insisted on postponing his wedding until after the war, she had not pressed him further. But now, when she saw Abhimanyu with Uttara, sober and mindful before the big day, she suddenly felt unsure about involving the children in the bloodbath that would follow. But keeping them away, she knew, was not a solution either. Only two warriors in the land of Bharatavarsha were abstaining from the war—Balarama and Rukma, Rukmini's brother. She did not want the world to remember her sons along with the two. With another fond glance at her five children, Draupadi forced herself to walk away.

To her surprise, she found the tent of Yudhishtira empty. Concerned, she hurried to search for him. The tents of the other four Pandavas were empty as well. At last, she found them all together by a fire lit on the banks of the lake.

'How will you face the battle tomorrow without a good sleep?' she asked.

Yudhishtira's response was a detached nod. He moved aside on the boulder he sat on, making space for her.

'Anything of concern, Samrat?' she relaxed only after seeing all the five shake their heads.

Why aren't you all sleeping?

The question remained on her face.

'The wait of fourteen years has come down to a single night, Samragni,' Yudhishtira replied, staring into the flame at the centre. 'But battles don't leave one the same. Especially, battles of this magnitude, which bring almost all the warriors, kings, warlords, and soldiers of Bharata to the cusp of killing or dying. This might be the last time we will see each other as we are, our spirits unscarred by whatever tomorrow holds in store.'

'Battles scar only those who either fight for selfish ends or those who have a narrow understanding of dharma, Samrat,' Draupadi protested. 'I trust none of you are after vengeance or have to be reminded of the nuances of dharma.' Considering their faces devoid of any expression, she continued, 'If vengeance was all we wanted, we could have extracted it the day Bhanumati begged us to save Duryodhana from the Gandharvas.' She smiled. 'Or when Arjuna faced the Kuru host and overwhelmed them single-handedly. We were not short of opportunities to pay them back.'

Sahadeva smiled at her as he would at a child. 'If they knew what this meant, we would never have seen this night, Draupadi.'

With an emphatic nod, she replied, 'We knew then that they would neither comprehend, nor acknowledge our restraint. Still, we did what we had to do, Sahadeva. It is this very conscience that they will lack when their weapons rise against us tomorrow.'

A drum sounded, announcing the second quarter of the night. Instantly, everyone turned towards the sky to check the movement of the stars.

'Face it and fight till the end, sons of Pandu,' Draupadi continued, partly concerned at the mixed reactions. 'Let us not forget, even for a single moment during the course of war, that we are not fighting for the kingdom, not for vengeance, not against our kith and kin, but for the honour of every man and woman who invested their faith, wealth and labour on us when we built Indraprastha. Fight to reclaim the lost honour in the eyes of those innumerable dead soldiers who fought alongside you, to establish the empire of dharma. Fight to restore that faith our subjects have in us. Fight for the victory that we owe them!'

Thirty-six

Bhishma's Secret

The darkness under Yudhishtira's eyes was worrying. After nine days since the war had started, the losses were heavy. Arjuna had lost a son of his—Iravan, by a naga woman who had faithfully sent her limited resources to fight along their side. Draupadi heard him recount how the togetherness of the father and son had been limited to a couple of days.

And it was just the beginning.

King Virata had lost both his sons. Even the bubbly and endearing Bhuminjaya who had not tired in his efforts to motivate the soldiers. Seeing Abhimanyu console the distraught Uttara, Draupadi could not help worry. It was not about personal loss, but about the grim pain of sacrificing the younger generation when their fathers were alive. Lighting the pyre of one's dead father was an inevitable pain that every man had to go through in his life. But lighting the pyre of his son is something no man can ever be prepared for. The tenets of philosophy, motivational axioms from the ancient texts, loving and consoling words from those who had experienced similar pain—everything seemed to fail when each of them, right from Arjuna to the lowliest soldier, combated their respective losses.

'Every life lost is a debt we have to repay, Draupadi,' Yudhishtira lamented. 'The fact that Bhishma is alive is the cause of demotivation for our men!'

It was a chilling transformation from being a loving grandson to waiting for the death of a beloved elder. Yet, his words were not laced with anger or hatred. Draupadi had inquired about how the other side was faring, and their condition was not better either.

'Only Arjuna can rein in Bhishma's mad run. Only Bhishma can hold back Arjuna's progress. But when they face each other, they fall weak and take out their fury on other warriors,' Yudhishtira narrated.

'Krishna was so badly wounded that he took up a weapon himself, unable to let the carnage go on, Draupadi. He had to be coaxed to back off.'

Draupadi rose from her seat and hurried to Krishna's tent. Not finding him there, she rushed to the makeshift stables erected to rest the horses and found him tending to them. She noticed other caretakers pause in their tasks just to see him in the act.

Watching him soothe the fatigued steeds was a sight that could melt stones. Draupadi waited until she saw him clutch his own right shoulder, still bleeding from one of the wounds of the battle, possibly by Bhishma. He had not even bothered to apply any medication. Walking up to him and patting one of the horses, she held his arm, smiling. 'Come Krishna. The horses deserve better than a wounded sarathi.'

Krishna's characteristic smile was absent. Graveness lingered in his eyes even when he let Draupadi lead him towards his tent, instructing the other caretakers to finish tending to the steeds. Neither of them spoke until Draupadi ensured that the medication was applied in a judicious quantity. She could see why Yudhishtira was annoyed at Arjuna's weak resistance to Bhishma.

'So, Arjuna's best does not come out when the grand old man comes in front of him,' she remarked.

'The strongest of walls too have their cracks, Draupadi,' Krishna said.

'What did you call me?' Draupadi almost jumped.

'Enough theatrics,' Krishna finally beamed. 'That's my territory.'

Draupadi relaxed and bade the physician to leave. 'Sakha, we need a Bhishma to counter Bhishma.'

She was about to lie back against the mound of wolfskins, but Krishna suddenly tugged at her arm, pulling her to her feet. 'What is it?'

'We are going to find a solution to this dance of death called Bhishma,' he declared, wearing his upper garment and handing her another shawl. 'From Bhishma himself,' he added.

It was a sheer leap of faith that made Draupadi agree to what many would have called a ridiculous idea. Before long, they reached the camp of Hastinapura, and stood at the entrance of Bhishma's tent. It wasn't that Draupadi was afraid to face Bhishma, but having taken the bold step, she needed the encouragement from Krishna when she entered while he stood guard outside. The man of a terrible oath sat in a meditative pose, eyes half closed.

'Greetings, Grandsire,' she knelt on the floor before him.

'*Deergha Sumangali Bhava!*' came the absent-minded response. Bhishma had probably taken her for a laywoman who had strayed into the camp.

'How can those words come true if my husbands cannot protect the soldiers faithful to them from the onslaught of the enemy's commander, Grandsire?' she rose and looked at him, prepared to meet his gaze if he opened his eyes. 'Isn't a king who cannot protect his soldiers from the enemy better dead than alive?"

Bhishma opened his eyes. The streak of recognition brought a momentary spark in his eyes. 'So, the sons of Pandu have again sought the refuge of their queen,' he laughed.

'The household of Pandu has learnt to survive without needing refuge, Grandsire. From assassination attempts to abject inaction of capable elders, we know the futility of seeking refuge,' she looked into his eye, the spark in hers daring him to laugh again.

'A wife never brooks a word against her husband. And you have five good ones,' Bhishma smiled—this time, a warm one. 'My apologies, child. This old man never had a woman in his life to gauge one well.'

'I wish you indeed had one, Grandsire. The descendants as well as the empire needed the care of such a woman to not end their existence in a carnage like this,' Draupadi rued. 'Before we lose ourselves in an intellectual exchange, the outcome of which will not matter, Grandsire, I seek to know what can stop your onslaught.'

Bhishma's eyes widened. 'For someone who once ruled over Bharatavarsha, I expected better from you, Draupadi. Or is it that grandchildren always falter in front of their grandfather? What kind of an enemy blurts out his own death secret, my child?'

'The one who realizes that he had a huge role to play in the deterioration of the empire he claimed to serve with utmost devotion,' Draupadi retorted. 'How long will you make the soldiers of Bharatavarsha pay for your mistakes, son of Ganga? And there are way too many, right from abducting unwilling princesses to staying silent when your word was the most required!' Draupadi's eyes blazed. 'I know you are wise enough to gauge your own role in this war that is claiming the lives of five whole generations of warriors, Grandsire Bhishma. Pray, show me a way to end this sooner.'

Bhishma sighed and rose. 'I am called Bhishma, child. And true to my name, I shall continue being the terrible old man on the field! As long as I face a *man!*' He considered her intent gaze, unflinching at what he had declared about himself. 'I understand what my inaction cost, daughter of Drupada. Go, my child, you have the solution hidden in my past *actions.*'

Draupadi lowered her gaze for the first time, pondering over the cryptic solution Bhishma had given. Bhishma touched her head, in affection and apology. 'You have everything in your hands, Draupadi. Go, ask the naughty boy outside, who brought you here in the first place. Tell him to end my predicament soon. Tell him I am counting on him.'

Draupadi's put her hands together, as she still battled the riddle. She had spoken about his past *action*, that of abducting the princesses of Kashi, Amba, Ambika and Ambalika, against their wishes. Ambika and Ambalika were married off to the much weaker Vichitraveerya, who had not lasted even for a year after his wedding. The women then had to endure *niyoga* to beget Dhritarashtra and Pandu. And the story of Amba was even more heart-rending. Draupadi could never forget what the name of Amba meant in Panchala during her childhood.

The thought struck her just as she met Krishna.

Shikhandi!

She clutched his arm. He smiled, 'I had an inkling. I just wanted to confirm. Come, Sakhi, let us give the poor old man some rest. He has suffered enough.'

Thirty-seven

Dushasana's End

It was the afternoon of the fifteenth day of the war when Draupadi woke up. The mounting losses each day had robbed her sleep. When Satyajit had fallen to Drona's arrows on the twelfth day of the war, the grief that had churned through her had been beyond comprehension. She had spent the entire night consoling Drupada, but in vain.

Abhimanyu's tragic death in an unfair combined attack had followed the next day and the entire Pandava camp was numb. She heard that every single soldier on their side had shed tears. Uttara had been stoic while Subhadra had wept hysterically the entire night. Arjuna had taken the pledge to kill Jayadrata who had played a key role in isolating Abhimanyu within the formidable Chakravyuha. Subhadra had taken a vow of not having even water until Arjuna returned safely after killing Jayadrata. While the Pandava side had suffered Drona's onslaught, Arjuna and Satyaki too had massacred the opponents that day, raising the spirits of the camp. But grief had remained and had multiplied with the death of every family member.

The fifteenth day had been strange. They had lost Ghatotkacha in the night of the fourteenth day, and Drupada along with

Virata, early in the morning. Draupadi had suppressed her grief to console Uttara and had hoped to vent hers with her brothers when they returned that evening. But by sunset, Drishtadyumna had achieved in his own words, 'what he was born for'. She had numbly watched him celebrate Drona's death more than he mourned for Drupada. She remembered Shikhandi's sober demeanour after he had felled Bhishma. Dhrishtadyumna, on the other hand, was exhilarated. Later, she had come to know that Drishtadyumna had been distraught on the field after Drupada's death and had killed Drona at what many called a 'morally wrong' moment.

'The bloodlust has been unleashed way too much for anyone to bother about morals and codes. All we can hope is for the feeling of vengeance to get satiated by itself,' Yudhishtira explained.

'My entire life before I wedded you, I had dissuaded my father and brothers from pursuing the path of blind vengeance,' she sobbed. 'Fate has succeeded in making a mockery of all my efforts. My father and brothers stood by me! But I failed as a daughter and sister!'

'Stop blaming yourself, Draupadi!' Bhima had exclaimed, partly annoyed. 'More losses were incurred because some on our side felt weak with emotions when they should have been giving their best.' The jibe had been directed at Arjuna who had abruptly left the conversation midway.

The fractures in the relationship among the five brothers had started deepening. This was a greater loss. Only Krishna, she felt, understood what she went through whenever an unpleasant conversation took place among them.

'Have we failed, Krishna?' she had asked him once when they were alone.

'We succeed. We fail. We give in. We get back,' Krishna had responded. He had retained his prized equanimity while she felt lost. 'Depends on when we consider our fight ends, Sakhi.'

'It seems like our fight will continue till we die, Sakha,' she had rued.

'Then we have the luxury of not worrying about success and failure!' he had patted her cheek.

It had finally drawn a smile from her amidst the devastation that raged around. Holding his hand, she had whispered, 'Don't die. If you die, those five are better dead than alive. But I want to follow you before anyone of them can.'

'Now that makes it necessary for me to postpone my plans of dying!'

She had thrown the first thing she found at him. He had left with that teasing expression.

He knew it made her feel alive.

It was dawn again by the time her eyes closed. None of her attendants woke her up until the blazing rays of the sun shone through the hole on top of her tent. Neither did any of her husbands come to her before they left for the battlefield. She suppressed the bout of anger knowing that they had done so only to not disturb her precious sleep, which had become scarce nowadays.

Like every day, she remembered the names of each warrior who went to war and prayed for their victory and safety. About two weeks back, that list had taken her more than an hour and had tested her ability to remember. Today, it was not as much of a challenge to remember the handful who survived. Her heart missed a beat with each name.

How worse could it get before it was over?

Draupadi felt her energy drained even before she had gotten

out of bed. Subhadra came searching for her, bringing her meal along. Draupadi saw traces of annoyance on her face and asked her for the reason.

'It is Sudeshna!' Subhadra sounded indignant. 'She was blaming you for her losses. I gave her a piece of my mind.'

'Go easy on her, Subhadra,' Draupadi waved, too tired to analyse or conclude. 'She has lost her brothers because of...'

'Because they thought it is their divine right to force themselves upon unwilling women!' Subhadra interrupted. 'Don't ever say it was because of you, Sister!'

Subhadra, like her brother, could boast of an impeccable clarity of thought. Draupadi smiled and wondered where hers had gone.

'Any news from the field?' Draupadi asked, shuddering at the next wave of troubling thoughts.

'Someone lost his charioteer. Someone's horses were killed. Someone was wounded...' Subhadra recounted, taking no names. But the numb grief of losing someone dear came through. 'At the risk of sounding selfish, our husbands are alive,' she said and turned away.

Draupadi turned to her, 'What is it, Subhadra?'

'It is Uttara, Sister,' Subhadra broke into tears. 'She neither speaks, nor sheds tears. Eats almost nothing unless forced. Faints frequently. Do something, pray, do something.'

'I shall try talking to her again, Subhadra,' she assured her. A thought struck her. But she was not sure how Subhadra would take it. She was not even sure how Arjuna would react. But before sharing with him, she had to know Uttara's thoughts.

The sun had begun his westward journey and the day began to wane. Draupadi realized sheepishly that she had not bathed and walked towards the lake when she heard Bhima's exhilarant

255

voice calling out to her. Even before she had turned, she was conscious of her heart beating fast. It meant something! Her jaw dropped, seeing his hands covered in red.

'Bhima!' she shrieked, rushing towards the giant. 'How did this…?'

Bhima laughed aloud, seeing realization dawn on her face. Without further words, he held her head with his bloody hands and kissed her, not bothering about the onlookers. 'Guess whose blood it is!'

Draupadi stared at him clueless. What shocked her more was the blood on his lips, parts of which were on her cheek. Whoever was his victim, the joy Bhima felt was disturbing. Draupadi realized that her hands were shivering when she held Bhima's. 'Whose…blood…is this, Bhima?'

'Remember the cowardly rascal who dragged you by your hair in the sabha? Remember the scoundrel whose lowly conscience permitted him to tear your garments?' Bhima shook with rage.

'Dushasana!' Draupadi spoke in a whisper and saw Bhima's hands again. 'You killed him?' A momentary smile appeared on her lips but it quickly faded at his next words.

'Don't you remember my oath to tear open his chest, taste his blood, and wash your hair with his blood?' Bhima said.

Draupadi nodded, her face pale, imagining what Bhima would have done on the battlefield. Her jaw dropped on realizing that Dushasana's blood was all over her hair, her face and her clothes.

'I have kept my oath! Draupadi, I have killed him. I tore open his chest in front of that conceited Karna. I could hear Karna sob out of sheer helplessness. I could feel the entire Kaurava host go numb with fear!'

'Bh…Bhima!' she held his arms. 'Bhima, tell me you did not drink his blood.'

Bhima was about to say something when he noticed her shock. The fear he saw in her eyes in place of the jubilation he had expected injured him more than the onslaught of all the weapons he had endured throughout the battle at Kurukshetra. 'Draupadi!' he whispered, realizing the bitter truth. Speaking no more, he shoved her out of his way and proceeded towards the lake.

It took Draupadi a long time to recover. Her first reaction was to rush towards the water and wash Dushasana's blood off her. This brought back the memories of her first day with Bhima, the encounter with the Naga factions, and how he had ripped apart the miscreant who had violated the Naga girl. That was immediately after he had known about the heinous act.

This was a Bhima who had suppressed his rage for fourteen years! And the woman was her, who he loved!

Under the personification of violent retribution, this was a man who loved with all his heart. She could not let that heart be broken.

'Bhima!' she rushed towards the lake. It took her some time to find him. Submerged in water, chest deep, he was facing the other side. She saw the big wound on the back of his shoulder and cringed. 'Bhima!'

'It is all right, Draupadi,' he sighed at her. 'Don't come near me. You shall regret it. Again.'

'Well, I am coming!' she descended into the waters and hugged him from behind. She felt his muscles flex under her hold. He tried to extricate himself. He could easily have. But she held on with all her strength. 'Please Bhima! I beg you, talk to me.'

257

His response was only a cry of anguish before he held her arms again. This time, it was not to shake her away. 'How did I turn into this monster?' he felt her shaking her head vehemently. 'Don't deceive yourself and me, Draupadi. Vengeance has festered in my heart and has turned it into stone. I have become a mons...'

'No, you have not! In fact, you are the farthest from being a monster, Bhima. And your heart is not made of stone. You felt a woman's trauma. I have tried to harden myself against the memory, but you felt the hurt all along. You bore it more than I did. Because you have the heart to feel and empathize. You make me proud, Bhima!'

He turned around, tears freely streaming from his eyes. He held her close. 'You are too kind, Draupadi. But I know what I am. At least, I know that I am very different from the other four! Different enough to be an embarrassment at times!' After a pause, he suddenly withdrew. 'You haven't yet washed off that blood!'

'I said you make me proud!' Draupadi smiled, crying. It was a rare occurrence that she had let herself cry in front of any of her husbands, especially after the game. He knew he had breached a wall. Draupadi brushed the tears away and beamed. 'Yes, you are different from them. They are what they are and they continue to be what they are because you are what you are. Each of you owes yourself to the other four, Bhima! I love each of you for what you are!'

Probably, it was the first time that she had openly declared her love. He held her and wept aloud. Bhima seldom held back his emotions, whether it was anger, grief or joy. But this was the first time he wept like a child of five or six. Like a huge burden was off his shoulders. Draupadi knew that the

258

burden was hurting him more than wreaking vengeance against Dushasana.

It was about her!

At last, he felt he deserved her.

Thirty-eight

Uttara is Pregnant

The reduced number of tents in the enemy camp was a sorry sight. Draupadi remembered the vastness of the Kuru camp which had been enough to intimidate the most formidable of warriors, just seventeen days back. The number of tents had dwindled with each day. Today, it was not even a tenth of what it had been. Draupadi looked at her own camp and the situation was not very different.

In the enemy camp, only Duryodhana and a few of his brothers had survived, along with Karna, Shakuni, Shalya, Ashvatthama, Kripacharya and Kritavarma. The Pandavas too had suffered irreparable losses—the deaths of Abhimanyu and Ghatotkacha being the most emotionally devastating. No, there were more—where every man in family had perished. Mechanically overseeing the activities under her charge, Draupadi walked towards Uttara's tent. How would the child stand the loss of her brothers, father, and even her new groom, before she had even seen eighteen springs of her life?

She saw Uttara sitting on the bed, a ghost of her former chatty self. Draupadi walked up to the princess of Matsya and brushed her long hair that had remained without care ever since the day Abhimanyu had died.

Uttara looked at her, her eyes bereft of all emotions. Before speaking anything more, Draupadi reached out for the jar of fragrant oil and began to groom Uttara's hair, like olden times. She fervently hoped that the child would vent out her grief and try coming back to normal. But Uttara's disturbing silence continued. It was when Draupadi called the maid to get her the bath oils that Uttara spoke up.

'Don't they say that a widow is not supposed to adorn herself this way, Mother Draupadi?'

'Who said you are one?' Draupadi whispered, suppressing her own sob. 'You have been my daughter ever since I stepped into your palace at Matsya, Uttara. You shall continue to be a daughter. We shall find another suitable groom for you.'

Uttara shrank back from her and shook her head. Draupadi sighed, 'It has hardly been six months since you wedded Abhimanyu. Steel yourself and move on, child. I shall not let your youth go waste.'

'It shall not,' Uttara replied in a small voice. 'Neither will I marry anyone else.' When Draupadi turned towards her, Uttara's tears broke their dams. 'I bear Abhimanyu's child.' In the next moment, Draupadi enveloped her in her arms. Amidst the devastating dance of death, Abhimanyu's bride had showed them hope.

The five brothers needed to hear this!

Searching for a messenger to ride out to the field, Draupadi, to her shock, heard that Yudhishtira had retired to the camp because of the multiple wounds he had suffered in the hands of Karna. Rushing to him, she found Arjuna exiting the tent, rage rendering his face crimson. She called out to him but found him in no mood to listen.

She caught Krishna just before he exited and pulled him back inside. The sight of Yudhishtira covered in blood made her pause. But taking the medicine and salve from the physician's hands herself, she looked at Yudhishtira's disturbed face and then at Krishna. 'Uttara is pregnant with Abhimanyu's child!'

The change in the men's faces was palpable. Krishna's emotions were eclipsed as his eyelids closed.

In relief.

Yudhishtira smiled through his pain, even if it was just for a moment, and ordered for a celebration in the camp after sunset. Krishna's inscrutable but burdened smile told her that something else had happened. And that it was not pleasant. As if urging her to speak to Yudhishtira later, he took leave. Yudhishtira embraced him and spoke in a tone uncharacteristic of him. 'Steer the war to Karna's death today, Krishna. I have lost hope on him whose will to fight falters at the time of need!'

The sarcasm in his tone when he refused to take Arjuna's name was not lost on Krishna, but he chose to only nod and leave. But not before conveying something to Draupadi with his eyes.

I am with Arjuna. Take care of the emperor.

Draupadi first chose to turn her attention to Yudhishtira's wounds. They were the worst she had ever seen.

'Don't bother yourself, Draupadi!' Yudhishtira exclaimed, pushing her hand away. 'For all you know, I might be better off dead soon.'

'Samrat!' There was more anger in her tone than shock. It was not only uncharacteristic of him to wish for death, but also irresponsible in the present circumstances. Softening with some effort, she sat by his side. For the first time, he moved away, despite the heavy bleeding in his leg. He grunted aloud in agony and fell back against the cushions.

'Calm down, Yudhishtira! The pain shall subside.'

'Unfortunately!' he rued. 'My dying will result in a defeat. For all my wrongs, the least I can do is to cling onto this life and stop you all from losing. Though it kills me every single time when I realize that I have only been a burden to you all.'

After he was quiet, she asked, 'Who did this?'

Yudhishtira's face wrinkled. He hated to even utter the name. 'That very low life who, on that fateful day, called you a...'

'Karna!'

'I know he would have said none of that if, as Arjuna ranted, I knew "when to stop".'

Draupadi sighed, imagining the unpleasant conversation that would have taken place. No wonder Krishna had urged her to take care of Yudhishtira. 'And Arjuna told you you are a burden?'

'Not in exact words, but as the one who snatched the benefits of all his hard work, including you, his rightful bride. I guess he meant that!'

Draupadi felt the world go dark for a moment but steadied herself. 'I don't deserve this!'

'Yes, you don't! Not after destroying the life of your dreams under this meaningless pursuit of keeping us united!'

'I shall talk to him.'

'Don't!' Yudhishtira held her hands. 'He probably needed to vent. And this has everything to do with us and not you. Stay assured, I shall not let you down on this one, Draupadi.' He saw Draupadi swallow the lump in her throat and nodded with difficulty. 'Besides, this will be forgotten if he manages to get rid of Karna!'

'I heard that Bhima was about to kill him. But he was reminded that Karna was supposed to be Arjuna's "rightful game"!' she grinned, drawing a slight smile from Yudhishtira. 'Never feel you are a burden, Samrat. I can't overlook the fact that we were ruthlessly let down by your decision to play dice. But unlike what Arjuna says, there was no stopping once you started. Every next wager must have seemed small enough compared to what you had lost in the previous turn. It must have felt like the risk was worth it. Only to realize that it was wrong and too late,' she stopped, seeing him smile sadly.

'When Uncle Vidura told me that rejecting the call to play the game bore the risk of a war, I agreed to play the game hoping to avert the disaster. And now... Resisting fate often ends up enabling it to hit back, carrying more disastrous results.'

'It was not fate that you resisted, Samrat,' Draupadi shook her head. 'It was the truth that no amount of amicability from your side could fix the fractured relationship between you and the sons of Dhritarashtra. Hoping against hope that their hearts would change and throwing ourselves in the fray only brought more disaster upon...this land. Besides, our allies and theirs, many took sides to settle scores between each other. The disaster was waiting to happen, one way or the other.'

The messenger from the battlefield interrupted them with the message that Arjuna and Karna had met in a single duel. Draupadi saw Yudhishtira's eyes blaze when he rose to his feet, unmindful of his multiple wounds, and nearly collapsed under the excruciating pain.

With the physicians rushing in, Draupadi's full attention was on reviving him, rather than on the result of the duel. Somewhere in her heart, she felt sure that Karna stood no chance against Arjuna, given the fury with which he had left for the field. She wondered why Arjuna had vented out those abominable feelings after all these years.

264

Why did he not speak when he could have done so earlier?

The stab of pain got stronger as she dwelt upon it. Draupadi curled her fists, trying to squish the feeling. It shocked her that it still existed in the hidden crevices of her heart.

No! I love all of them!

Yudhishtira's condition stabilized and he was put to sleep. It was almost sunset by the time Draupadi had supervised the other activities of the camp, checked on the medicine supply and the recovery of the wounded. It was time for some updates from the field. But it looked like all the messengers were caught up on the field.

Arjuna would be in his best form.

She smiled to herself and walked back to Yudhishtira's tent. To her relief, his wounds had stopped bleeding and his energy was rising. The first to return were Shikhandi and Dhrishtadyumna, after facing mixed luck in the hands of Ashvatthama and Kripacharya. Her five sons returned in higher spirits, having defeated Shakuni, his son, and the other warriors. Draupadi debated on whether to break the news of Uttara's pregnancy and decided to wait for Arjuna's return.

The dust in the horizon rose, indicating the arrival of speeding chariots. The familiar banner sporting the intimidating face of Lord Hanuman was the first to break through the cloud of dust. The sounds of both the conches, Devadatta and Panchajanya, greeted her ears. Draupadi knew the result when she heard the triumphant call from the distance. She rushed back to Yudhishtira, waiting for the arrival of the victorious. A look at Yudhishtira told her that he shared her hope.

Before long, Arjuna hurried in, his face showing a strange mix of graveness and accomplishment. Yudhishtira rose, now without any help from her or the physician.

UTTARA IS PREGNANT

'Eldest, he is dead!'

They embraced. Draupadi sighed in relief. Krishna followed close behind and grinned at her. The camp erupted in cheer.

'Take me to the field! I wish to see his dead body!' Yudhishtira demanded, stunning every one. Bhima and Nakula readily escorted him, while Arjuna chose to retire.

Draupadi stared at Yudhishtira's departing form.

'War often brings out the worst in people, Sakhi,' Krishna remarked, reading her thoughts. Neither of them were new to celebrations that followed the death of an enemy. But going to see the corpse of the enemy warrior, and Yudhishtira, of all people doing so, was something different.

And disturbing.

'The emperor bore no hatred towards Karna. But that son of Atiratha had hurled the worst of insults that day. Worse than those that Duryodhana spoke!' Draupadi recollected. 'I thought Yudhishtira was immune to them. But now...'

'Don't, Draupadi,' Krishna squeezed her palm. 'Don't despair when it is expressed. Let the worst be purged out. Don't aid in suppressing it.' When they parted for the night, they both knew the relief each felt.

One man stood between them and the end of this destruction.

Thirty-nine

Victory at What Cost?

The day had started on an almost joyful note. Uttara's pregnancy seemed to have cheered the lowest cadre of foot soldiers as well. Subhadra, aware of how loved her Abhimanyu was, had made sure that the sweetmeats prepared on the occasion reached everyone in the camp.

The warriors had left for the battlefield in high spirits. Even the perpetually sullen Sudeshna had cast off her melancholy to celebrate her daughter's news. If something had felt unusual to Draupadi, it was Kunti's lack of jubilation. How many women lived to see their great-grandchildren? Draupadi was not sure she would. She did not understand why Kunti, instead of being a part of the joy, chose to stay back in the tent, not agreeing to see anyone, including her and Subhadra.

The messengers kept bringing updates from the field. Yudhishtira had killed Shalya, the king of Madra. Draupadi remembered how much Shalya's last minute defection to the other side had hurt Nakula and Sahadeva. They had faced and bettered him multiple times throughout the war but had stopped short of killing their maternal uncle. Today, that put an end to their suppressed agony. Just as she was fondly thinking of them, the messengers brought the news that the twins had killed the wily Shakuni, and his son, Uluka. The Panchala princes and her five sons had taken up the job of holding off Ashvatthama, Kripa and Kritavarma, while Bhima killed the rest of the sons of Dhritarashtra.

Offering the customary rewards to those who brought the news of victory, Draupadi's thoughts went back to Kunti. When she ventured into Kunti's tent, she was shocked to find her mother-in-law grieving.

Like she had lost someone dear. Who could it be?

They had all mourned Abhimanyu and Ghatotkacha alike. She could not think of anyone on the other side who could have been the recipient of Kunti's affection. Kunti's grief was concerning, but Draupadi was unsuccessful in finding out the reason. With the routine duties of supervising the camp waiting for her, Draupadi went back. The workload had decreased greatly, given how men fell in the war. The concerns in the early days of war had been procuring weapons back from the field and deploying smiths to sharpen them in order to ready them for the next day. But in the recent days, it was all about preventing the outbreak of any unforeseen disease caused by the decaying bodies on the battlefield. Both sides were working to ensure honourable funerals to their respective martyrs. But the number of deaths overtook the number of chandalas who assisted in disposing off the bodies. Meanwhile, as the queen, Draupadi took all the care she could to prevent an epidemic.

In the early hours of the afternoon, she heard that Duryodhana had fled the battlefield, and that the Pandavas, with Krishna and his cousin Satyaki, had gone in search of the enemy king.

A new complication!

She cursed Duryodhana in her mind for delaying the

inevitable. After letting his whole side be massacred, right from his grandfather Bhishma to young children and dear friends, she had at least expected the eldest son of Dhritarashtra to put up a valiant fight as the last man standing. But as Krishna had pointed out, the war had indeed brought out the worst in everyone. For Duryodhana, it perhaps brought out his cowardice.

Fatigue had begun to claim her limbs and Draupadi tried to get some rest in the afternoon. Sounds of jubilation from the Panchala groups gathered momentum. She learnt that most of the Kuru army was disheartened after Duryodhana deserted them and that some of their foot soldiers surrendered while others chose to leave the field. There was still no sign of the five brothers or of Krishna and Satyaki who had accompanied them in their search for Duryodhana. Guru Kripacharya had withdrawn from the battle, angry and disappointed with his pupil, and Ashvatthama had gone to persuade him to come back to the field. Something about this news made Draupadi uncomfortable. More than half of the camp had started celebrating the end of the bloody war even before the enemy king had been killed or captured.

It was a familiar sense of foreboding that Draupadi felt. Her sons convinced even Subhadra, Sudeshna and Uttara to join them but she was far from feeling triumphant.

Like she had lost everything. But war of this scale does take its dues.

Draupadi kept debating with herself, looking frantically for the Pandavas and Krishna to return. Her eyes remained fixed on the paths leading to their camp. Even the messengers got tired of her incessant queries. Sensing their restlessness and longing to join the celebrations, Draupadi chose to not send them again for updates. The sun set and darkness only encouraged the drunk soldiers to celebrate louder.

VICTORY AT WHAT COST?

The sound of conches blaring from a distance caught her attention even amidst the noise and Draupadi rushed toward the entrance of their encampment. It was the lusty note from Bhima's Paundra.

The war had indeed ended!

⌢

Draupadi lost count of how many times she tossed in the bed. The fact that she slept in the deserted Kuru camp as the conventional conventional symbol of the victor, had a part to play in her sleeplessness. Not that she had ever slept well a single night since the war had started. But today seemed different. She had hoped for a good night's sleep in the empty camp, away from the noise of celebrations in her own camp. But the noise raged inside her mind. It was past midnight when she felt Yudhishtira's hand upon hers.

'Samrat?'

It was hard to make out his expression in the dark, but Draupadi guessed that Yudhishtira was smiling. 'Sleep deserted you too?'

Draupadi sighed and lifted herself up against the giant backrest of the spacious bed. Duryodhana had indeed looked after his comfort well, even during the war.

'The tricky thing is that I don't know what robs me of my sleep. We could have very well stayed back at our camp and joined the celebrations.'

'Theoretically, *this* is our camp now, Samragni.'

It was Draupadi's turn to chuckle. 'This deserted camp?'

'An indication of what we will rule over from tomorrow.' His hand clutched Draupadi's again, the grip strengthening, 'That's what he cursed before dying!'

'The instances of a dying man blessing his enemy in history can be counted on the fingers, Samrat,' Draupadi proceeded to feel for the lamp beside the bed. She suddenly clutched Yudhishtira's hand. 'Samrat, where are your weapons?'

Sitting up at her cry, Yudhishtira retrieved his spear from under the bed. 'Here, close to me, love. Draupadi, what's the matter?'

The relief in her sigh was palpable. 'Your commander-in-chief never keeps his within his reach. Sadly, his nephews seem to have taken after him. Almost every other night, I used to wake them up, telling them to keep at least one weapon handy, just in case!'

'Samragni, the war is over.'

She felt Yudhishtira reach out to hold her and pull her close, to rest her head on his lap. Mixed emotions washed over her at the intimacy that had surfaced after fourteen long years.

As if he had considered himself unfit for it until the war was over.

She did not resist. There was that nagging sense of foreboding that she first wanted to get rid of. She lay on his lap trying to find the root of the feeling.

'Draupadi. I risk disappointing you again. But shall we crown Prativindhya and retire back to the forests?' he asked, knowing that the question was not to her taste.

'Will the forests give you peace, Samrat? Rather, has anyone found peace after abandoning a child dependent on him or her for their survival?'

Yudhishtira had to admit that she was right. 'I agree, Draupadi. It will be cowardly of me to abandon this broken land this way—to gamble it away after uniting the Janapadas with high hopes of establishing dharma, and now, to abandon

271

it after this devastating war. Prativindhya will die of shame for being my son,' he felt Draupadi's hand upon his lips.

'Don't be harsh on yourself, Yudhishtira. Trust me, there will be enough people to do that job.' She tried to laugh but could not. The very thought of facing the elders at Hastinapura made her tongue go bitter. After years of arduous exile and the devastating war, being blamed for this destruction was the last thing they deserved. But that was all that they could expect.

Yudhishtira rose to his feet. 'Let me see if Krishna is feeling sleepless too,' he said. Draupadi felt grateful for the initiative. Talking to Krishna was all she needed. He would uproot that feeling of loss within no time. Yudhishtira returned with Krishna sooner than she thought.

'We could have called you in earlier if we knew that you were not sleeping too!' Draupadi moved back on the bed making space for Krishna while Yudhishtira brought one of the torches.

'Your dear sakhi still loses her sleep over whether our weapons are handy while we sleep, or try to sleep,' Yudhishtira quipped, lighting the lamps inside the tent.

Krishna stared into space while acknowledging both. 'Our samragni is one of those for whom the war does not end tonight, Samrat.'

'A war worse than this awaits us at the capital, Krishna.'

'You are intuitive, Samrat,' Krishna remarked. To Draupadi's surprise, he was unsmiling. It was uncharacteristic. But for the moment, she wanted to chase the looming melancholy away.

'Here we stand, at the threshold of another barren land. Like we stood in front of the burnt Khandava, years ago,' she reminded them. 'Can we make Indraprastha happen all over again? This time, it is the whole Bharatavarsha we are talking about. And to begin with, some long-deserved cheer. Samrat, Krishna, Uttara carries Abhimanyu's child in her womb! The child has not seen a single pleasure due to her. I would like to see her married again. To Prativindhya? With her consent, of course.'

Yudhishtira beamed at the idea. Both looked at Krishna. But to their dismay, his face remained blank. 'The deaths have been far too many. The mourning, I am afraid, will drown the sound of any celebration, Samrat.'

Draupadi sensed the stab of pain in Krishna's eyes. At the moment, they reflected the ordeal of every soldier who had perished or bled in the war. She almost felt small for suggesting the idea of a wedding. But how was one supposed to make a start? The question remained in her mind. The distasteful quiet followed—till an ear-splitting cry was heard.

'Subhadra! Wasn't she supposed to be in our camp?'

The three of them sprang to their feet and rushed out. Subhadra's cries were calling out to Arjuna, Krishna, and Draupadi, and they had gotten louder. The other four Pandavas and Satyaki too woke up and rushed out of their tents. Reaching the entrance of the encampment, they saw a lone chariot followed by a couple of horse riders.

Draupadi saw Prativindhya drive the chariot that carried Subhadra and Uttara. When the chariot halted, Subhadra was the first to get down, but collapsed to the ground before she could help Uttara. Prativindhya carried Uttara in his arms and descended the chariot. But the very moment they reached him, he too collapsed, barely giving Arjuna time to support Uttara, who was heavily wounded. Draupadi screamed, now, seeing the gush of blood from her son's back. Prativindhya pulled out the dagger that was stuck there and cried out. Yudhishtira held him close, suppressing his distress. More horses came. Some without riders. Some with mutilated bodies.

'Shatanika!'

'Sutasoma!'

'By Mahadeva, tell me that is not Shrutasena's body!'

Draupadi stood rooted to the spot. Her limbs did not know which son to rush to, while they fell like fruits from a tree. She heard Yudhishtira cry out Prativindhya's name more than thrice.

'It was Ashvatthama. It was deceit!' she heard Prativindhya struggle for words. 'The soldiers who surrendered, they actually attacked us in the dead of the night!'

She heard Nakula shout out Shatanika's name loud enough to be heard by the gods above. She saw Bhima hug Sutasoma's limp form, words and voice, both failing the giant.

'Uncles Drishtadyumna and Shikhandin, both told us to escape while they fought off Ashvatthama and Kripacharya,' Prativindhya's words now faltered, losing coherence. But she could hear him. Very clearly.

'They are all dead! Ashvatthama massacred them all— Yudhamanyu, Uttamaujas. We escaped only to save Uttara and aunt...'

Draupadi walked up to Yudhishtira who was holding Prativindhya. The boy's face was covered with blood. He looked apologetic the moment he met his mother's gaze. 'I should have kept my weapons handy. Forgive me, Mother.'

She stared at the face, which would now never talk to her, and then, at Yudhishtira's, pale with numb grief. Spurred by something within, she dragged Prativindhya's body away from his reach 'It was the thought of this child that made me ask for your freedom that fateful day, Yudhishtira!' her voice broke at every syllable.

'All of you, don't even dare to touch my sons! Don't touch them till you vanquish Ashvatthama! The war is not over!'

Forty

Empress Again

Placing the corpses of each of her sons by the pyres was the last thing that Draupadi had imagined fate would make her do. Other than Subhadra and Uttara, only two others had survived the massacre. Kunti who had gone to visit Grandsire Bhishma and the charioteer of Drishtadyumna who had gone to the lake to bring water for the horses. Tears refused to flow out of her eyes. As if all emotions within her had died with those who had perished. When she dragged herself to check on Uttara, her state bothered Subhadra more than Uttara's.

'Gather yourself, Sister!' Subhadra pleaded, embracing her. 'We both have lost our sons, but think about Uttara. The child is handling the trauma better than us, Sister. We need to take care of her and her child!'

Draupadi looked at her and nodded, but said nothing. Subhadra hurried back to tend to Uttara and Kunti. Draupadi saw the sun rising in the horizon. Drishtadyumna's charioteer told her tearfully that the whole camp had been set ablaze. Even the animals had perished in the fire. The whiff of the dying fumes now came up to this camp, stinging their nostrils. That was all she had of her brothers who had survived through the eighteen days of war.

'That son of Dronacharya is even more monstrous than his unruly father. You should have thought before sending the five brothers in his pursuit. They are all we have!' Kunti rued before fainting.

The possibility of Ashvatthama bettering all her husbands had not occurred to Draupadi. Even if he did, she knew she somehow had to protect Subhadra and Uttara. And the heir of Abhimanyu. She was ready for that. She remembered the various discussions she had had with her sons throughout the course of war, even the minor ones where she had scolded them. Most of it had occurred the previous day when she had rightly been sceptical about the celebrations being premature. Even Subhadra had pacified her by saying the boys needed some fun after enduring the long battle. She should have forced them to come to the Kuru camp at night. She should have sent them on some errand right after the war, or even midway. Perhaps, on the day the rules of the war were made, they should have decided to not involve the children at all. Perhaps the God of Death should have claimed the Pandavas and herself, and spared the children. Each thought wrecked whatever remained of her already battered heart. Yet, no tear made its way through her eyes. The memory of the ten-year-old Prativindhya clinging to her lap when all his brothers were fast asleep kept flashing in front of her eyes.

By late morning, even Uttara had recovered, and she tried to lead Draupadi into the tent. But seeing her, the princess of Matsya chose to stay with her, near the dead bodies. They held hands in silent camaraderie.

'Those monsters did not even think of sparing women, Mother Draupadi,' Uttara narrated, controlling her tears. 'Your son shielded me and took the spear on his back. You must be proud of them, Mother.' Draupadi's form shook once. But no words came out of her. 'I want to name my son after your Prativindhya,' Uttara said, hoping this would move Draupadi. But her mother-in-law only shook her head in mute disagreement.

The clattering sound of the horses on the rocky path commanded their attention. Uttara pointed at the familiar banner that was leading the rest.

Draupadi saw the five brothers get down their chariots, along with Krishna and Satyaki. Involuntarily, her eyes sought Bhima, who dragged along a bound Ashvatthama. Her lips instantaneously curved. The valour that each of them had exhibited when their sons had died—why had it not surfaced before death had claimed the young ones? It was a question that would forever remain in her mind.

She looked at the son of Dronacharya, once a name that had caused fear in every soldier in her army. 'Welcome, Guruputra,' she smiled. 'Come with me.'

Yudhishtira caught her arm, surprised at the undeserved hospitality. She gently extricated herself and led the way, not glancing at any of the stupefied faces around her. Staying dangerously close to Ashvatthama, she even waved Bhima away when he stepped between them. Leading the way further, Draupadi pointed to where she had carefully placed the corpses of the Upa Pandavas.

'Did you see them fight in the war, Ashvatthama?' she asked, her smile not fading. Seeing his lack of response, she introduced each of them by their names. 'They must have fought well for you to think that attacking them in the dead of the night was preferable to facing them on the field.'

'Draupadi, what are you up to?' It was Arjuna, but he was held back by Krishna.

'Guruputra, when the celebrations of victory started yesterday, I was told that you escaped alive. I was initially relieved thinking that we could talk peace with you and secure your tutelage for the children.'

Ashvatthama collapsed to his knees on hearing that.

'Ashvatthama, in the eighteen days of war, did you see them running away from the field even once?' Hope rose in her eyes when she asked the question. Her smile only became more pronounced when he shook her head. She moved towards the youngest, Shrutakarma. 'Even he, the youngest. He was never fearful, was he?'

Sahadeva rushed to Draupadi's side and shook her, as if reviving her from a spell. 'Tell us to kill him and get done with it, Draupadi! I beg you, don't do this. This abomination of a Brahmin does not need to certify our sons!'

She pushed Sahadeva away, mildly annoyed. 'As their parents, we must have always felt defensive and hopeful of them, Sahadeva. But the son of Drona, as the opponent, must have a more accurate assessment. Are you, as a father, not eager to hear his feedback?'

'There were no flaws in any of them!' Sahadeva held her close. 'You are stronger than this, Draupadi. You steered us out of impossible situations. Don't give up now! You are going mad!'

When his voice broke, Yudhishtira intervened, turning her to face him. 'Samragni, you have an entire orphaned land to mother,' he pleaded, cupping her cheeks. Her eyes, however, showed no grief. Patting Yudhishtira's hands, she turned back to Ashvatthama.

'You are a fighter superior to your father, the great

Dronacharya, Ashvatthama. You would have been a superior teacher too!'

'Sakhi!' Krishna stepped in between them. When she met his gaze, the first trace of bereavement surfaced in her. 'Your husbands need you.' Inching close to her, he whispered, 'You are all they have. They can't bring up Uttara's child like you would.'

'You know me too well to despair like this, Krishna,' she replied, the first stream of tears springing out of her eyes. Wiping it away, she shook her head and turned back to Ashvatthama. 'Guruputra, my Arjuna who wrought havoc in the armies of every opponent he faced, he is still known as the best of Drona's disciples. One seldom thinks of him without taking his guru's name. I pity you, Ashvatthama, you have lost so much.' Brushing the hair of dead Prativindhya, she sat by her dead sons. 'My sons, they would have healed the pain of losing your father. They would have served you, looked up to you, made you known for great things. But today, you lost it all. You immortalized yourself as the midnight murderer of defenceless children. Worse, you will have to live with the pain. Live long. Very long!'

Tears did flow out of her eyes, but she was a picture of composure. Subhadra tried to lead her inside. She stopped by Krishna. 'Sakha, the brothers might break down in the middle of the cremation. Console them well.' Tears blinded her for a moment when he brushed her hair. Apart from the grief, he betrayed pride at her equanimity. 'As for Ashvatthama, yes, feed him after the cremation and let him go. Let him leave the borders of Bharatavarsha. We have a whole empire to take care of and leaving a murderer loose is not a good start.'

There were gasps of disbelief from her husbands. But none

of them contested her decision. Moving into the tent, Subhadra wept, holding her. This time, she broke into sobs too.

⌣

The winter solstice was fast approaching. A month had passed after the war. Performing the final rites seemed like a never-ending season of painful rituals and the Pandavas took care to not differentiate between friends and enemies while offering the final oblations. It did take a toll on Yudhishtira's strength. However, his unflinching stance throughout the war was admirably consistent, much to Draupadi's surprise. What hit him hard was the revelation that Vasusena Karna was the son of Kunti, born to her when she was an unmarried maiden, experimenting with things she was not supposed to.

On hearing this, Draupadi had felt indignant at the beginning. Karna had been the one who had aimed more insults at her than Duryodhana. He had been the one who had killed Ghatotkacha and had broken Abhimanyu's bow from behind.

It had taken her weeks to convince Yudhishtira who suddenly gave in to the new-found grief. The worst part was the distance he maintained from Mother Kunti after getting to know the truth.

'Leave him alone, Draupadi. It takes a bewildered teenager who is pregnant with child before being wedded, and a paranoid mother of five fatherless children surrounded by enemies, to understand what I went through,' Kunti remarked and retired to her room.

Draupadi's admiration had only grown for the old woman. How would Kunti have felt when her own estranged son added to the strength of those who endangered her other sons' lives? There had been many opportunities when she could have broken down under the pressure of motherhood. But the very same motherhood had kept Kunti away from sharing her secret. She went to assure her support to her mother-in-law when Kunti revealed another shattering secret.

'I had met Karna before the war started, Draupadi. I begged him to change sides. But he was too loyal to Duryodhana. Still, he promised to spare the lives of Yudhishtira, Bhima, and the twins. Arjuna was the one he could not stand,' Kunti narrated.

Draupadi for the first time felt unsure at the revelation. Karna had indeed been a man of his word, sparing their lives as he had promised. She still remembered the excruciating pain that Yudhishtira went through, being injured by Karna. She could not place whether it was his nobility or sadism. At least, when one of her husbands decided to spare the opponent's lives, they would, she thought, show more compassion. Terrifying thoughts about Karna did not leave her the entire evening.

It could have been far worse.

She sadly steeled herself when thoughts of her dead sons revisited her and prepared to face another night of convincing Yudhishtira to shed his melancholy and take up the reins of the kingdom.

'There will be blame. There will be curses. We might have to grovel before the undeserving and spend aeons trying to convince them to start afresh. It takes a warrior to fight till the end. But it takes a true leader to convince people for a new beginning. You alone can do it. Bharatavarsha needs you, Dharmaraja Yudhishtira.'

Conclusion

Into the Future

'I remember the day of the coronation, Janamejaya,' Uttara's tone had paled into a whisper, heavy with the myriad emotions that she alone was aware of. 'Bereft of any festivity that the sons of Pandu truly deserved, amidst hushed decrying by those they considered their own, Emperor Yudhishtira was crowned. He took the responsibility of the land that almost despised him for the war, driven by the inspiration that Mother Draupadi was an embodiment of. It indeed takes a true empress to see hope after the gruesome end of countless lines of Kshatriya clans.

'I remember the day your father, Parikshit, was born. The midwives pronounced him a stillborn and the entire family was heartbroken. It was only Mother Draupadi who kept her faith and mine as Uncle Krishna resuscitated him.

'And I remember the day they all left, never to return. The three and half decades of their committed reign had transformed the empire again. Like they had transformed the once dreaded wilderness of Khandava into the magnificent Indraprastha,' Uttara leaned against the wooden backrest of her seat. 'Her ichhashakti, or driving desire; Uncle Krishna's jnanashakti, the power of wisdom; and the Pandavas' kriyashakti, the will to see her vision take shape in reality—the triad—is something that would remain unique in all the ages to come. I pity those petty minds who blame her for the war.'

Seated on the floor by her feet, Janamejaya kept staring into Uttara's lost eyes. A cool breeze blew, signalling the sunset. One of the attendants of the rest house stepped in to light the earthen lamps. 'Grandmother.' He gently patted her knee. 'She was indeed a true empress. Any other woman in her place would have weakened and our history would not have been the immortal tale that will survive the test of time.'

'She was a walking challenge to the regressive forces that subverted the code of dharma to suit their narrow means and ends,' Uttara smiled, setting her greying locks right.

I still miss her loving touch when she combed my hair. She did that until the day she left for the forests, never to return.

Only Uttara knew what it meant to be a daughter to the unforgettable empress. Her tale threw up a new facet of hers every time she remembered it. For the good of the empire, she hoped that the knowledge of this timeless tale would disseminate before any mischievous distorting forces took over.

At least, the look on the face of the new emperor, the great-grandson of Arjuna, spoke of a determination that set her mind at ease.

Acknowledgements

Presenting an immortal tale like *Mahabharata* cannot but need many hands to shape it. It has been a great experience working with the team at Rupa Publications. I thank the commissioning editors, Shambhu Sahu and Rudra Sharma, for their continuing support. Aparna Kumar has been a great editor and it was a pleasure discussing *Mahabharata* with her as we progressed with the editing of the manuscript. I am grateful to Mugdha Sadhwani for the impressive work on the cover.

I am fortunate to have parents like Usha Krishna Swamy and Krishna Swamy Kumar who have brought me closer to the ancient knowledge of India since childhood. The opportunity to write *Draupadi* knocked at my door when I was on the threshold of motherhood. Writing this manuscript would not have been possible without the love, care and support of my mother. She was my inspiration, my hustler, my babysitter, my reader with unique inputs, and much more. My father Sri Krishna Swamy Kumar has been a pillar of support, ensuring I got the best ambience to write this manuscript. My husband Arvind Iyer believed in my writing even when I lost belief in myself.

Dear daughter Abhirami, thanks for those punctual naps that gave me the much-needed time to write!

I owe a major part of my writing career to the support

extended by Indic Academy, founded by Harikiran Vadalamani. I am grateful for the insightful interactions with the members of Indic Academy, including scholars, senior authors, editors, reviewers, bloggers and some great friends.

I am grateful to each of my readers and friends who motivate me, promote me on social media, and are now an inseparable part of my life.

Finally, I thank my Ishta Devata, Krishna Vasudeva, for powering me through this storytelling journey. It is hard to imagine writing a story without him. I pray that he fills joy in the life of every reader who reads the book.

ACKNOWLEDGEMENTS

References and Inspiration

—*The Mahabharata,* translated by Kisari Mohan Ganguli.

—*The Mahabharata*: Critical edition, translated by Dr Bibek Debroy, Bhandarkar Oriental Research Institute.

—*Andhra Mahabharatamu* and *Andhra Mahabhagavatam* : Tirumala Tirupati Devasthanam editions.

—*Krishna Charitra* by Bankim Chandra Chaterjee, translated by Alo Shome.

—*Krishnavatara* by K.M. Munshi, Bharatiya Vidya Bhavan.

—*Parva* by S. L. Bhyrappa.

—*Krishna, the Man and His Philosophy* by Osho, Jaico Publishing House.

—Talks and discourses on Draupadi, Krishna and the *Mahabharata* by various gurus and scholars including:

Bhagawan Sri Satya Sai Baba

Brahmasri Samavedam Shanmukha Sarma

Brahmasri Garikipati Narasimha Rao

Swami Chinmayananda

Brahmasri Chaganti Koteshwara Rao